D1535031

PRAISE FOR *CICADA SEASON*

"Mindy Steele burst onto the Amish fiction scene with her invigorating, uplifting stories and she hasn't slowed down. Her stories bring a fresh view to the Amish world, and her readers are hooked from page one. She's a heartfelt author who creates characters you want to be friends with and communities you want to belong to. If you see a new Mindy Steele book on the shelves, grab it now! I promise, you won't be disappointed." ~ Patricia Johns, author of *Jeb's Wife*.

"Mindy Steele is a welcome addition to the Amish romance genre. Readers will love both her and her books!" ~ Jennifer Spredemann, USA TODAY bestselling author of the Amish Christmas Miracles Collection

"Mindy weaves a beautiful story of love that only comes after Hannah learns to trust Leon. I love Mindy's writing style! She has a way of making her characters come alive on the pages. I didn't want the story to end." ~ USA Today bestselling author, Tracy Fredrychowski

"From tears to laughter, Mindy Steele will evoke every emotion possible in the reader. Steele's writing captures simplicity, and yet her characters have incredible depth. To read a Steele book is to make new friends." ~ Vicky Sluiter, author of *Oliver's Moving Day*

Cicada Season

A Miller's Creek Series, Book 3

MINDY STEELE

Vinspire Publishing, LLC
www.VinspirePublishing.com

To Cody and Jordan,
because you make me laugh watching your love story unfold.

Glossary

Ach	Oh
Aenti	aunt
Bopplin	babies
Blut	blood
Bruder	brother
Daed	dad
Faul	lazy
Fraa	wife
Freinden	friends
Froh	happy
Geh	go
Gott	God
Griddlich	cranky
Grossfeelich	one who thinks they are of more importance
Gut mariye	good morning
Haus	house
Ich bin sorry	I am sorry
Ich kann naett	I can not
Jah	yes
Kaffi	coffee
Kinner	children
Kumm	come
Liebling	little one
Maed/maedel	girl/young woman
Mamm	mother
Mammi	grandmother
Mei	me
Narrisch	nervous
Nee	no
Onkel	uncle
Ordnung	Written and unwritten rules in an Amish district

Schee	pretty
Schwester	sister
Sohn	son
Wunderbaar	wonderful
Youngie	teenager

CHAPTER ONE

Hazel Miller looked up from the table of fudge cooling at Miller's Bakery when the bell over the door jingled. At this hour it could only be one person, Hank Fisher. *Persistent Hank Fisher. That's who he was*, Hazel determined.

A person could set her watch by Hank's day. Ten minutes before six he walked into the bakery for a sweet roll and *kaffi*. By six-thirty, he walked out, went two blocks down the street where his wood shop was, and worked until eleven. At that point, one could watch him, brown bag lunch in hand, stroll to the bench at the park across the street. Ducks who called Twin Fork Lake home often waddled out of the water and squawked for whatever he didn't finish. Hank always had plenty to share.

By eleven-thirty, he was back to work in his woodshop when the bakery was in its biggest rush of the day. Then at five after five, every day without fail, Hank stood outside the bakery window until Hazel looked up and waved. Well, she didn't always wave, but after two years, it was rude not to wave considering he never left out that part of his routine. It wasn't Christian to be rude and not wave at the poor man, Hazel reasoned, for she was a reasonable woman after all.

She gave the bakery case a good study and noted each tray full of baked goods. It was when her eyes landed on the four long rows of sweet rolls that her thoughts shifted to Hank again. Why did the man torture himself with sweet rolls and *kaffi* every morning? It was simply an unhealthy habit. Just because he didn't pack around extra pounds didn't mean all that sugar and caffeine were good for him. She retrieved a knife from the drawer to her left, letting out a frustrated huff.

A man his age should watch his diet more closely, she thought while cutting the freshly cooled batch of chocolate walnut fudge to ready for packaging. Hazel shook off the care. Hank Fisher's diet was none of her business.

Behind her, Rose, her mother-in-law and half-owner of Miller's Bakery, pushed another cookie tray into the oven. She was nearing eighty-two and baked from dawn to dusk. It was becoming hard not to notice Rose's struggle to pull heavy trays from the ovens. No matter how often Hazel wanted to tend the duty for her, she'd learned a thing or two about older women. Well, women older than her. Never get in their way. No one wanted to feel they had nothing to offer. Hazel had plenty to offer, and as the weather warmed and flowers bloomed, she was ready to do what she did best.

"How are all my *schee maedels* this day?" Hank greeted as he reached the counter and removed his straw hat. Bits of sawdust from whatever he was making currently floated about, catching the early morning light seeping through the front glass windows. The strong scent of cedar filled her nostrils.

Oh blunder.

Hazel adverted her gaze quickly when Hank floated her that signature good morning smile. Forty years ago, such a smile might have made her blush by the bushel. At sixty, the idea of blushing was utterly ridiculous.

"Now, Hank Fisher, I ain't been a *maed* for as long as you ain't been a gangly *bu*." Hazel snipped while shaping fresh boxes for the fudge she was so well known for. Hank chuckled. He had a good chuckle, strong, deep-throated, and never at the expense of others. He was like that when they were young too, always polite and always smiling. Even the loss of his *fraa* ten years back barely dented his happy nature.

Being widowed herself, it was nice to see smiles on another. Since the loss of so many two years ago when a building collapse took the lives of the men constructing it, Hazel believed such smiles were the healing sparks on broken hearts. Few understood the power of a simple smile.

"I was all sticks and limbs rightly so." Hank shrugged. "Glad you still remember it," he added with a hint of flirtation. "But you're still as *schee* as always."

For a man, he was sure acting like a *youngie*. Hazel waved off his unwelcomed compliment and went to fetch more boxes. It wasn't proper to say such things in public. The man may have a nice smile and two healthy rows of teeth, but he had no sense when it came to stroking an old woman's vanity.

When she returned carrying a stack of unneeded boxes, Penny came waddling in. She was barely a *maed* of fourteen when Hazel and Rose had hired her to help at the bakery. Having a soft spot for the downtrodden, Hazel felt pulled to reach out and help the young girl who had lived a hard life. In no time, Penny had proven a natural at everything she did. She no longer looked like the shy, sad faced *maedel* responsible for putting bread on her *mamm*'s table. Penny had grown strong under Hazel's wing and the raven-haired *maedel* was now blissfully married and as round as a watermelon.

Pride was a sin, but Hazel couldn't help but feel the swelling of it every time she saw the Lord's will fulfilled. Hazel loved baking, but it was her God-given talent to help others she believed truly fed those around her. Some called it meddling, but the Lord knew better. Hazel was simply a tool of the maker, and Penny and Luke happily wed and expecting their first child was proof of that fact.

"*Gut mariye*. You look as if someone just baked you a pan of frosted brownies." Hazel couldn't ignore the extra glow of joy wafting off her help. Penny shed her shawl and traded it for her apron hanging on the hook nearby before waddling over.

"I could eat a whole pan." Penny chuckled. "Who knew happy felt this *wunderbaar*. I am the happiest woman in all of Miller's Creek. Luke is the best man I have ever known. I think I love him more today than I did yesterday. I can never thank you two enough for meddling."

"*Gott*'s doing, my child. Not *mei* or Rose's," she said humbly. Hazel was just doing her duty, the way she saw it. God gave her the gift of seeing the needs in others. Then He gave her bright ideas and well-honed planning skills to see those needs fulfilled. It was a rewarding calling, matchmaking. Seeing others happy and loved was more important than feeding a hungry belly. Love was the greatest joy one could ever be gifted. And between her and God, Hazel was determined not a soul in all Pleasants County would be without it.

"Well, *Gott* must be pleased at how well you listen to Him. Does that not make four weddings you two helped along?" Penny grinned playfully.

"Twelve my dear," Rose said assertively. She shuffled to the counter. "We have been at it for a spell." She pulled out a sweet roll while Penny poured a cup of *kaffi,* and they both handed Hank his morning regular. Hazel bit her tongue from suggesting Hank try something different, and healthier.

"A dozen? Well, you two have been…busy."

Hank winked Hazel's way before sinking his teeth into his sweet roll like a man who never had one. Was it really this hot in here for late April?

"First was Hazel and my Joseph," Rose began, smiling at her daughter-in-law. "Oh, don't give me that look. You think *mei sohn* fell in love with you for your baking alone?"

Rose teased. "Then there was," Rose paused, searching the blank air for her next match made well. "Oh, I reckon next was Frannie and Gabe Mast. Though I don't think Gabe has ever forgiven me for that one." Hank and Hazel chuckled.

"Why?" Penny asked curiously as she donned her work apron next. Hazel tied it for her as Penny tucked a few wisps of her heavy dark hair back under her *kapp*. Never a girl was born with more hair than flesh than Penny Milford.

"Frannie can be a bit harsh with her words and Gabe has taken more tongue lashings than stripes on a hitching post." Hazel clarified. It wasn't gossip if one just answered a question, Hazel reasoned. "Don't forget Sarah and the Bishop's son, Mark. That boy was a hard egg to crack." Hazel stepped back to her boxes, avoiding Hank's gawking at her.

"That he was." Rose waved a crooked finger. "Thought we'd have to have poor Sarah learning to plow a field to get that one to look around and take notice. Fella had the attention span of a squirrel."

"You matched me *sohn*, Abner." Hank said. "He told me how you two would make him take Cilia home from every gathering."

Hank sounded thankful, but the loss of his daughter-in-law was still fresh. Abner and Cilia were a perfect match until God called her home. No one knew how sick she was until cancer had ravished her completely.

Rose reached across the table and patted Hank's hand affectionately. Hazel wanted to do the same, but when he looked up at her, the pain of Abner's loss so early in marriage reminded Hazel of losing Joshua and her gaze dropped. She had no way of knowing *Gott*'s plan in full, just the parts He wanted her to know. Still, guilt was there tapping her with a finger for matching two people who never had the chance to build something together.

Sensing her thoughts, Hank said, "He had her for a time and loved her. We cannot ask for more."

Hazel's head lifted in the profound faith of his words.

Hank was right. Whether it be five years or fifty, love was there, present and felt. Hazel would give Abner his time, but a man who still grieved after five years was one who loved deeply. It would take a special *maedel* deserving of Hank's son.

"Who else have you matched?" Hank's voice lifted as he broke eye contact with her, obviously hoping to divert attention to another match and not one so close to his heart.

"We matched Lewis Milford and Jenny Schwartz," Hazel said with a certain pride. "Rose was doubtful of that one, but *Gott* knew those two needed what the other had. And so, as it was, they did." Hazel shrugged.

"She actually waved at me the other day," Penny put in. "And when Luke and I ate at his *mamm*'s last week, Jenny sat quiet the whole meal. It was a miracle if I ever saw one."

"And let us not forget you and Luke. The Lord sure was right about you two," Hazel said.

"He sure was." Penny confirmed with a gleaming smile.

"*Ach*, I remember now, Millie and Eli Troyer," Rose said finally, recalling another blissful union they helped along. "Remember how Millie's *mamm* was set on her marrying Noah Weaver?"

"I remember taking her *mudder* to that garden show in Ohio with the lot of us." Hazel chucked before turning to Hank to further explain. "Phyllis complained the whole way, but we do what we must for the sake of love." Hazel shrugged.

"We readied a picnic for Millie." Rose leaned on the counter. "Later on, it was that same spot Eli built their house beside his family orchard." Rose's face fell into a frown. "Poor Millie, she and the girls have been working to the bone since Eli passed with the others," Rose said sorrowfully. One could not think of one loss without thinking of the many.

Eli Troyer had been one of the many locals, some Amish and some *Englisch*, working together on the five-story office building in the center of town. Through poor judgment and the pressures of reaching their deadline, the concrete had not set well, and the walls crumbled and collapsed, taking iron, wood, concrete, and men down with it. Thirty-one men lost their lives that day and forever changed the lives of so many. Hazel shoved off the shiver of the memory that day evoked. The loss was so great the small community never truly recovered.

Women were left to carry burdens alone or move away to new communities where relatives could take them in. Then poor, desperate, Nelly Raber had gone and placed an ad for husbands in the Budget. Her innocent intentions to help those dear to her had turned into a flood of lonely men coming like a swarm of locusts ready to set up new homes.

The local ministers had debated Nelly's act of goodness as sinful, but thankfully a scolding was all she received. Desperation always left a sour taste in Hazel's mouth. But it was all old news now, the way Hazel saw it. There had been some matches made out of the ordeal, not that Hazel would have matched them, but still, loneliness and need were present in Miller's Creek. Hazel preferred listening to God and good old fashion common sense herself. And God told her who needed the most attention of late. Hazel already had that plan in action.

"Well," Hazel began in a slow, drawn-out tone.

"Let me guess. *Gott* is giving you another great idea," Hank said with a grin.

He should wear brown more often. It brought out his eyes.

"Well, you know we still have a debt to pay." Hazel reminded Rose of their promise made to the youngest Troyer girl. She'd helped them when they needed her. In return, Ivy Troyer only asked that Hazel and Rose help find husbands for her sisters.

"If my old eyes aren't mistaken, Addie doesn't need your meddling. I see those long looks she and that Milford boy toss at each other," Rose said.

"Ivy has two sisters, ain't so?" Hazel grinned cunningly. "And you should know she and that one are merely *freinden*."

"Hannah Troyer is too busy to focus on any poor fella. And with that temper, she might just bite one's head off." Rose protested Hazel's current endeavor. "Youngin thinks she has to run that whole farm herself. I blame that for her temperament. Too stubborn to ask for help and too fussy to take it when it is freely given." Rose waved her boney finger.

"She so enjoyed teaching," Penny said.

Hannah had been teaching scholars for two years before the death of her father. It was obvious to all who knew her that the root of Hannah Troyer's current behavior was spun by grief.

"I think it weighed on her, giving it up," Penny said.

She and Penny had been friends since they were *kinner* Hazel knew.

"Best to see to another," Rose advised. "That would be a task for sure and certain."

"And who doesn't like a gut challenge to keep the blood flowing," Hazel said with a devilish grin.

"You remember how she bloodied Leon Milford at volleyball last year?"

"Three times." Penny reminded Hank.

"Few like a tempered sort who'd rather pick apples than bake them. Hazel, my dear, you might not be listening to the Lord on this one."

Hank's suggestion earned him three huffs and a piercing grey stare. "She is a fine baker I have you to know, Hank Fisher. And who gets to say one soul is less worthy of love than another. Besides…" Hazel shifted and stiffened her shoulders. "I reckon he's green broke. Now, that Milford could use a bit more training." Hazel pointed out, confident in her choice, or the Lord's choice need she remind them. It was His idea, after all, to put the thought in her head.

"He? You mean Leon Milford? That's who you think to

match with Hannah?" Penny's voice hiked a few octaves.

"You think it not so *gut* a match?" Hazel folded both arms over her chest and waited for Penny's reply.

"Leon is very cocky and wonderfully competitive. He likes attention and crossing lines," Penny said. "Luke says himself that his *bruder* will never marry or settle down. Leon likes his life the way it is. And since Lester met that *Englisch* girl that has everyone up in a bee's nest, Leon is the talk of all the single *maedels*. He's been courting like it's a sport."

It was no secret to Hazel the Milford fella was always carting around a different *maedel*.

"Hannah won't compete, I know that sure enough. She doesn't play anything she won't win, and she doesn't even like Leon." Penny's voice hitched again.

Hazel padded Penny's shoulder. "Which is why he's perfect." Penny gave her a doubtful look. "Who doesn't like a *gut* game? And no one should win all the time," Hazel said. "A man should be humble, not boastful." It was true and no one argued the fact. "A woman should be humble as well. It does no good for two nice-looking young folks to be wasting their time when they are of age to marry and do as the Lord asks. I told Irma just last night how hard them girls work and how poor Millie can't be lifting apple crates at her age come fall." Hazel told Irma Milford a lot, which helped get things into motion.

"Her knees give her fits something awful too. And Millie says Hannah hits the bed so hard at night she won't even let a fella court her. And there are a few trying, according to Millie you know." Hazel leaned closer. "Can you see any of them appreciating her calling? Hannah loves the land and the Lord. Not a one of them vying for her interest are farmers." It was ridiculous to think of Hannah Troyer matched with anyone other than a man who could appreciate the orchard as much as she did.

"Leon isn't either. He might help with milking and carpentry, but he is not made for such a life as one who toils in dirt and waits for a bounty. He is not one who carries patience."

Penny continued to try to persuade Hazel from taking on this particular match.

"I think he would prefer something in town. Perhaps working with Lewis in the shed shop. We can't dare to consider this idea."

Locals always referred to the small building factory as the shed shop.

"Maybe we should let Hannah choose one of the men already sweet on her. I heard that Milford boy likes to dabble in mischief," Hank said as if he was part of the group.

Was he a part of the group? Hazel shook her head. Matchmakers weren't men and he was certainly not part of the group. His opinion meant nothing to what the Lord had in mind. She ignored his comment.

"*Jah*, I agree with Hank. Leon is the last person that should be helping Hannah at the orchard. They will fight like cats and dogs until one of them kills the other."

Penny tried again but Hazel wasn't buying the excuses.

"If she liked them fellas, she would have courted them already. Hannah isn't one to hold her thoughts in and has a smart head on her shoulders. No, it's settled. Leon needs a few lessons in putting others first, and Hannah needs help and to learn she can't do everything alone. *Gott* did not want us alone and sometimes lessons need taught. Leon ain't dumb. He can learn and she can teach him all he needs to know, just as she taught little Gideon to stop pranking others at school. She is a good one for handling rascals." Hazel held up a hand to quiet any further objections. "There is no talking the Lord out of something He already has in the works."

"The Lord?" Hank protested with a frown.

"You know I wouldn't meddle in others' love lives, Hank." Hazel shot him a stubborn glare. "Of course, the Lord. As His child, I shall always do His bidding."

"Well then. In that case, He told me to show you some-thing today." Hank said, a hint of something impish in his smile.

"He did, huh?" Hazel wasn't quite convinced and cocked her brow.

"Pick you up at five. He really wants you to see it." Hank pushed his empty napkin and cup toward Penny and winked.

"Now, Hank Fisher, I can't be running off when I got hearts to mend and a bakery to tend to, and you can't be using the Lord for foolishness when He has work to be done too."

Hank donned his hat and went to the door, paying no mind to her at all. He opened the door and stepped out. "Five sharp, Hazel Miller. Be ready."

The door shut and Hazel was left standing in its wake. A little nervous butterfly fluttered in her stomach. How did one prepare for what they didn't know was coming?

CHAPTER TWO

Leon Milford whistled a little tune while he unhitched Marva, his black mare, from the buggy and urged her into the pasture. Winter had warmed up and birthed a perfect spring. Taking a deep breath, he filled his long-dormant lungs with a burst of a new and awakened energy. Each day posed a new challenge, a new chance, and he was never one who liked missing out on either.

Today, Leon had helped his *onkel* at the dairy. Normally, it was Leon's elder brother's duty, but Lester was sort of unreliable these days. Leon wondered just how long Lester would keep up these disappearing acts. Leon shrugged off the disappointing thought. Lester was not baptized, so what could Leon say. Freewill was granted to all and Lester knew very well the consequences of lingering behind his.

At least *Onkel* Hank made the work swift and the conversation fun. And it never hurt to be spoiled by your favorite *aenti* either. There was always plenty to feed a man's appetite. *Aenti* Emma was by far a wonderful cook.

Leon lifted the small box filled with fresh donuts and a still fully intact pie from the back of the buggy. He'd been tempted to give the pie a taste, but it would only spoil his appetite for supper. *Mamm* hated when he did that even now that he was grown. So, he only ate two donuts on the ride home. Running a sleeve along his face to hide any evidence, Leon tried not to worry over his wandering sibling.

Leon disliked secrets, but he was keeping Lester's tucked tight in his pocket. After their eldest brother had his bout with the outside world, their parents didn't need to know Lester was dating a girl that was not Amish. What was it with his brothers when there were plenty *maedels* more than happy for their attention right here in Miller's Creek? And who would have thought Lester would be fixed on *one* girl? Leon shook his head at the shock of it.

Rumspringa, or runaround years for Amish youth, was permission to test the world, not necessarily jump in head first without a care. Leon was beginning to have doubts his *bruder* would even attend baptism classes with him this fall as promised. Was it from growing up under the strict bishop of their last community that birthed such rebelliousness? Leon could hear the old bishop now, preaching his hell fire if one merely looked him in the eye. A blade of grass was never cut that Bishop Brennon didn't approve of first. Strict, that's what he was, and no one dared question a bishop, one chosen by God.

Moving to Miller's Creek was the best decision his family ever made, Leon felt. If Luke had never fallen in love with Penny Miller who knew what the future held for the Milford brothers. Now two years later, with fresh air, a new life, and abundant freedoms, Lester had gone rogue. It made absolutely no sense.

Lester smoked cigarettes, drove cars with his *Englisch* friends, and now was courting Faith. Leon met her once. Not that eye-catching and a little wobbly in Leon's opinion. Yet somehow, the woman got a finger hold on his brother and wasn't letting go.

He peeked into the barn as he strolled by. Lovis, the youngest Milford, and *daed* were feeding the hogs. *Two hundred of them*. It was a noisy exchange from the dairy farm they once had, that was certain, but Leon knew *daed* liked trying something new too. Perhaps that's where Leon got his restless yearnings.

Mamm called that restless spirit high-strung with endless energy. Leon liked to think that was more good than bad. Never settling to one thing gave a man plenty of adventure the way he saw it, keeping his interest piqued.

He glanced over the yard, lush grass painting it emerald where just last fall the ground was bare from too many basketball games and ached to see it worn again. Hopefully, Luke would give him a go at basketball this evening after the birthday supper. Levi too, if he cared to lose again Leon chuckled. Rarely could any of his five *bruders* beat him at anything. With the exception of marrying, that was. Leon was far from being dragged down that particular path.

With donuts and pie in hand, he aimed for the house. Twenty-one felt good and he and his twin anticipated all their favorites for supper tonight. *Mamm* never skipped out on spoils for birthday suppers. Hopefully, Lewis's *fraa*, Jenny, didn't bring her chicken casserole again. It apparently was her signature dish. Lewis didn't mind it, but if Leon had to eat those dry cracker pieces and crusty cheese chunks again just to be polite, he was going to hurl.

Luke's *fraa*, was a different sort altogether. Luke was smart marrying that one. Not only could Penny bake like his *mamm*, but Penny would soon add another Milford to the family. Just the thought of being an uncle lifted his spirits. Leon could stand an adventure like that. *Favorite onkel*. He liked the sounds of it already.

Suddenly, as he slipped into the house, the idea of *kinner* sparked in his mind. Leon liked *kinner* and a man could get used to coming home after a long day to a warm meal and a pretty smile awaiting him. Yeah, if Leon ever changed his mind, about marrying that was, a Penny was a good choice; quiet, meek, and keeping a man's belly full. No way would he spend a lifetime with a Jenny. No man wanted an opinionated woman who couldn't cook a simple casserole.

With another year under his belt, Leon accepted he was required to find permanent work. There was nothing he couldn't do, but Leon required something different. Not a life of routine, boring him into an uneventful existence. He needed substance to feed his hungry nature, a challenge meeting him every day. How was an Amish man ever going to find that? Until such presented itself, he would just keep helping where he was needed, and shifting through the single *maedels* of Miller's Creek. Eventually, he would find one that suited him, right? Problem was, none of them had. No stranger to working hard at something, Leon figured if she was out there, he would find her eventually.

Late afternoon light filtered into the windows, casting brilliant beams over planks floors and bare white walls. *Mamm*'s voice sounded from out back, clucking at one of the hens that followed her relentlessly for scraps. A peek out the kitchen window revealed he had been right. He chuckled at the sight, ignored the slowing growing scents from the oven, and aimed for a shower. He needed to go wash up and ready for an evening of family, food, and hopefully basketball.

After a shower, the greatest blessing his family had ever been permitted to have since their former community didn't permit indoor plumbing, Leon put on the light blue shirt *Mamm* had gifted him this morning. He stepped out into the hall and collided with Levi. His twin was wearing his shirt.

Levi's wrinkled expression said just what Leon felt. Why women insisted twins dress to mimic the other was ridiculous. It had been fun when they were *kinner*, but now it was a bit disturbing. Yeah, one of them needed to marry and get out soon or this fetish of *mamm*'s would ensure not a single *maedel* in Miller's Creek would take them seriously at all.

"We match, again," Levi ground out the words, clearly not pleased either. They looked so little alike, aside from light sandy hair and *mamm*'s blue eyes. Leon was taller like

Luke and Lewis, whereas Levi could be Luke's twin in every other way, such as build and temperament. Leon slapped him on the shoulder and laughed.

"It makes her happy, so we do it." Leon shrugged, pasting on a quirked grin. He would never break *mamm*'s heart by mentioning it even if he would rather step back into their room a fetch the green shirt he often wore to *singeons*. "But I do look better in this shade." Leon slapped Levi on the back of the head and darted off down the steps before Levi could return the jab. Levi never resisted a good chase and Leon could hear his twin's footsteps closing behind him.

Reaching the kitchen, they skidded to a stop at the sight of Irma Milford and that all too familiar wooden spoon extended in her hand.

"You two are getting too old to keep pestering one another and running through the house like untamed critters." Irma's words snapped.

She was barely five feet with light hair, a few threads of white scratched in, but adorable when riled. Still, she had no difficulty bringing mischievous boys to a halt with one stern brow and that wooden spoon. Getting her exasperated just to see her expressions explode was a duty each of her six sons took on equally. Leon had learned to outrun his *bruders* early on. Not because of his competitive nature, but he respected the fact that *mamm*'s aim with a spoon was dead on target.

"Never too old to pester my favorite *bruder*." Leon punched Levi on the shoulder and ran to cower behind *mamm*. Hopefully, it stirred him up for a wrestle before supper.

"Thought I was your favorite," the deep voice filled the kitchen, forcing everyone to attention. Lewis stepped into the house with Jenny shadowing behind, and that all too familiar glass dish. Leon's face dropped into a frown, and he growled inwardly. If Leon wasn't mistaken, *mamm* was growling inwardly too. She must not be a fan of Jenny's chicken casserole either.

"Your Lovis's favorite. He's still too young to know any better. I tell him *daed* found you on the side of the road, and that one still claims ya," Leon teased, sending Lewis chuckling. Lewis was the only one of the Milford Half Dozen, as the community called the six sons belonging to John and Irma Milford, to have dark hair and dark eyes. All the rest of them looked like *mamm*, though it was clear he was a favorite even if he did run off for over a year before Luke drug him back home to join the church.

Maybe Lester was just following his footsteps, dodging the plain life and being reckless while he could. Leon felt better considering that some just needed to see for themselves the world was a scary place outside the community before coming to their senses. *Lester would never abandon his Amish faith completely.*

Lewis kissed *mamm* on the cheek as Jenny moved in to do whatever she did in helping with supper. It was best not to give her too much eye contact unless one wanted to be pulled into long conversations about who was courting who, who bought a new buggy, or any other nonsensical gossip.

When Luke and Penny arrived, Leon went out to greet them. Luke was everyone's favorite. Leon's spirits lifted immediately to see Penny had made a few dishes herself. Now he wouldn't have to live off whatever *mamm* was stirring on the back of the stove and chicken casserole.

Leon helped his sister-in-law down from the buggy. She was much too small a woman to have a belly that huge, he thought. Then again what did he know about such matters? *Poor woman.* She looked tired, but her smile told she was as happy as a pig in mud to soon be a mother.

A couple arm wrestling matches and an hour later they all sat at the family table. Leon's frown dipped to his collar bone when Jenny sat her casserole directly in front of him. She did that on purpose, he recognized. He reached over, tempted to move the casserole elsewhere, when Lewis kicked him under the table, connecting with his shin. Leon swallowed the yelp, leaving the concoction where it sat. He sure did love his *bruder*, but there was no way he was eating that. Brotherly love had limits.

"Is Lester not joining us for a birthday supper?"

Daed aimed the question toward him. Leon paused, unsure how to respond. He hadn't laid eyes on Lester in three days. Lewis darted a look to Luke then to Levi before all gazes settled back on Leon. How he was going to respond, Leon hadn't a clue.

"Luke and I tried speaking to him, but I cannot say it did any *gut*," Lewis said in a barbed tone. Not another word was mentioned over the matter and all heads lowered for prayer. Adding Lester to his silent prayer, seemed best, though Leon suspected he wasn't the only one. Perhaps it was best Leon seek his brother out and remind him of his responsibilities. Whatever was going on couldn't be more important than family, and certainly not a woman.

After the birthday meal and four games of basketball, which proved Leon still had the upper hand over his brothers, Leon settled on the porch steps with *daed*. He needed a break and refueled on another slab of Penny's chocolate pie with that mile-high meringue that had been teasing him since Luke carried it in the house. He had managed one bite of Jenny's casserole in hopes of not receiving another shin kick but gorging himself on everything else seemed the only way to get the taste out of his mouth.

"You're getting older," *Daed* said, watching the game continue in the front yard.

"That's what *they* say," Leon said, swallowing a healthy bite of chocolate and sugar.

"What? Who says?" *Daed* lifted a puzzled brow.

"Never mind," Leon shrugged. Some of Lester's silly *Englisch* sarcasms were rubbing off. "*Danki* for the buggy," Leon offered as he glanced towards the barn. Two new courting buggies sat side by side, winking at him to enjoy the days that would soon follow. No more sharing with his brothers, Leon grinned. "I guess that set you back, buying two at one time." It had always been like that; he and Levi gifted the same presents. When finances were tight, it only made the twins feel guilty for being born the same day. "That's what happens when you have twins." Leon sat down his empty plate and patted his father's shoulder.

"It does." *Daed* popped a toothpick in his mouth, probably from eating too much chicken casserole, and began picking away. "Just wait until you have a turn at it," *Daed* jested.

John Milford was a sturdy man who often looked more serious than he really was. Truth was, Leon's *daed* had a sense of humor that rarely could be matched.

"I'm never having twins." Leon couldn't imagine buying two of everything. He ran his hand through his sweaty hair and watched Levi dunk the ball over Luke's head. His quiet twin was either improving or just getting tired of losing. The sun's descent was always spectacular on this side of Sugar Mountain. One day he would have a porch, aiming it for such a display each evening.

"Never say never. Runs in the *blut* heavy enough, yet." If that was the case, Leon was not having *kinner*. Nine sets of twins had been born in *mamm*'s family line. *Nine*. Not odds to wager his future on.

"Best to stay a bachelor then." Leon smarted off and stretched to help settle his tightly filled middle. Had he really eaten three pieces of pie already?

"Not the right way of thinking, and…" *Daed* turned his gaze on Leon, "…it's time you find work outside of here and maybe find a pretty gal like your *bruders*."

Leon had been thinking on such things himself these days, but hearing *daed* say it made it sound more like an obligation. Obligations strapped a man down and left him little room to maneuver. Leon like moving too much to be strapped down.

"I just turned twenty-one and know plenty pretty gals,"

Leon was never short on that order. The girls were always batting eyelashes and begging him to take them on buggy rides. He obliged of course, but as pretty as they were, none of them held his interest. "And Lewis can't get me on over at the building factory until next year." Leon shifted and gave his father a sidelong look. "Have you had this talk with Levi as well? You know we both had a birthday today."

"*Jah*. He is already thinking as I am. He might just find something he can be better at than you." *Daed* smirked.

Leon cocked a brow and stared down to his *daed*. There was no way his twin had an interest and Leon not know about it.

"I reckon one day he was bound to," Leon said still unsure of the topic.

"I have made some decisions," *Daed* said.

Leon swallowed, hoping whatever *daed* had on his mind currently, it wouldn't disturb his plans to keep helping his *Onkel* Hank until a job opened at the shed factory.

"Levi will work for Hank mornings and evenings and Luke during the day." *Daed* turned to face him. "It will be a fair wage for him, and you won't have to make excuses for Lester any longer."

The sour mixture of cheese and chicken rose into Leon's throat. One bite and Jenny's casserole was making him ill.

In the background, Penny's laughter clattered from the kitchen, followed by *Mamm*'s. In the front yard, Lovis and Luke fought for control of the ball while Levi cheered the youngest on from the sideline. Leon looked around, nervously adjusting the tightness in his shirt. He disliked disappointing his parents and clearly, *daed* was disappointed that he had kept secrets from him.

Leon spied Lewis strolling behind the barn with Jenny. He yanked his gaze away. No one wanted to watch that. They had been married a year and still acted like teenagers when they thought no one was looking.

"You knew about me helping with Lester's duties?" *Daed*

nodded. Leon sighed heavily.

"Lester has always been a bit restless, but I trust he will return soon. He is a *gut sohn* and I know his heart for the Lord and his family is strong. I had hoped at his age he would have settled down by now, but some take longer to become men."

Daed pinned him with a glare that almost suggested Leon fit that same category.

"So, what am I supposed to do about work if you gave all mine away to Levi?" Leon asked, ignoring the unsettling in his stomach from this terribly uncomfortable conversation.

"You have a job, full-time," *Daed* said. "Your *mamm* has a friend in need. *You* will lessen that need. It's a fair wage, free meals, and something…different."

Leon perked at the last word. *Daed* knew him all too well, and Leon could handle…different.

"Will it be carpentry or cattle? You know I don't mind either, but outdoors is better for my…" What did one call it?

"Extra pound of energy," *Daed* said with a chuckle. "*Jah.* You will be doing a bit of everything. That is why it is perfect for you. In fact, I am well pleased and think it a perfect match for you and all your many talents."

Leon liked the sound of this new job better and better by the minute.

"You will be working for the Widow Troyer, mending a lot of things neglected, and helping with the fields and orchards. You will not run out of work any time soon." *Daed* laughed again.

Air stilled and gravity enhanced threefold as the words took long to sink in. Being one who didn't succumb to natural forces so easily, Leon shoved himself from the porch and got to his feet against the resistance. *Daed* just knocked all the air out of him with that one, but he was breathing now. *Don't overreact. Don't overreact.* Of all the friends *mamm* had to have, Hannah's widowed mother just had to be one of them.

"Not the birthday I had in mind. You can have your buggy back." Leon's words strangled out. No courting buggy was worth such trouble.

"Then how will you get to work each day," *Daed* looked up at him with a twinkle of mischief in his eyes. Just like Lewis, he could be stern and amused in the same sitting.

"I cannot be working full-time, part-time, or any time with that *grossfeelich* redhead. She busted my nose." He didn't like the sound of his voice raising an octave, but it couldn't be helped.

Daed's face cracked open and spilled out into a deep roar of laughter. The sound disturbing echo traveled over the front yard before dying out. The basketball ceased bouncing and the kitchen grew eerily quiet. Was this punishment for helping Lester?

"Hannah Troyer is not one who thinks herself better than others. She's just better than you are at volleyball, and a great many other things I suspect."

The insult landed harshly. "Wanna bet? If memory serves me, I let her win. Not my best moment since it backfired." Leon's voice ebbed. He had a reputation to uphold but letting Hannah beat him, thinking it would have earned him some kindness on her part, had been misplaced. "Some *maedels* don't appreciate a gentleman when they see one." In the yard, Levi and Luke tried stifling their laugh but failed miserably. Leon shot them both a sharp glare just as he did anytime either of them thought to bring up the sore topic.

He could remember it all fresh. When their family moved to Kentucky from Michigan two years ago, Leon couldn't wait to set his eyes on the land and fresh faces. Hannah had caught his eye faster than a sparrow swallowed a gnat. She was the most beautiful, energetic, and alluring thing Leon ever had laid eyes on. He wanted nothing more than to get to know her, see if there was an interest beyond attraction between them. But that spark blew out in ten seconds flat when she busted him with a volley, not once, but three times at his first youth gathering. The woman was lethal. Leon had hoped for sweet.

"The family is in need of help. You *will* take the job and help these women if not because the Lord wills it, then to make your *mudder* content. She frets over Millie something terrible."

"That's not fair." Leon countered, sounding more childish than ever.

John Milford stood, unaffected by his son's protest. Raising six sons had made him immune to complaints. He plopped his toothpick back into his mouth.

"You are grown enough to see to your chores and Lester's. I reckon your man enough to handle one woman just fine." John pinned him with a fatherly glare.

This *was* punishment after all.

"I have helped many and would never disobey you, but I am not the man for *this* job. Levi would do just as *gut* as me." Yes, Levi could take on apple picking with the best of them the way Leon saw it.

"*Nee*, Levi has his work, now you have yours. And you'll not say another cross word about one of the Troyer women. Hannah lost a father. They have over a hundred acres of trees, bees, and berries to tend to. I suggest if you are afraid of Hannah, then you will have plenty of room to keep a distance."

Daed was only adding fuel to the fire. Leon clenched his teeth to hold back what his tongue had to say on the matter. He had never talked back to his parents before and was already pushing limits he knew better than pushing.

"I cannot do this." Leon tried one last time for mercy.

"I thought you could do anything."

Daed smirked, feeding Leon's own words back to him with a shovel. Leon should have never been so boastful. Since he had been old enough to spout the words, Leon had always insisted he could do anything.

"You have proven *gut* at carpentry and milking and even working a field. Now let us see if you can grow an apple."

Daed was not normally sarcastic, but Leon couldn't help but note, he was pretty good at it currently.

"You can put away a bit for your future while helping out another, like four women who shouldn't have to do the work of ten men."

His final word spat, John lumbered down the porch steps and joined the boys at basketball. Well, now he was just being cocky, Leon thought watching over him.

Leon plopped back down on the porch and dropped his head in his hands. He had no choice. He might have to take the job, but he didn't have to like it. And if Hannah Troyer even tempted to touch a ball in a one-mile radius of him, he would just have to hint to Jenny the Troyers were in need of food for the next month. That would teach her.

CHAPTER THREE

Hannah slipped her brown chore dress over her head and secured the pins across her chest. Then she donned her apron and bound her hair into a tidy bun. Covering her hair with her prayer covering always required more pins than her siblings had to use. More often than not, she wished for a thinner head of hair than the dreadful curly locks inherited from *daed*.

She ran through her mental morning list. She had morning milking, hogs to feed and water, and horses to tend to before the light broke over the eastern hill. Today she would have to watch over the farm stand for an hour while Addie checked her bees. Then *mamm* needed to go to the local bakery to deliver her jams. Hannah blew out a breath. She needed to plow the pumpkin fields too, all before nightfall. Her shoulders grew heavy just thinking of the full day ahead. For every chore she crossed off her list, three more awaited her, but *daed* would expect no less than her best and that is what she would give him.

Complaining did no one any good, so she didn't waste time on it. *Daed* had worked hard to build this life for all of them, and she would see it tended to. But it took a lot of work to fill his boots. And what big boots they were. Eli Troyer was a man made strong, made for hard labor, and despite running a full orchard and raising hogs, he worked outside the home too. His energy would never compare to another. If only she had inherited that trait as well, she wouldn't be so tired all the time.

She thought of her father. Hannah missed his laugh and that wide smile and deep chuckle, strong and soft all in the same timbre. No man would ever compare to him nor hold such a place in her heart. Her father had consumed all its chambers and then took it with him. Despite keeping memories buried deep, they surfaced unbidden some days. She remembered every detail of the day the building in town collapsed two years ago next week as if it was new and fresh. Even *mamm*'s cries still stung in her ears, remembering when the bishop came to tell them Eli had been one of the men who lost his life in the disaster that shook whole communities in the fall.

Then there had been her students. Many had lost a *daed* or *bruder* and all their eagerness to learn when life had delivered its hardest lesson. The blank looks on her student's faces sometimes sneaked into her dreams. She regretted not being there to help each of them continue to heal, but her family needed her. The orchard needed her.

She swallowed back those menacing emotions that memories delivered. She couldn't take one step in any direction and not find part of her father there. His passion for the orchard had spilled over her the first time he sat her on his shoulders and walked her through the trees. Three generations had worked this land and she would not let it end with her.

Taking a deep breath, she forced back the unbidden thoughts as she crossed the barnyard. A whiff of spring blossoms flowered the breeze as she hurried through the morning chores. She loved everything about the orchard, *even the bees*, she chuckled to herself. Hannah would never admit that to her sister Addie, but Addie's hives were the heart of their good fortune, gifting them plentiful trees, berries, and gardens. Even the neighbors benefitted now that the hives had grown to thirteen.

Once she scratched off the first chores of the day, Hannah entered the kitchen with a ready-for-the-day attitude and a weak pail of milk. *Mamm* was setting crisp bacon on the table as her youngest sister Ivy finished frying the last of the eggs.

"Old Nell is drying up," she said, not one for flowery good mornings. "We should speak to Hank Byler about getting another," Hannah suggested as she set the pail on the counter. She reached for the homemade soap bar to wash her hands and turned on the faucet. *Mamm* was strict about clean hands.

"Should we get rid of you when you're old and of no use anymore?" Ivy asked with a look of horror on her ivory features.

Pale as a batch of boiled eggs with hair more carrot than strawberry, like Addie's, Ivy was a sensitive sort when it came to God's creatures. If only Hannah's fourteen-year-old sister spent more time tending the animals she might think differently about feeding one that served little purpose. *No practical sense*, Hannah mentally clipped.

"Didn't say we'd get rid of her. We just need a younger one for milk." Hannah ignored the oncoming Ivy pout that was predictably present. "Nell is up in years and milking her is cruel." Hannah argued. Ivy closed her mouth on further complaints and nodded. Surely, she appreciated Hannah not wanting to send Old Nell to an early grave for a few spurts of milk. *Which is what a good farmer would do,* she reminded herself. Though few suspected her heart to be soft after life had hardened her wonderfully so, Hannah's heart was indeed made of tenderness.

"We don't have the finances for that, Hannah," *Mamm* muttered in a low breath.

Hannah finished washing her hands and plopped into her chair just as Addie lumbered into the kitchen, donning her chore apron.

"I'll figure something out," Hannah muttered. Millie's tense shoulders relaxed. It was no secret *mamm* trusted her decision making. In fact, *Mamm* had left all decisions up to Hannah now that *daed* was gone.

"*Gut mariye* sleepy head. You know if you woke before the chickens my chores would go a bit faster. And that barn stinks bad enough to make a skunk proud. You have to do your share around here, Addie." Hannah scolded her sister as she poured everyone a glass of milk.

"You had me out stacking wood past dark. I'm tired, Hannah." Addie pouted and plopped in a seat like a dropped sack of horse feed.

Addie didn't know what tired was, nor was she built for hard work, thin as she was, but Hannah appreciated anything she would give, even if it had to be prodded out of her.

"Well, I didn't ask you to bust it, now, did I?" Without a man present to help with such things, Addie didn't say another word on the matter. Of course, she didn't want a single one of Hannah's chores. A few local men had tried catching Hannah's eye from time to time, all offering to lend a hand. Her stiff shoulders said she should have taken them up on their offer but doing so would only give them the wrong impression. Hannah would much rather chop wood all day than give the wrong impression. Troyer's Orchard needed no man running it. Hannah didn't dare flirt with fanciful thoughts of opening her heart to any man. She'd not risk a man taking over the orchard her father worked so hard to build. *Not happening.*

After the silent prayer, Hannah started passing around bacon, fried eggs, and biscuits.

"I think I have an answer to part of our troubles," Millie said as she smothered jelly on a warm biscuit.

Had the deacon finally gotten to *mamm*, convincing her

to sell? His eagerness to see them sell and move into a smaller house was a bit disturbing in Hannah's thoughts.

"We ain't selling. I know Deacon Miller thinks it best, but we can't." This was one subject Hannah would never cave in to. Her sisters shook their heads. Good, they all agreed. *Mamm* wouldn't go against all three of them if they stood their ground.

Since Thomas Miller drew the lot becoming Miller's Creek's deacon, he made it his mission to voice his thoughts freely. He even dared to have poor Nelly Raber shunned for placing that stupid ad in the Budget for husbands after so many Amish men were killed. Hannah agreed it was a foolish act, but Nelly had meant well. A great many women were made widows that day, like her own *mamm*. It was an act of love that drove her to it. Thomas just had an itchy mindset.

"I would never sell, no matter what Thomas says. He is just too bold for words, that one." Millie said. "I heard he even made a scene at the bakery last week. Told poor Rose Miller she was too old to work and needed to move in with family for her final days because she didn't fetch his order fast enough." Millie huffed. "Who tells a person such a thing?"

"Thomas Miller," Hannah answered before swallowing down a mouthful of eggs. "So, what are these answers you have?"

"We need help."

That was an understatement, but Hannah didn't want help. Pride was sin, yes, but it was her orchard.

"You are working too hard, all of you are." Millie took a drink of her milk. "I spoke with Hazel last night at the quilting bee. She suggested I hire help, a young man to do the heavy lifting. Maybe fix what needs fixing around here." Millie scooted her chair back, the legs scraping the wooden floors as she went to fetch more milk for her glass. "It would be nice to have a man around. Do the hard stuff," Millie said, shaking her head.

Addie and Hannah shared glances. Hazel Miller was devious at matchmaking, but her heart was pure marshmallow cream. Hannah continued to listen, knowing full well Hazel wasn't trying to push *mamm* to remarry so soon.

"No man in all Miller's Creek can out work Hannah." Ivy teased Hannah. "If they did, she might just have to marry him." Ivy chuckled awkwardly.

Hannah wasn't that strong, just stronger than most women and all the boys she went to school with. She never was dainty like *mamm* or her siblings. Yeah, *daed* blessed her with many fine traits, muscles included.

"I think that's a great idea, *mamm*. Can he at least be handsome? One gets wonderfully tired looking at Hannah day," Addie said, bouncing in her seat. Seemed energy had found her all of a sudden.

"Hush, Addie. You and Ivy are being pests, and when there's work to be had, you're never about," Hannah said.

"I think Hazel was right. She knows about these sorts of things," Ivy said.

Hazel was a baker, not one who knew the ins and outs of owning an orchard. Hannah turned toward her youngest sibling. Why did Ivy look so flush? Hannah studied her intently until her face reddened and she had to look away. Ivy was always up to something. Hannah was certain of it. As a girl, Ivy could come up with silly ideas to get a new toy or a bigger bed. She knew just how to make their parents cave on her wants even if she had to resort to holding her breath. This was that same look.

"Well, I don't know if he's cute, but I hear many think those Half-Dozen are handsome," *Mamm* said.

The room fell deathly silent. Hannah forgot all about Ivy and the appetite she had worked up this morning as the subtle hints grew into a disturbing truth. The Half-Dozen *mamm* referred to was the silly name all the community called the six Milford brothers now living in Miller's Creek. Hannah stumbled to her feet.

"You aren't thinking to…" Hannah took a breath and held it two years. At least it felt that long. How could *mamm* suggest one of those Milford's helping? It was unthinkable. She closed her eyes, not willing to read *mamm*'s clear expression. *Think before you react. Think before you react.*

Maybe she was overreacting. Hannah did sport the habit. She would remain calm. There were six Milfords, she reminded herself. Lovis was young, Ivy's age. He could help through the summer until school started again. It was a perfect job for him. There was also Levi. Quiet like Luke, and Addie could swoon over him all day. In fact, hadn't she caught Addie staring at him from time to time during church Sundays? Penny had told her plenty about Lester being gone more than about, and Lewis and Luke were freshly wed and working full time. That ruled three brothers out fairly quick.

Hannah swallowed down the thorny thoughts parading around in her head and forced her eyes open. *Three brothers unavailable, and three capable.* She could live with those odds. Until you took the math further and Hannah realized she had a one and three chance that the wrong Milford might land at her door.

"Which one?" It was all she could muster to say.

"*Ach*, one of them. Leon I think it was," Millie said. She waved a hand as if that name held no meaning whatsoever.

Addie's sudden burst of laughter had to be tapered down behind two hands cupped over her mouth. Ivy cowered behind her plate, suddenly succumbing to silence.

Hannah simply stopped breathing. Who needed air now that the world had just collapsed? *Mamm* was hiring the most handsome one of them all. Too bad he was the rudest, most prideful, pigheaded flirt in the lot.

"Any of them, but that one. I cannot work alongside Leon Milford." Hannah said in a slow drawn-out manner.

"But I already hired him." Just then a knock sounded at the front door and sent hot coals to travel through her veins. This wasn't just some teasing joke provoked by her sisters to lighten an ordinary day. This was real and happening no matter her thoughts on the matter. Today was the second worst day of her life. Everything about this day, this season, was going to be a complete and utter failure. How could she even think to pay the bank, buy a cow, raise hogs and gardens and berries, and then harvest a full orchard with that man standing in her way?

Hazel Miller, Hannah mentally screamed the name. Hannah had half a mind to drive to the bakery herself and ask Hazel what she was thinking, putting such ideas in *mamm*'s head.

"Hannah, don't just stand there. See who has *kumm* and welcome them." Millie waved her forward and resumed eating as if they had company every day.

Hannah huffed in a most unladylike manner and stomped heavy-footed to the door. She took three slow, shallow breaths to calm herself, though they did little good. Just the very thought that Leon Milford might be standing on the other side of this door had every hair bristling.

CHAPTER FOUR

Leon slapped his hat against the side of his dark trousers as he strolled up to the front door of Millie Troyer's two-story white clapboard house. Each stone he crossed over from the driveway to the house fueled his temper. Being an obedient son was a hard chore. With heavy footfalls, he stomped onto the long porch as if attending his own funeral. He shoved his straw hat back on his head with a bit more force than needed. He was a charitable sort, especially to poor widows with *kinner* needing help. But this wasn't just any family, now, was it?

Something brushed his trouser leg, and he glanced downward to find the sorriest-looking animal to ever be created. The patchy black fur ball purred around his leg. Leon studied it, trying to determine whether to pat it or nudge it away with his boot. It looked to have all sorts of strange diseases. A scrawny cat, black as night where hair was present, and if the critter was born with a tail, it had certainly lost it along the way. Probably in the same place he lost half of that left ear. Despite concerns of rotting flesh diseases, Leon let the critter purr about. What stood on the other side of this door was far more dangerous than a rabid beast.

Fist already clenched, Leon made three loud thuds on the front door and took a self-preserving step back. It was best to be prepared for anything when one found himself at this door. He had about a one in four chance of *that one* answering the door. Normally a confident man, capable of handling an array of situations well enough, right now he didn't so much like his odds.

The door jerked open, stealing his next breath. Leon knew the Lord must have decided right now would be a good time to make him accountable for painting Tabor Lewis's horse two summers ago, because sure enough when the white door with two little glass windows opened, there stood the redhead who gave him three busted lips and a bloody nose that same year.

When their eyes collided, they both let out a sigh. Why a woman who looked like that never smiled was beyond him. Leon stiffened and gathered his wits. He was raised proper, knew how to be polite, so he forged a smile. She didn't deserve his smile, but *daed* wouldn't have it if he was rude from the start. He should at least attempt being civil.

Bold green eyes narrowed on him, her best attribute in his opinion, always making her stand out in a crowd. Leon knew the signature look. Even in the absence of a volleyball, he took another step back.

"*Ach*! I was hoping this was a joke."

She stomped her foot like a three-year-old and Leon wanted to join her. She folded her arms and glared at him. Hannah Troyer was still cute, even when she stomped her foot like that. He had managed to avoid her like the chicken pox for two good years, looking over her during Sunday church, and not giving her the time of day if she even dared attend a youth gathering, which was rare now that most of her closest friends were married. But right now, Leon was having trouble *not* looking at her. She wasn't just cute anymore. She was stunning.

Her plain brown chore dress did wonders for those green

eyes, enhancing them strangely. That wide mouth, often going, pinched tightly. Upon closer inspection, a slight hint of lavender lay under each eye, fury or weariness, he wasn't certain. He shook his head. This was Hannah and those natural soft features wouldn't work on him a second time.

Summoning his reserves, Leon met her glare and stepped forward. The disapproval he had detected in her voice snapped him out of his own infatuation. He had a job to do. *Ordered to do.*

"If it was a joke, then we have both been played equally." Despite her very harsh behavior, Leon had never said one unkind word to her. Why she had marked him an enemy from the first day he laid eyes on her, he hadn't a clue.

As they stood there in lingering silence, he recalled that snowy Thanksgiving weekend he first laid eyes on her across the volleyball net. She glanced his way, and he was momentarily stunned. She wasn't just pretty, Hannah was beautiful. Bright green eyes and dark auburn hair, too thick for one little prayer covering to hide.

In return for his best smile, she busted his lip and cheek, and before the end of the next two volleyball games, bloodied his nose. Here he let her win the game just because Leon Milford was no quitter. For his fortitude, two weeks later after his wounds had healed, the woman decided he needed another busted lip. Well, he wasn't a slow learner. She was lethal, a wolf in sheep's clothing. Unfortunately, as he stood there seeing her up close, he was having a hard time reminding himself just what she was.

"I see some things haven't changed." His eyes swept over her, keeping his tone deep and steady. "*Daed* said you needed help." He took another step forward until he could smell *kaffi*, very strong *kaffi*, and bacon. His stomach begged for attention. He was far too upset this morning to even consider eating and now regretted it.

"Not from you," she said sharply.

Unlike most of the opposite sex, Leon didn't exactly

tower over her. She nearly met him eye to eye. Why did that strike him as nice? A man could get an awful crick in the neck staring down all the time.

"I assure you I wouldn't be here otherwise." Then something else hit him, a light flowery fragrance, sweet and completely opposite of the woman wearing it. He held his breath so as not to breathe it in, distracting him, and instead focused on her *kapp*.

"*Gut*," she turned with a shudder, gripping the door handle as if contemplating giving it a good slam. "We at least have one thing in common."

That and they both could play a strong game of volleyball.

"And it seems I have no choice but to let you help." She spied the mangy cat he had forgotten all about. Probably finding him a perfect victim to share fleas with.

"Come, Tom," Hannah said scooping up the mangy critter with a tenderness that surprised him. "You, Leon Milford, can go wait by the barn. We," she affectionately nuzzled Tom who seemed an unwilling prisoner to her affections, wiggling for freedom, "are having breakfast. I will give you your orders after we have had our stomachs filled."

Before Leon could counter, the door slammed, hard. *Daed* said meals were included while he worked here. Leon growled out as he stepped back from the door that now looked like two eyes instead of windows, mocking him. Hannah was probably feeding his breakfast to Tom, the flesh-eating, disease-ridden mongrel, who was also getting more affection in one moment than Hannah had shown him in the two years he had known her.

Dark clouds that had hoovered all morning floated overhead as he marched toward the barn. He might as well unhitch Marva while he waited. It was sure to be a long day and there was no sense in both of them being uncomfortable.

"*Narrisch* woman thinks to order me about," he muttered making quick work of setting Marva out to pasture. Pushing his new buggy to the side of the barn, Leon grunted again. *Daed* had no idea what he was doing making him come here, asking him to work beside Hannah Troyer for a full season.

"Might as well let it pour and drown me now before she finishes breakfast and does it for ya. We both know it was me and not Lester who took the wheel off the deacon's buggy," Leon argued heavenward. A good confession might earn him some mercy because it was clear he had earned punishment for all his foolishness over the years.

At the time, removing the deacon's wheel right before a downpour seemed noble. Thomas Miller had the harshest tongue Leon ever met. The way he spoke to others earned him a good lesson in manners. Plenty were suspected of the foul deed against the elder, but Leon was never convicted.

"And I acted alone in that manure incident." Leon removed his hat and waited for a good washing, but none came. Instead, the clouds parted, and light showered the earth. That wasn't expected. Was this mercy? If so, Leon would take it and hope it lasted more than a day. "*Danki*," he said, looking upward. *Mamm* always said the Lord had a sense of humor and had no problem expressing it from time to time, but even He knew some days a man needed a handful of mercy.

Leaning on the barn wall, Leon peered over the landscape. The Troyer house centered everything. A typical Amish home with no shutters, two stories, and a black roof. The porch wrapped around so one could view all the happenings about. If he had a house, Leon mused, this is what it would look like, with exception of disease-ridden cats and front doors that watched you from all directions. He really didn't like those windows in the door staring and shifted his gaze.

Beyond the yard and down the drive sat a roadside stand. Little more than a tarp and a few nailed-together boards really. Many Amish farms set up stands nearby selling what they grew for extra income. Leon smirked, trying to imagine

Hannah sitting in the summer sun long enough to sell anything. She had the ability to stand still about as well as a grasshopper. Well, maybe they had two things in common, but Leon didn't dare tell her that.

The barnyard was made up of a maze of lots and gates. Not a one hung straight, and the muck was thick on the hoof. Besides Marva, three other horses munched on some sparse hay. He studied the old worn-down gelding looking to be on its last leg, but the two huge Belgium's looked healthy enough to give a four-team plow a challenge. Nothing lacking there, the two animals were in prime shape. A misshapen chicken coop with a caving roof sat near an old garden plot. He searched the sky again. Weather was clearing. Maybe he should turn the earth now in preparation for planting. Everyone knew Millie sold produce as well as apples. They would need to get the garden out right away if they expected to fill their cellar for winter.

May was planting season and here not a blade or spade had touched it. *Mamm* had lettuce and beets in the ground. A couple high pitched squeals broke the air. *Hogs*, probably inside the barn. From the smell of things, he wasn't ready to find out.

The door of the house opened. Hannah led the gaggle of women heading his way. Her arrogant strides defined her overly confident attitude. Millie sported an old gray chore dress and slight limp he had noticed before. She was near *mamm*'s age. He suspected an old injury had been recently disturbed by the rapid changing of the weather. Another reason the Troyers needed his help, *daed* had said. He swallowed down all the reasons to walk away now and settled that God always knew what He was doing even if Leon hadn't a clue.

Addie, the middle Troyer, was eighteen and probably wouldn't get much taller than her five-five stature suggested. Leon was sure his twin had a crush on that one. Levi, like Luke, kept secrets like his life depended on it, and in a house of six *bruders*, it often did.

Ivy, the youngest, nearing fifteen and the same age as Lovis, was catching up to Hannah's five-foot-seven inches fast. All that stretching gave her the look of a hitching post.

Leon still wasn't certain he was the man for this job, but as the women drew closer, he considered his father's words again. Eli Troyer, a man he never met, had left behind a lot of responsibilities and these four were now responsible for a farm and running an orchard that by first impressions alone needed immediate attention. A hundred-acre orchard, he reminded himself. They did need his help, however limited it was. Leon knew nothing about running an orchard.

Leon shoved both hands in his pockets and studied the approaching woman from under the brim of his straw hat. She was not a delicate creature, nor one who expected more from others than she was willing to do herself. He'd heard the whispers. Many thought Hannah Troyer stubborn but she was admired. Her way with *kinner* and her dedication to her family's orchard had earned her respect. Leon thought her determined, surprisingly athletic, and curvy.

He hiked a brow. Very curvy by the way the fabric of her dress strained so perfectly against her movements. He was not a man who generally ignored God's *gut* works. A beautiful sunrise, the way the wind danced over pasture grasses in autumn, or the glorious scent of rain on a summer afternoon.

Hannah held a few Godly traits herself. If only the Lord could work on her temper as much as He had the rest of her, Leon would be more appreciative.

As if sensing his thoughts, her gaze narrowed and locked on to him. Yes, determined was that look in her flashy emerald stare. He stiffened as she marched straight up to him leaving not even a foot between them. His heart climbed into his throat when she shoved two strong hands on those curvy hips. She was still utterly breathtaking, even with that defiance trying to stab him.

"Hannah!" Millie called out in a tone that could shatter

glass.

Did she fear Hannah would bust his nose again?

"It's fine *mudder*, but he will hear me out."

Leon fought the urge to chuckle. She hadn't a clue how adorable she looked, standing there all mad with no cause to be.

Why did Hannah dislike him so much? After all, he had let her win that volleyball game, and Leon had never let anyone ever win without earning it. When he offered to fetch her a hot cocoa, you would have thought she was allergic. Leon had seen her drink plenty since. She should be thanking him and not staring at him like a vacuum salesman. Well, if Leon could get past this uneasy first day, he had a whole apple season to find out, and as he looked down at her, something shifted. A churning, hankering for complete attention.

"First, just because you are the only man here does not mean you will bark any orders."

Her sharp words collided with his intake of breath. Her sun-kissed cheeks held a strawberries and cream tint of temper. She had a couple of freckles on the base of her small and perfectly straight nose.

"I figured you would do plenty of that," he said coolly. "For both of us." Her eyes flickered in surprise. Was she blushing? No chance. Flustered could easily be mistaken for blushing, he reasoned. Tempting as it may be to boss her around just for the fun of it, what did he know about apples except never to eat one with a good-sized hole in it or you're bound to find out what hollowed it out. Leon had worked on dairy farms, construction crews, even did a bit of horse breaking and shoeing, but when it came to fruit and trees, or this woman, he was a man without an oar in the middle of a lake.

"*Jah.*"

She lifted her fists from her hips and crossed both arms over a rather healthy chest. Leon quickly jerked his gaze away. *Mamm* would tan his hide for being so bold. He dared a glance upward. Still no rain. Leon could get used to all this mercy he was receiving today.

"And you will learn and work hard. There will be no time for fooling about and causing troubles."

What kind of trouble could he cause on a hundred acres of trees?

"If we can work sunup to sundown, I expect you to keep up, or at least try to do so."

Her challenging last words jerked his mind back from wandering blissfully. The left side of her plump lips curled upward in a menacing smirk. She was most definitely challenging him to keep up with her, a woman. It was laughable, but it would do no good laughing at Millie's daughter right now. *Mamm* would tan his hide for that too. Perhaps *daed* knew what he was doing, after all, sending him instead of Levi. Leon could spend an entire summer watching a pretty *maedel*, learn something new, and by the end of the season perhaps he could conquer one of them. A man needed a good challenge to fend off the mundane, did he not?

"I'll do my best to be a good student, Ms. Hannah." He folded his arms and gifted her his most signature grin that said, 'challenge accepted.' That sudden look of surprise on her face was worth surrendering the thought that this was a bad idea. The rest of her family sidled beside her, each pasting on an 'I'm sorry' expression. Leon suspected they did that often.

"I won't have some dairy farmer who puts manure in the bishop's buggy for sport killing our trees and destroying hives."

She was livid, and he hadn't even started working yet. No *maedel* had ever dared snarl at him that way. Well, his *aenti* Fran, but she didn't count.

"And all buggy wheels are off-limits too."

How did she know about that one? He managed to hold on to his blank expression. Thomas Miller hadn't a clue it was him so how could she know? Hannah jabbed her finger in his chest to look more threatening. She was clearly not finished in her rant but winced with the contact. Leon almost felt sorry for her. She should have known he wasn't made of lazy and biscuits.

"And you can forget all about that ad Nelly Raber put in the *Budget* a ways back. We all know what brought the lot of you here. We are too busy to be concerned with husbands."

No ad brought any of them here. Leon opened his mouth to set her straight, but Millie beat him to it.

"Hannah!" Millie scolded. "That is no way to speak to others. Leon, I'm so sorry. Our Hannah has just taken care of things a spell now. She is very *passionate* about the orchard."

"Passionate?" About the orchard or her dislike of him? That big 'why did she hate him' hung there and he wanted to pull it down and make her look at it. If he knew what he had done, he could apologize, and his summer might go a lot smoother.

Millie patted his arm. "We are blessed John and Irma could spare you. Your *mamm* says you help Hank every day and you helped your *bruders* build their houses. Even the Bishop had nothing but *gut* things to say about you bringing in his corn last year when he was answering the many troubles."

Leon dared a glance at Hannah who didn't seem one bit impressed by all his goodness. No one needed to know he helped the bishop harvest his fields as a silent apology for the sins he had yet to confess to.

"Rose and Hazel have asked our Ivy to come help at the bakery for a spell," Millie added then turned her attention toward Addie. "Addie tends to the vegetable stand and has her hives. Hannah has all the rest of it," Millie made a dramatic wave of her arm over the area.

Leon couldn't believe one woman was doing all of this alone.

"Then I am glad to help." He ignored the revelation that Hannah was doing all the hard labor. At least he could offer her some relief. Now he was coming to suspect such labors had a part in her natural foul mood.

"Hannah will see you know what is needed of you. We have much to do ourselves today."

With that Millie, Addie, and Ivy turned and strolled away as if it was just a regular day, leaving him with Hannah, alone.

Silently, Leon suddenly prayed for rain.

CHAPTER FIVE

Leon followed Hannah inside the barn. The stench that had only teased him earlier hit him like a throat punch, evidence Hannah and her sisters cared more about apples than cleanliness and animal health. Tom the cat was a prime example.

"I do the milking, but Addie is responsible for the barn." She winced. "*Ach*, and Gab and Samson and Old Ben need not your hand on them. They do not like strangers," she said. Suddenly, milking cows twice a day without so much as a day off didn't sound so unappealing.

"I know nothing of apple growing and berries, but I can handle three horses just fine. The old one needs some tending to." Sensing another snarky remark, Leon beat her to it. "Unless you want me to sit back and wait for you to do it." His brow lifted sharply. "I can *kumm* each day, earn a wage, and watch you do all the chores."

"Or you could just not come at all," she countered.

They both knew that would only infuriate their parents. The only thing they seemed to agree on was that they were stuck in this situation, together.

"You can clear the barn. Addie is lazy; she rather read about life than actually be part of it." Hannah rolled her eyes.

At least it wasn't only him that sparked her unpleasantness. So that wasn't a real "no" about the horses, and it seemed Addie was to blame for all the gnats swarming about. Hannah liked control more than *daed* liked fresh donuts.

"Mind you stay clear of the hives. My sister doesn't need you pestering her."

"Pestering her?" Leon titled his gaze on her. Ignoring his question, she came to another stop in the center of the barn. Three stalls lined the right, about thirty young hogs filling one to capacity.

"I don't think I need to tell you what needs done here," she said a bit smugly. "From what very little I know of you, hog pens are nothing you can muddle up."

Since the contract to many families in the area was for hogs, Leon figured anyone could manage thirty with little issue, but he didn't miss the insult she was tossing his way. The sudden thought to kiss her smacked into him. It would sure put an end to all those insults hurled his way. He quickly shook off the foolish thought. Kissing Hannah Troyer might be tempting, but a man would pay harshly for quieting her.

"I'll try not to take offense to that one."

"Ivy tends to the chickens so don't bother," Hannah continued not missing a beat.

Oh, he would bother. That coop was an accident waiting to happen. He understood assigned chores just fine, but no one looked over a need such as a falling roof and ignored it because it wasn't their responsibility.

"I can handle all this well enough." No stranger to the goings-on of a farm, Leon figured two good days would have Addie's laziness remedied, Ivy's chickens safe, and one old horse walking straighter again. "But I have one question." His restless spirit always fed him with an eagerness to learn new things and cleaning a barn long past due wasn't his idea of interesting. Hannah spun around and let out a huff.

"Already? Guess that was to be expected." She came to a halt.

"Do you have a day of rest of hurling insults? I can return then." He schooled himself to practice patience, but it was getting masterfully hard with insults heaved his way so frequently.

"Is that your question?"

She made him want to pull his hair out. "Hannah, I'm here to help, not to be your student. I know my way around a farm well enough, so show me what I don't know, perhaps with a little less vinegar," Leon didn't raise his voice, but it held a hint of authority in it. They had to establish some peace somehow. She stared at him as if contemplating her next sarcasm. He hadn't planned on a stare-down with a woman today, but he wasn't flinching even if one of the hundred swarming gnats dove straight into his eye.

After what seemed like a lifetime, she blinked and began moving through the barn pointing out things that needed to be brought to his attention.

"A few boards need replaced there and we have a manure pile around back." Hannah tried on a look that wasn't shameful by lifting her chin. "The manure spreader broke long ago, so it's past due."

Leon held up a hand.

"I can remedy that too. Shall we go see what you want tended to elsewhere?" Leon waved her on. Surely, she could smell the strong pungent odor too. He would open all the doors he could find and start with the barn before ever turning earth regardless how late the season was getting.

Next, she showed him the large parcel he would need to plow soon for pumpkins.

"I usually have it plowed by now."

Leon flinched as Hannah's words sounded more like a confession than a fact. "You?" He said too quickly. Didn't someone from the community do that for her? He hardly believed Hannah had plowed this much acreage alone since her father's passing. Then again that would explain why she could spike a ball harder than Luke. Still, something inside him twisted, trying to imagine her handling plow and team. Leon knew well the feel of leather chafed on callused hands, but women were meant to stay soft and never need to carry such burdens, for God had already seen that they had plenty enough as it was.

"I reckon you can handle it."

She sounded pained, almost hesitant to give up the chore, but her chin lifted with that common arrogance she liked to flaunt in front of him. All he thought he knew about this stubborn woman vanished with that hesitant look. He moved in a step closer, giving her his full attention as she slipped out of the barn.

"This area drains well and since the pumpkins need so much nourishment the manure pile isn't far off."

Leon gave the parcel a long look. The farm looked more than a hundred acres already without a view of the orchard over the rise of two hills.

"A perfect place to hide a body," he muttered, and to his surprise, her lips quirked a grin. He would do well not to give her any ideas. They made their way toward the back of the house.

"We sell our fruits, honey, and vegetables from summer to early winter. The *Englisch* love to come fall harvest time and buy all the apples and pumpkins we can grow. Aside from the obvious apples, honey is our best seller, and we keep Hazel's bakery shelf full when we can."

They walked to the bottom of a hill with barely a few cedars and oak.

"Beyond there is the rest of the orchard. We grow over nine hundred trees in a handful of varieties. I figure you will be busy enough until harvest so no need for you to concern yourself seeing my trees and trampling Addie's dandelions."

Leon sensed she was very protective of the orchard. He

noticed how her right hand tightly gripped her dress skirt as they walked along uneven earth. Hannah Troyer knew the meaning of bare-knuckled. Those chafed knuckles were proof she was working her fingers to the bone. Leon was tempted to reach out and take a closer look. It looked painful, the reddened scrapes. The sight tugged at his soft core.

"I noticed the berries. You must have worked hard keeping them tamed and tied up so well. *Mamm* looks forward to them every year." She didn't slow her steps at the compliment.

"*Daed* loved them. He thought they would make a great addition." Her voice lowered at the mentioning of her father, a hint of melancholy in her voice. "I love them even more than chocolate. That's what *daed* always said." She cleared her throat, obviously not meaning to speak so privately with him.

Leon floated her a gentle smile, mentally noting to add chocolate to his list of things to do here.

"Every little bit helps…financially speaking." He still couldn't wrap his head around how they had gotten by for two years relying only on themselves. He could barely deal with doing the same thing after just a handful of months.

"Addie is our bee charmer. Ivy helps with the jellies and gardening and housework and now I guess working with the local matchmakers." Hannah rolled her eyes again and let out a weary breath.

She was clearly concerned with how she was going to manage so many tasks with one less sister about.

"Well, I will be here to help lessen the load so there's that."

"Indeed," she muttered. "You will be fed your meals and pay comes on Fridays. I'm sure you can make more elsewhere and should consider looking elsewhere for it."

There it was…an out. Hannah was giving him a reason to walk away. A smart man would tip his hat now, turn on his heel, and run, not even walk, away. It was a rundown farm with more work than he could finish in one season alone if he were being honest with himself. And her, he mentally added, distracting and bruising him every minute he was about. But Leon couldn't do that now that he had seen firsthand why the Troyers needed help. Hannah clearly was over her head here.

"It is a fair wage. I think I'll give it a go." He leaned closer. "Even if Tom, the flea-ridden cat, gets my breakfast." Another sneaky grin split her lips. She had an endless supply of them.

As they strolled back around the house to where they started, Leon eyed the barn with fresh eyes. A few missing boards around the back, a flap of tin banging in the breeze, and if a rooster once centered the weather vane on the roof pitch, he had flown away long ago. A small wooden shed between the main house and barn looked ready to cave just like the chicken coop. The house clearly needed a fresh coat of paint. All things he could remedy the way he figured it.

"What are you building over there?" The concrete pad sat dormant between the barn and pumpkin field.

"That...is none of your business." She said between clenched teeth and stomped away.

Whatever was started there, it was clear she was ready to see it finished. Most likely something Eli had begun to build before he was taken from them. Another prick to the heart he felt seeing one woman trying to follow in the footsteps of her father. That was it, he settled. Her anger was mirrored in heartbreak and her stubbornness was simply the need to see that everything her father had built remained true to his works.

He took a breath and recalculated his early misgivings. Attention was sorely needed here before things fell into worse disarray. Leon wouldn't state the obvious, but he could roll up his sleeves. He would patch the barn, fix the coop, and clean up the muck. He could freshen the appearance, plow some earth, and maybe learn a thing or two about orchard growing. He could also keep a close eye on Hannah Troyer, in case she tried working herself to the grave. Watching her wouldn't be as much a hardship.

After reciting a list two arms long, Hannah left Leon to his own devices and went about her day. Avoiding him wouldn't be hard if he could manage following orders. By evening, she had all the berry canes tied securely, trees in three lots sprayed a second time considering the overly wet start to the season they were having, and a casserole cooking in the oven. No, she needed no man's help. Hannah could, and did it all just fine, she settled as she strolled into the kitchen. Opening the oven, she sneaked a peek. Ivy preferred a delicious golden-brown top. It had a bit more to go so she turned her attention to finishing the dishes Addie left behind and wondered if all middle children foolishly never finished anything they started.

She pondered the whole misguided arrangement her mother placed on her. She wouldn't argue that help was a blessing, but why him? She peered out the window as she ran a dishcloth over and around the insides of the last pot, stained by years of jam and jelly making. The warmth of the sudsy water calmed her nerves as well as any hot bath after a long day. In the backdrop of an early sunset, she caught the flicker of movement and turned her attention toward it.

Leon shimmied up the ladder like an ant on a stick and began ripping rusty metal from the chicken coop. *That wasn't on the list*, she mentally seethed. She should have known he couldn't follow simple directions. He would wear out quickly. Leon was accustomed to sharing his chores with five brothers. And, she mentally noted, if she threw plenty of labor his way, he would. A greedy smile spread over Hannah's face as the thought matured. *Mamm* said he was her to do the heavy stuff, did she not?

Content with her new idea to make Leon's employment here short-lived, Hannah continued to watch him as he tugged on another strip of metal. His reach was mildly impressive. If she had the time to tackle such a chore, she would have at least taken the screws out first, but she'd give him marks on trying. He could quite possibly hold five *kinner* and not drop a one with arms so lengthy. A damp streak of darkness ran down the center of his back as he muscled the stubborn metal into submission. In a surprisingly quick yank, powered by a strong body and too much over-confidence, the sheet of metal released its grip from the rafters. Hannah's breath hitched and the dishwater grew warmer, not colder, as she securitized his methods. Good thing she was immune to things as petty as looks and muscles. A weak woman might find those abilities admirable, the man handsome, and worthy of second looks. But not her.

"That'll be yet the cleanest pot I ever owned."

Hannah jumped at the sound of her mother's voice. She dropped the pan and let out an unbidden yelp. Embarrassment brushed her cheeks as she gathered the pot from the floor and tossed it on a towel for drying. Turning, she found mamm *and* her sisters standing in the doorway wearing those same foolish grins that had over breakfast this morning.

"It's not nice scaring a person you know," she said.

"Addie," *Mamm* said moving further into the kitchen, "*geh* call Leon for supper. A man that works hard has earned a full plate like as not."

Wunderbaar, Hannah thought on an eye roll. *Mamm* was going to feed him after all.

"I must see to something," Hannah stuttered and aimed for the kitchen door. There was no way she was sitting at the supper table with Leon Milford.

"But what of your supper?" Ivy pulled the casserole from the oven. Hannah's stomach roared in protest for her need to fill it, but she would not surrender. *Mamm* had chosen the wrong man to help, and as much as she wanted to see the look on Leon's face when he spotted the casserole, she knew some victories weren't worth the trouble.

"It cannot wait. Save me some." She tossed the words over her shoulder and hurried out the back door and in the opposite direction of the chicken coop currently being disassembled. The further she put herself from Leon Milford the better.

Leon stepped inside the Troyer kitchen as the aroma of fresh bread and warm chicken immediately engulfed him. He kicked off his boots, soiled from cleaning stalls all morning, to keep from dropping a clump on what looked to be freshly polished kitchen floors. Growing up under Irma Milford, Leon had learned a thing or two about how not to offend.

With a quick scan of the spacious room, he noted Hannah wasn't present. Was she still working in the orchard? "Chicken coop should be finished before dark. *Daed* has some wire left over from ours. I'll bring it tomorrow and expand the run after I finish mucking out the rest of the barn." Millie waved him forward.

"*Danki,* Leon. You are such a hard worker and a *gut* man for helping us."

Millie shouldn't compliment him. If she knew he had been contemplating between kissing her daughter and burying her in the manure pile all afternoon, she wouldn't think him so good.

"Sit here," Millie pulled out a chair at the head of the table. Leon hesitated to take it.

"Go on. It is proper as you are the only man among us."

It felt very improper and a lot like intruding. The head of the table belonged to Hannah's *daed*. Ivy smiled as he lowered himself cautiously into the wooden chair. Did he deserve such a place as Eli Troyer's? He thought not. *Onkel* Hank spoke often of the man. They had been friends, but

Leon never had the privileged to meet a man many called a working machine with the softest heart. As the women worked setting the table, not one eye shot him a look like he was invading some sacred place. The Amish believed when one was called home, he had served his purpose.

Leon had seen the aftereffects of many struggling when thirty-some men had been called home in the same breath.

Hannah's family all took a seat, and still, she was nowhere to be seen. Leon shifted uncomfortably in his chair. To add to his unease, Millie nodded to him to begin the silent prayer. It appeared she was not joining them for supper. Setting aside how much that troubled him, Leon's throat grew terribly thick. He had never led prayer before. Swallowing a nervous fret, he lowered his head. After a few moments of clarity for his current situation, he cleared his throat as *daed* often did to indicate the prayer was over.

"Where is Hannah?" Leon couldn't help but ask. It wasn't right for her to skip out on a meal Millie must have rushed to prepare considering she had been gone most of the day. "Does she not share her supper with her family?"

"Not today," Ivy blurted out, an exasperated look on her face as if someone had just taken the last piece of pie and she hadn't had her share yet. Addie kicked her under the table to hush her. Suddenly, it was all clear. Hannah wasn't eating because of him. Food was energy and she needed her share. From what little he had witnessed today; Hannah couldn't afford to miss any meals. As Millie lifted his plate and began filling it with something from a large white bowl, Leon made a mental note to mention such to Millie after supper. No more missing meals for her daughter or he would eat on the porch.

When Millie placed a full plate before him, Leon's stomach lurched in rebellion, souring immediately.

"Hannah made it. She thought it to be a favorite of yours," Millie said.

"Of course, she did," Leon said offering a fake smile.

Lifting his fork, he grudgingly began dissecting the chicken casserole. *How did she know?* For a woman who declared no use for him, Hannah sure knew plenty about him. He wasn't sure if that was a good thing or not. Well, if he could force himself to eat Jenny's, then he could force himself now. Taking a forkful, he bravely shoved it in his mouth as eyes watched him in curious delight.

Tender meat and creamy flavors, perfectly blended, kissed every taste bud. Leon closed his eyes, let the ingredients blend and swoon him. Hannah's chicken casserole made a man thankful to have a mouth. He chewed slowly and then swallowed. "Now that is a chicken casserole." He blurted out, helpless against it.

Giggles erupted around the table, and feeling a bit foolish, Leon laughed too. And was it his imagination or was Ivy particularly invested in his approval of the casserole. He shrugged off the thought. On his third helping, Leon was tempted to talk Millie out of the recipe. Some women clung to recipes as if they held some secret, but Leon was fairly certain he could wiggle this one out of her. Jenny could sure use it he thought as he scoffed down his plate and helped himself to a second helping.

"Where's Tom? Doesn't he live inside? I haven't seen him all day." Leon scooped up another forkful.

"Tom?" Addie chuckled as she stood to retrieve a pie from the back of the stove.

Cutting him a healthy slab and placing it before him, Leon wasn't sure he had much room for more, but he was never one to resist chocolate.

"It's Hannah's favorite," Addie muttered.

He didn't dare mention it was his too.

"That cat isn't permitted indoors unless I have need of him. Eli never stood for animals in the house," Millie said.

That confirmed that Hannah had indeed fed the beast his breakfast. *Ach*, he would certainly not be eating inside anymore.

As thick, smooth chocolate slid down his throat, Leon pondered over Hannah's reasoning for disliking him. He was likable. All the easy chatter over supper tonight proved that well enough. She hadn't been courting when they met, so that hadn't been the cause for her dislikes. In fact, Leon pondered, Hannah hadn't courted anyone in the time he had known her.

Just then the main subject of his current thoughts came in the back door. The women stood and began clearing the table, but Leon lingered, purposefully. She avoided eye contact and went straight to the sink and began running water. Was she still not going to eat?

Gathering his plate and fork, Leon carried them to the sink. Suds were collecting as her fingers toyed with them like a curious explorer checking the depths. He slipped his plates into the water and put both hands on either side of her, blocking her in. Hannah stiffened and he couldn't help but take in another breath of her as he leaned close to her ear. Apple and lavender made for an alluring aroma, setting him on edge, and he whispered. "Supper was *appeditilich*. You should share that recipe with Jenny since you're close friends." And he stepped away, leaving her to ponder over her newest attempt to rid herself of him.

Chapter Six

There was a reason Hannah seldom helped Addie with the hives. Bees sting. And nothing spurred a bad day of moods and tempers faster than having one find just enough leg to land a good one on her.

"Aggh! Addie, your bees are acting up again." Hannah said as pain shot threw her limb, suddenly wishing she had an allergy that might send her to the hospital and away from honey bees and Leon Milford. She should have never taken Penny's advice about her Leon problem. His dislike for Jenny's casserole backfired terribly. In fact, Addie said he had three helpings. Well, so much for fixing his most hated dish. She would have to think harder if she wanted to rid herself of him because food most certainly wasn't going to work.

"Well, it's not like I can make them mind. Stop stomping around and getting them upset," Addie fussed, her voice strained by the confines of her protective veil.

"Well, they get on my last nerves." Hannah snapped out her words and marched a good distance from the nearest hive.

"I think you have a man problem, not a bee one," Addie

muttered under her breath.

Tired and out of sorts, Hannah was apparently transparent too. Leon would be here every day for every week, until the end of the harvest. How could her nerves not be rattled? What had *mudder* been thinking, hiring him? Leon was overly confident to a status of cocky. He pranked and blundered his way into the community's good graces because he had a nice smile. Worse, she couldn't find a lazy bone in him. In just a few days of torturing her with his presence, he worked nonstop on the duties she'd given him, and she hadn't been light on handing them out either. Keeping him well out of her hair apparently wasn't going to last long. She sighed heavily.

Spring rains meant an extra spraying for the apple trees to avoid worms and disease, and she still had rows and rows of spraying to do. She didn't dare ask him to help her. He would probably think her weak and fragile like those *maedels* he wasted his spare hours on.

"I'm mad at both today," she said. "Can you believe he wanted to use some homemade grass killer instead of mulch on the berries and hasn't a clue how to walk from the barn to the pumpkin field without trampling at least a hundred dandelions on the way?" At the sound of actually having a bee in her bonnet, Hannah jerked off her protective head covering and watched a lone warrior fly off without a care for her. It would be best to remember not to bathe in *Mamm*'s apple blossom water the night before helping Addie with the hives. Bees loved the scent, and she was lucky she only got one sting for her idle brain. Having Leon here was simply too distracting.

She sat at the base of the old sycamore to give her leg a study. Usually, they wore *Daed*'s britches anytime they handled the bees, but *Mamm* insisted it was improper while they had Leon present. *Another reason he shouldn't be here*, she added to the long mental list she was forming. Couldn't everyone see he was making life harder, not easier? It was too hard to concentrate knowing she had to see he didn't kill everything she worked hard to keep living.

"Well, he is trying, even with all your fussing. And he asked before spraying, so he didn't almost do anything." Addie defended Leon, pumping another puff of smoke into the current hive she was inspecting meticulously. "And Ivy's chickens ain't ever been so happy."

"As long as Ivy's chickens are happy," Hannah said sarcastically, clutching a hand to her heart for dramatics.

"The barn is as clean as the kitchen floor. The horses are all wearing new shoes and both the pasture gates now hang straight." Addie reminded her.

"Anyone could do those things. Even Andy Weaver and Tabor Lewis could shoe a horse and hang a gate proper."

"He whistles while he works," Addie said with a sly grin. "*Daed* used to whistle."

Hannah shot her sister a don't-you-dare glare. Leon was nothing like *daed*.

"We need his help, Hannah. Don't go ruining it," Ivy said, appearing out of nowhere.

That only meant it was already evening and the day had gotten away from her.

"Why are *you* defending him?" Hannah narrowed her eyes. Just because Ivy had grown another three inches didn't call for her to be defiant.

"I think him kind and hardworking." Ivy shrugged. "He fixed the barn roof and helped Addie move two hives to the sheriff's farm without being afraid of getting stung." Ivy smiled, unaffected by Hannah's foul mood.

Her light green eyes danced with something mischievous. Ivy was always planning something, like saving poor sick cats or giving dead ones proper burials. Tom was just unwilling to die but Hannah wouldn't make a fuss. Tom had cleared the barn of unwanted rodents. Anything brave enough to go in there and eat a meal earned his keep in her way of thinking.

"And if he ain't fearful of the bees then you don't have to help Addie no more. You can finally take Tabor up on his offer for a date now that Leon is here."

Where had that come from? Hannah had no interest in a man who could talk the leg off a mule. And since when was Ivy interested in Hannah's love life?

"Leon isn't afraid of bees because he's too dumb to be afraid," Hannah said, hiking her dress skirts and inspecting her newest punishment. She really hated bees. Now apples, they didn't bite back. "And I don't want to spend time with Tabor so don't you be getting any thoughts in that head of yours about that. There is no time for such nonsense."

Addie moved closer, lifting her veil too as the three congregated at the fallen log.

"Leon is making things easier even if you're too stubborn to admit it. Maybe you could try being nice. You know, love your enemies and do good. Perhaps you can even muster up one of your smiles you save for a rainy day."

Hannah all but laughed out loud. Addie was just being unreasonable.

"Watering a rock won't make it soft." Hannah countered and got to her feet.

"Don't we know it," Ivy said.

"He is strong, is he not? Handsome," Addie said. "He looks so much like Levi."

Addie's voice trailed off. Always full of romantic notions and never on the task at hand.

"*Jah*. Did you see him tackle the roof?" Ivy asked, looking directly at her.

"He likes showing off. And *gut maedel*, especially one who is still in school, shouldn't be looking. You two should be ashamed, talking nonsense." Hannah fetched her protective head covering. "He's not that handsome. He is a know-it-all male who thinks he is better than a woman at everything."

"So, he's like you then, just backward." Addie continued to poke, one hand on her hip.

"Finish your chores and ready up," Hannah ordered. "The gathering starts at seven." Hannah no longer attended gatherings for the youth. Not since her best friends Lydia and Penny off and married two of the Milford half dozen. The Milfords weren't all bad, just Lester and Leon. Those two liked admirers and were so full of themselves that if one tipped over just a quarter, pride would simply spill out thick as mud.

Gatherings and *singeons* were for those looking for matches. Hannah had no such interest, but as Ivy grew and Addie blossomed, Hannah didn't dare let them wander far from sight. As eldest, it was Hannah's responsibility to see over them.

At a quarter past seven, Hannah stood alongside Addie and her friend Kay as the Reihl's backyard began filling with all the eager youths of Miller's Creek. Many stretched out their *rumspringa* time for as far as they could as she noted a few faces her age and even older. Hannah barely touched the given freedom it offered. She had secured her salvation at the age of seventeen by taking her baptism. As eldest, setting the proper example to her sisters had been expected. She could still recall the look on her father's face the day she took her baptism. It spoke volumes of how he felt about her choice. She never regretted choosing so early in life to join the church. She had never cared for worldly ventures, just a peaceful life at the orchard.

However, at seventeen, with so few men her age baptized too, courting had been out of the question. Baptized members and unbaptized members weren't permitted to court one another. It didn't bother her, those rules, for her life was the orchard.

"You want to stop for a treat first?" Kay asked the sisters, though her eyes were eagerly roaming over a gathering in the front yard. Kay's *mamm* always served the same staples of cookies, lemonade, and *kaffi*. It was no secret either that Fiona Reihl had no baking skills but loved trying any recipe put before her. Hannah preferred all her teeth, and they all ventured closer to where a few boys were tying up volleyball nets in case Fiona insisted on Hannah tasting her newest concoction.

"Hannah."

Hannah and Addie turned as Tina Raber and Mirim Stolfus strolled toward them. Just a few years younger than Hannah, Tina was small, with dark, thin hair that could be held by the security of a single pin. Her cute pudgy nose made her childlike and it was no secret she loved pink. Hannah suspected she currently sported pink toenails under her shoes. The foolish *maed* regularly kicked off a shoe in church just to be rebellious and flaunt them.

Mirim was fair-haired with dark blue eyes, and a crooked nose she broke falling off a fence when they were *kinner*. The dress she wore, a pale mint green, made her stand out among the others. There was always one who stood out in every crowd, and now that Jenny Schwartz married, Mirim was that girl. Old Order Amish didn't usually permit such colors, but for those not yet members of the church, they couldn't very well chastise it either.

"Never thought to see you here," Mirim said, looking oddly disappointed.

They weren't close friends, but that look struck Hannah as peculiar, since they had always been at least kind to one another.

"Addie wanted to come," Hannah said.

"I missed the last gathering." Addie looked about. "I see many have *kumm* this time about." Kay agreed with a nod.

"I hope *mamm* made plenty *kichlin*," Kay said worrying her lip. Hannah assured her that Fiona need not worry about her cookies no matter how many attended this evening.

"You think the Milfords will *kumm*?" Addie asked, her gaze continuing to rifle the area.

"If you are speaking of Leon and Levi, they seldom do anymore," Mirim said with a pout. "Tina only comes to spy a look at them."

Hannah ignored Mirim's open remark and took a quick scan of the turnout. Hopefully, today was regular and not one of the seldom Mirim was speaking of. It was enough she had to see Leon at the farm.

"As do you," Tina jabbed her friend with an elbow playfully. "Is that a new dress?" Tina aimed the question at Hannah.

"*Nee*," Hannah said simply. If she had a new dress, it would be for church, not a youth gathering. Last thing she wanted was attention. Few understood her love for the orchard. If she agreed on a ride home, it could lead to courting, which might lead to something more. She was married to the earth, the apple trees, the patches of dirt labored by her father and his father before him. Both Mirim's and Tina's gazes swiveled between sisters.

"You know if you two made an effort—" Tina began when Mirim jabbed her.

Hannah wasn't sure if it was payment for the earlier jab, or to stop Tina from saying something unkind. Neither were purposefully vexing, though Hannah did find their forward tongues and one-track minds a bit to stomach much of the time.

"Well, *you* both look as *schee* as a flower garden." Hannah complimented them, adding her kindest smile. It was no secret these two were here scoping out for matches. Trouble was, they had each been seen with at least a dozen different partners in the last year. But the compliment worked and both grinned widely, having their vanity fed. Hannah remembered the sweet humble friends of her childhood but now noted these weren't those playmates she had grown up with.

"Perhaps you should try harder." Tina's beady eyes trailed Hannah's blue dress with a look of distaste. "Then mayhap someone will give you a ride home without fear of getting his face bloodied." Tina twisted her skirts and amusingly sashayed off, Mirim faithfully behind her.

"They envy you, *schwester*," Addie remarked with a hint of humor in her voice.

Just then, someone cleared his throat.

"You two going to play?" Addie quickly asked, looking over Hannah's shoulder.

Turning, Hannah found Leon and Levi Milford standing directly behind them. Hannah's throat swelled and her cheeks warmed about three shades. Had they heard the conversation with Tina and Mirim?

The twins really looked nothing alike, despite their strange attempt to always wear the exact same shades on each given day. Leon stood much taller, his shoulders broader, and his grin was way too confident looking at her like that. Levi's smile was subtle, bashful, and aimed straight for her younger sister. Hannah had no qualms with that one, and hopefully, if Levi held an interest in her sister, he would make it known sooner rather than later. Leon on the other hand for all she cared could go drag some other weakminded *maedel* into his buggy seat where his reputation could remain intact.

"Depends."

Leon grinned at Addie's question, but his gaze followed the length of Hannah's dress, a simple shade of chicory blue until he met her eyes with something akin to interest, and maybe a smidgen of danger.

The man was skilled in flirtations. At least that's what she told herself when a shiver skidded over her. His gaze pinned her tighter, making her self-conscious and she resisted the urge to brush her hands down her dress.

"You playing?"

It had been two years since teaching him a lesson in being prideful, and he was most certainly due.

"*Nee*, I just came for Addie, not to participate like you," Hannah said, lacing her reply in a sting of bitterness. Of course, Leon came to show off and flirt with any girl willing to find his energy infectious. Which it most certainly was not.

"Then *jah*, Addie. Levi and I are most certainly playing," Leon said matter a factly.

He aimed for the nets without another word. Gut *riddance*. It seemed Leon wanted no more to do with her than she did him. So why did that make her feel burnt?

"Ignore him. I think you should play." Addie said as she wrung her hands anxiously watching the *bruders* walk away.

Hannah knew the habit, one Addie often displayed when she was excited, but playing volleyball would only tire her and make an early morn harder than they were already.

As the twins marched toward the net, Tina and Mirim ran up and tugged them the rest of the way. It seemed wherever a Milford went batting eyelashes followed. Hannah couldn't dispute that Irma and John made handsome sons.

Allowing curious fascination to take hold, Hannah watched a group assembled for a game. The community grapevine had been all abuzz about Lester of late. Penny all but said Luke had been worried sick his older brother was wandering off too far to be reached. He had been gone for more than a week with no word to his family. As Penny's dear friend, Hannah ought to inquire. Surely, there was no truth behind the rumors Lester was living sinfully with an *Englisch* woman in town.

Tina Raber sidled closer to Leon. She shot a look over one shoulder toward Hannah, a smirk of mocking thrown purposefully her way as she locked an arm around his and tugged him toward the net. With a sudden thought, something inside Hannah alerted. It was not her way to be proud, boastful, or competitive, but as Tina gave her a second glare across the yard, Hannah realized she was merely human and maybe enjoyed a good challenge as much as Leon. She might not be looking to win any favor with a man she disliked but wiping that smile off Tina's face would be fun.

"Just one game," Hannah said. "And if I play, then you

play too." Hannah wasn't the only Troyer who had mastered the game. *Daed* thought it important women were strong, smart, and capable. Even at volleyball.

"I was hoping you would say that," Addie said greedily, her light green eyes glistening with joy. "And I am pretty *gut*, so don't be hogging the ball,"

Addie marched ahead of her. Hannah tapped down a grin as Levi stood there, ball in hand, waiting as if knowing they would join after all.

CHAPTER SEVEN

"Glad to see your aim has softened."

Leon rubbed his left cheek as he followed Hannah to a table of cookies and drinks. Hannah poured them both a lemonade, her focus more on her sister playing a fourth game and flushing every time Levi looked her way. Where was all that energy when Hannah needed help with chores? Hannah glanced over one shoulder, surprised that neither Tina nor Mirim were anywhere in sight. They had been glued to Leon's heels all evening.

She had to admit, keeping up with Leon for three whole games was a workout. But that red spot on his cheek, matching the fading day to the west, was worth all the sore limbs she would have come morning. She handed over a glass and Leon took it. He swallowed it in one long, desperate gulp. A bead of moisture slipped down the red of his face and guilt stabbed her for hitting him. She was getting too old for such childish games.

"I always hit what I aim for, but you did fix the barn roof and Ivy says her chickens lay more eggs for being so happy," she said and grinned. He frowned and laughed uncomfortably. Both their gazes shifted to the sunset. Red and orange hues predicted a soothing night of frog song and cool air. She looked forward to a good night's sleep. Hopefully, Addie wouldn't want to stay too late.

"So, if I add fresh paint to the house, will that earn me a year of peace?"

She wished his voice didn't affect her, but it did.

"You ask for too much, Leon Milford." She jested and sipped her lemonade slower than she liked. No man liked a woman who gulped down her glass like a famished pup.

"Looks to be Levi and Addie are getting to know one another."

Hannah was thinking the same when Levi touched her sister's elbow and guided her back to another round of volleyball that was commencing.

"I know a few fellows who might not like my *bruder* right now." Leon expelled a chuckle.

"Are you jealous of your *bruder*?" Hannah studied him closely. Of course, Leon was jealous that one girl here barely noticed him. He could have his pick of any girl in Miller's Creek and Addie was certainly the prettiest one of all. Addie's hair was the perfect shade of strawberry, kissed with light blonde strands, and not a curl sending it into a tangled disaster like her own. Addie's skin bore barely a freckle or a blemish.

It was all making more sense now. Leon spent a lot of time helping Addie with the hives. No one liked getting near those temperamental bees of hers. Was it possible he set his sights on her sweet sister? Well, that was not happening.

"Jealous?" Leon pinned her with his deep blue eyes. "I wouldn't think to court Addie."

His defense insulted her more.

"And why not? She is more attractive than most you find company with and has *gut* heart," Hannah said.

"*Jah*, Addie has been blessed with fine looks and is kindhearted."

Leon crossed both arms, his grip on his empty glass

tightening. Why was he smiling at her like that? Something inside her twisted, but she fought the need to draw attention to it. Indigestion perhaps.

"You don't deserve a woman like my sister. Tina suits you just fine," Hannah said sharply, looking away.

"Tina suits none. She has a bad reputation, and I learned my lesson with her two years ago. And courting your sister is farthest from my thoughts."

What did that mean? 'Courting is farthest from my thoughts.'

"For a man who doesn't court, you sure spend your time in the company of many," she said.

"Taking a girl home and seeing if you have a thing in common is not courting," Leon said, his tone surprisingly calm after her jab.

His gaze refused to flinch, sending an uncomfortable itch over her.

"What about you? Any poor guy taking their chances and giving you a ride home tonight?"

"Are you trying to be sarcastic, or do you just enjoy ruffling my feathers?" His smile reached his eyes, and she stubbornly awaited his response.

"Just curious if you are riding home with anyone," Leon repeated but he did seem to like ruffling her.

Hannah felt he was holding back from saying more. Letting her shoulders relax, she was glad he had no interest in her *schwester*.

"I have my own buggy and Addie to see over." And if she did flirt with such an irrational idea as letting someone drive her home, it was none of his business. "Why are you even here talking to me? Don't you have someone to work your charms on?" she asked smugly.

"You find me charming?" The veneer of Leon's overconfidence was leaking again.

"Hannah, there you are."

Hannah jerked her head around as Tabor Lewis

approached. His dark blonde hair looked freshly washed, peeking out from under his hat. He had asked her repeatedly to attend tonight's gathering and she declined him each time. She always blamed the orchard and her responsibilities to her family for not coming. Tabor had a reputation, and her father would never want her courting a man known for ignoring the rules. She should tell him her sister was the reason she had attended but her mouth had run dry.

"Ivy told me where to find you. I thought you said you weren't coming." Tabor's glare shifted to Leon.

"Leon," Tabor said dryly.

Leon nodded politely as Tabor addressed him. There was no friendship between the two ever since Leon painted Tabor's horse with white paint. Hannah was one of the few who knew why. Tabor had once had an interest in Penny Lapp, her dearest friend, the same time Luke Milford had. Leon and Lewis had more than once sent Tabor a message to find another interest. It was cruel, Leon doing Tabor that way, but Tabor and Penny would have never suited, not with Penny's eyes set on Luke like they were. And Luke deserved her. Penny had endured more hardships than Hannah ever had. Too bad there weren't more Luke Milfords out there. That would almost change Hannah's thoughts on marrying.

"I couldn't let Addie come alone," Hannah strangled out. It was unsettling standing between two men with obvious dislike between them.

"Addie is of age and old enough to be responsible for herself. You told me you would not attend another gathering."

His tone was sharp, sending the hairs on the back of her neck bristling.

"Hannah is eldest and she's capable of changing her mind if she sees fit," Leon said surprisingly.

Hannah watched him dig in his heels and for a moment the two men only glared at one another.

"So is telling the truth," Tabor said quickly. "May we

speak?" He looked down at Hannah. "Alone?"

Before her mouth could offer a reply, Leon cut her off. These two were truly getting on her nerves.

"We were kind of in the middle of a conversation."

Leon glared over her head to see if his words hit their mark. Tabor's dark eyes narrowed. Hannah had no intention of listening to their quarrels.

"You're a fast talker. I assumed you were done by now and ready to move on," Tabor said.

His darkened gaze gave him a devilish façade. The Lewis brothers were known for their short tempers and long Roman noses. Tabor only stood out from the brood because of his forward honesty. Hannah liked honesty, forward or not, and that's why she chose to call him a friend. Right now, Hannah was finding him oddly intimidating.

She peered at Leon's blank expression again. Yes, this was Leon Milford. He painted horses, removed buggy wheels, and pulled off pranks like a boy with no desire to grow up. Tabor was safer to spend the next hour talking with, even rattled as he was to find her talking with Leon. No blue eyes looking inside her, no smart comments to rile her, just plain old, brown-eyed Tabor.

"*Jah.* You may have a word." She handed Leon her half-empty glass and quickly followed Tabor a short distance away.

Leave it to Tabor Lewis to spoil a perfectly good evening. Hannah had said nine words to him, and barely a one held coldness in it. When she offered him a glass of lemonade, Leon found himself pleasantly surprised. It felt like progress. A good game always lifted his mood and it seemed he wasn't alone in that. Whatever caused them to barb at one another, it felt like they had reached a truce over lemonade.

And what made her think he had an interest in Addie?

Men didn't court the sisters of… *Of what?* Leon wasn't sure what Hannah was, but suddenly not knowing stirred the thought. 'Don't you have someone else to charm?' She said that, out loud, and his heart sank in his chest when she did. There was only one girl here Leon wanted to charm, and she disliked him something terrible. *Why?* His reputation was not a false one. And now it was burning him. Hannah thought him a man of little morals but hadn't a clue Leon's morals were grounded and rooted deep. But she would, he settled, setting their empty glasses back on the table.

In the play of shadows, he watched protectively as Tabor hoovered over her. Leon would give him no warning that Hannah didn't like being thought of as meek and submissive. She most assuredly wasn't Tabor's type. She was a girl with a stubbornness that had held her family above water for two years. Hannah didn't waste time on silly things like courting and batting eyelashes. Hannah held a category all her own.

Tabor led the way, and to Leon's shock, Hannah followed. They approached Addie, stopped to talk briefly, and then aimed for the barn. Leon's lower jaw went slack as Hannah obediently followed.

"She's gonna let him take her home," he said aloud not minding who was listening. The very sight pitted Leon's guts. Tabor wasn't known to be the most honorable man in Miller's Creek, and if Hannah knew what was best for her, she would turn around and come back to the yard. She was about to make a big mistake. Leon waited and watched, trusting those good senses Hannah was born with would kick in, but when they disappeared inside the barn his feet acted first, and Leon started marching their way.

"Hey *bruder*," Levi said, halting his purpose. "So, Addie is letting me take her home and I thought…" Leon let out a ragged breath at the registering of words. This night was only getting better and better.

"So, you want me to take one buggy since Hannah just

went off with Tabor?" Leon finished his twins thought just as he often did. Right then, Tabor and Hannah rode out of the barn in a newly polished courting buggy and off into the night.

"*Jah*, and Tina is hoping you will ask to take her home. I think Mirim is too." Levi grinned sheepishly. "So, you can take your time and I will wait with Addie for you to get there and pick me up. No hurry on my account."

Leon growled inwardly. He had thought he was over his fascination. Leon was pretty sure he was until he knocked on the Troyer's front door. He had no interest in Tina or Mirim, but it was clear as mud that one redhead with a sharp tongue might have just wrecked his world or opened his eyes to it. That was left to be determined.

"I'm not taking anyone home," Leon said between gritted teeth. "See ya at the Troyer's." Leon headed for the barn to hitch an old, worn gelding that probably would kill them both before the night was over. And if he beat the Troyer sisters home, a good talk with Ivy might be in order. After all, she had told Tabor where to find her sister.

A handful of stars blinked, multiplied into a hundred. If Leon cared much for starry nights, the slow pace he was traveling with one beat-down gelding would have gone a little more pleasant. Currently, Leon was more focused on brooding. The night was filled with frog songs and a sky created for romance. Would Tabor dare take Hannah to the lake to watch stars tonight? Would she let him? He tightened his grip on the reins as he dug to understand what went through the woman's mind. Leon retraced every word that had passed between him and Hannah. He calculated and re-calculated what he could have said differently. The woman just had a habit of tongue-tying him.

It was the pranks, Leon concluded. That's what gave her such a low opinion of him. But that was two years ago. Maybe it was time Hannah Troyer got to know the real him.

CHAPTER EIGHT

Hazel greeted them as Ivy followed her mother into the bakery this morning.

"*Gut morgen,* Millie. Glad you spared Ivy again to help out an old woman."

The warm fresh scents of sweetened breads filled her lungs and her mouth watered. Ivy never dreamed of working outside of the family farm, and here she was surrounded by sweets, fresh faces, and plotting with the best matchmakers in all of Miller's Creek.

As she approached the long wooden counter over a glass display case, Ivy's mouth watered again. Fresh bread, cookies, pies, and fudge spread out like a Thanksgiving meal. She loved baking almost as much as she loved Hazel and Rose. They were funny and never scolded Ivy for her love for soft fragile creatures. Yes, teaming up with two was going to be interesting, and as long as Leon was helping Hannah, it would grow more interesting still.

"She can be helpful in a kitchen, but I warn you, keep her away from your best flowers," *Mamm* said with a rare light-hearted laugh.

Ivy had noticed lately *Mamm* was smiling more and more.

Life had certainly been tedious these past two years, but she had so missed the joyous mother she had before the accident.

"Thought they were weeds, not zinnias," Ivy muttered, ducking her head and scurrying into the kitchen to find her work apron. She never was much for growing things.

"I hear Addie is adding to her honey business," Hazel said.

Addie's hobby was doing well and adding to the extra income Ivy was making four days a week at the bakery, they were both contributing to the family finances. Hannah wasn't the only Troyer who could make an income, Ivy mused. Hannah was just the best at fretting about money. She always barked about making ends meet and did her best to work them all to death to do it. Thankfully, Hazel's plan was working like a charm. Now that Leon was there to help, Hannah would be too focused on him to care if floors were scrubbed on a Thursday morning or that laundry hung first thing Monday morning. Ivy disliked floors and laundry and *Mamm* didn't mind at all which day of the week one washed linens.

"*Jah*. Sheriff Corbin planted beans this year and thought it was a *gut* idea to add the hives to help their crops. Addie charges a small rental fee, which the sheriff was more than happy to pay."

"She is *schmaert*, that one," Hazel said.

"*Jah*," Millie said, leaning forward a nudge. "Addie likes using her head over hands any day."

The women chuckled, and Ivy simply rolled her eyes. Addie was good at getting out of chores. If she put half the time in doing them as she did getting out of them, a lot more would be done.

"Corbin has always been most kind to our communities." It was true the local sheriff had a soft spot for the Amish. Ivy recalled them sharing more than one meal at her family table after *daed* had been killed. He had earned the respect of many, paying private visits to each family and he more often shopped at the market for his goods than he did the local grocery stores.

"I do think well of him," Hazel said with a smile.

She pointed to a few pans of freshly risen dough for Ivy to go ahead and put in the oven. She needed little encouragement to know what to do. The women were good teachers compared to living with a schoolmaster under her roof, and it seemed Ivy had found something she enjoyed more than plotting with the local matchmakers. Baking brought communities together. Hazel had been right about that.

"And what of our Hannah these days?" Hazel prodded further, lifting a thin brow. "I see so little of her since she left teaching to tend to the orchard."

Millie sat primly on one of the stools at the counter where patrons often lingered for a cup of *kaffi* and sweet indulgence and let out an exasperated breath. "She won't rest," Millie said as she removed her black bonnet, setting it on the seat to her left. Under a crisp white prayer cover, *Mamm*'s hair revealed a few silvery strands.

"I fear I have leaned on her heavily since Eli left. I blame myself for her weariness. For too long, I just couldn't accept Eli was gone."

Ivy said nothing but remembered well the days of *mamm* lying in bed crying. It was true Hannah had to become both *mamm* and *daed* overnight. Ivy felt a pinprick of guilt over it all now. She could have been more helpful, accommodating, to her sister's plight. With that thought, Ivy decided she would bake her a chocolate cake, chocolate fudge frosting thick as freshly churned butter. That would surely put a smile on her sister's face.

"It takes time to accept what we wish we didn't have to shoulder, and Hannah is a dutiful *gut dochder,* but she does work too hard. Such a life can make a soul bitter," Hazel said. "That's why I suggested the help."

Ivy bit her tongue, wanting to add she had come up with

the idea to get her sisters married off, not Hazel.

It was Hazel that believed Leon was the one God thought a good fit for her sister. Hazel was old, which meant she was wise. Ivy had whispered a thousand prayers over the years and not once had she heard even a mutter. What did she know, her fourteen years not even filled in yet? As far as she was concerned Leon wasn't her choice at all. Tabor was already interested, moving things along so much faster and all.

Ivy closed the oven doors and made herself useful cleaning up the morning dishes. The way she saw it, getting two folks to like each other who clearly didn't, would be a real chore. Good thing she had help.

"Are you matchmaking or trying to give my Hannah some rest?" Millie asked, breaking Ivy out of her thoughts.

"Cannot the two things be done at once?" Hazel asked with a cunning grin.

Mamm thought on that for a moment.

"He has done much. Repaired the barn and old chicken coop, plowed fields and sowed most of the seed, and now he wants to build the building Eli started but never finished. I had to tell him we had not the funds for such," Millie said and smiled. "It is *gut* to have a man about once again. Eli would like him. He is not at all as I have heard rumored."

"Leon is a man of many talents, and we both know better than to listen to the newest gossips," Hazel's homespun humor added.

"He could have given my Eli a challenge at chore time, more so with Hannah always fussing about with him. I'm surprised he hasn't quit yet," Millie said.

"My Leon is no quitter. He would butt heads with a storm cloud if it dared spoil a sunny day."

Irma Milford appeared out of thin air, and Ivy watched as she moved up and sat next to her *mamm*. Ivy should be washing the stack of dishes piled up but decided now would be a good time to clean the cookie glass case, staying within earshot.

"He gets it from his *daed*. He too knows how to see a chore down through."

Irma floated *mamm* a tender smile while Hazel automatically poured both women a fresh cup of *kaffi*. It was habitual when Hazel wanted to chat with patrons for longer than a minute.

"He had made a difference, *jah*. We have very much liked his company too."

"When Leon was little, he thought to follow his older *bruders* at everything." Irma shook her head. "There were times that was a trial, but it serves him well now. John and I worried he would be the one to give us our most worries, aching for adventure and all things new, but I see the man he has become, and my worries are no longer."

"He is learning a lot of new things," Millie said.

That was the truth. Like not crossing Hannah when it came to simple tasks such as which bugs to kill and which to leave be.

"I don't think my eldest is the easiest…to work alongside."

"I'm glad he is there to help lighten your load. Your family has been through much. Leon knows this." Irma patted *mamm*'s hand. "Your Hannah has a lot on her shoulders, and we all know how we women can be after no rest." Irma chuckled and leaned into Millie. "My Leon has a *gut* heart, but he was also born with a thick skin thanks to five *bruders* always poking. He won't take to heart her words."

"That's wonderfully *gut* to know. I'm ashamed by how fussy she can be, but I do understand what a weary mind presses on us. I hope he understands she wasn't always this way." *Mamm* sighed.

"If he doesn't, he will," Irma said.

Mamm immediately relaxed. Ivy too felt glad to hear it. Leon had every reason to be angry, considering how Hannah spoke to him. To know he had some insight into her hurt meant a lot.

"Some need a bit longer to grieve what is lost. Hazel has told me *wunderbaar* things about your *dochder*. I was a teacher for a time before Eli caught my eye. Penny too is very fond of her."

Ivy agreed Hannah could be wonderful, it had just been a spell since seeing it. Before losing *daed*, her eldest sister was fun and full of silliness. Her laugh turned heads, as did her ability to urge a smile out of the discontent individuals. Scholars had enjoyed her so much some cried the day she gave up teaching to take over the orchard. It was her determination to not fail that wore at her personality. Why she worked so hard to impress no one made absolutely no sense at all.

"Hannah didn't have older siblings. She was born stubborn." Millie added with a laugh.

It was nice seeing *mamm* chatting and laughing with others. Irma was around *mamm*'s age, but a bit brighter with life. Maybe helping get Hannah and Leon together would do more good than she first thought. Connecting families could possibly grow friendships.

"So, they are still at each other." Hazel huffed, setting two apple streusel muffins in front of each woman. "*Gott* has His work cut out for Him, He does,"

"Why Hazel, I see you *are* matchmaking." Millie pinned her.

"Not me but the Lord. I would not meddle in such things as to know the hearts."

Hazel upheld her position. She always deflected her agenda like that, and Ivy found it amusing.

"So, I see the rumors about the Miller matchmakers are true." Irma looked over her cup. "Did you and Rose have a part in my Luke and Lewis as well?" Irma asked.

"*Gott* was smart matching them and you will soon be a *mammi* for it."

How could Irma argue that, even if Hazel hadn't answered the actual question? Ivy stifled a laugh.

"*Jah*, He and you both did well with those two. I guess He will do well here too. What do you think Millie?"

Ivy jerked to attention.

"I think we are all servants and should do our part to help the Lord in His work," Millie said, and they all laughed.

What was happening? Did that mean Irma and *mamm* would help Hazel with her newest matching? Ivy hoped so. This was an all-hands-on-deck kind of endeavor to get Hannah and Leon together. Like oil and vinegar, those two.

"Tabor brought her home from the last gathering. Can't say I saw that coming. She never seemed to like that boy and he has come and paid a visit a couple times to get her attention." Millie wrinkled her brow.

"I heard Levi took Addie home." Irma sipped on her *kaffi*.

"You have *gut sohns*. I have a feeling one of them might win one of my *dochdern* hearts." Millie winked. "Is Levi allergic to bees?" Millie prodded with open-aired interest.

"Levi is not, and he sure loves honey." Irma giggled. "In fact, I suspect he has been lending a hand of late. His britches the other day were sticky as ever."

"I wondered how she got all those supers to the honey house last week. Each one weighs as much as she does and Leon was plowing fields all day," Millie's palm slapped the counter. "You can tell him he doesn't need to be sneaky about it. He can help Addie anytime. Or should we pretend we still don't know?" Millie shot a hand to her chest.

Ivy had wondered about that herself. Being gone so many days a week she hadn't even noticed that Levi had been sneaking about and helping Addie with the honey harvest. *Yes*, she mentally fist-pumped the air. Getting both sisters out of her hair was happening sooner than she anticipated.

"We should let nature takes its course. Addie might want to keep him her secret. Courting is private after all," Irma said. "I courted John for months before I dared telling my *mamm*."

"Well now, Irma Milford, I know a thing or two about *dochdern* hiding secrets, and I assure you that your *mamm* knew," Hazel said, speaking as a mother with three daughters.

"I never had *dochdern* and look forward to it."

"I look forward to *sohns*," Millie said in a dreamy tone.

Ivy was getting weary keeping up with who they were referring to. Hannah and Leon or Addie and Levi. Either way, the display case had never been cleaner.

"Well, *freinden*, I reckon we sit back and watch the Lord do His work unless nature sends a hailstorm, then we must see His plan through," Hazel said. She leaned on the counter as laughter spilled out through the whole bakery.

CHAPTER NINE

Hannah stared at the ladder leaning into the lush apple branches. She loved harvesting the apple blossoms, letting *mamm* steep them into a fragrant scent for bath water. Today, she wanted to simply crawl back into the bed and stay there all day. Days were getting longer and sleep shorter. A body could only go on *kaffi* so far.

Reaching her arms high above her, she stretched out the weariness as a cool morning breeze kissed her ankles. Her bare toes were still damp from walking through the dew-covered grasses ready for mowing. She inhaled the air, hoping it would entice her, but fatigue wouldn't allow for it. At least she was alone, here among the trees. Bees kept a safe distance, ignoring her presence. There were no chatting sisters, no *mamm* with worried expressions, and no need to fret what bills needed to be paid this month.

Daed would have never taken out a loan at the bank if he knew he wouldn't be here to see it was paid. The orchard's full potential would never be achieved. His dreams had been lost with him on that fateful day. Dreams Hannah had too.

Hannah tried not to imagine the sight of a full harvest filling baskets and racks in the new farm store he had aimed to build. The cider press alone would have generated a healthy income. *Daed* had wanted a place for charity auctions to benefit all the community. A store they could sell their *guts* on regular days. They had plans. Tours and pick-your-own fields the *Englisch* found to enjoy. Many sought out the simple life, the charm of being Plain.

Hannah chuckled as she climbed the ladder a bit higher. There was nothing Plain or simple about being Amish. It was obeying your elders and sacrificing for your family. It was submitting to God over selfish wants, working hard even when you didn't feel like it, and repeating each day on the next.

There would be no store and no auctions because before the first stone was set, *Daed* was gone, dead with thirty-one other men. May 31st, a date burned into her mind forever. Now two years later, the farm was in her hands, and it was failing miserably. Maybe he had more faith in her than he should have. Her failure brought forth shameful tears. Good thing no one could see her cry out here.

Leon breathed in the fresh air. Rains overnight mingled with the sweet scent of flowers, and the newness of summer, his favorite season of all. Summer meant fishing, long swims, and lots of sports. He thought of Lester. If only his brother would just come home, restoring what was normal. It hardened his heart to see *mamm* worried another *sohn* was tempted to jump the fence.

He climbed the hill Millie had pointed out as the sun rose behind him. Hannah's mother had been a book of information lately and Leon felt compelled to act after hearing about Eli's intentions of building a marketplace for all the local families. It was a good idea, and many would benefit from it. Joshua Schwartz had listened to Leon's thoughts until the end. Hannah wouldn't be none too happy about that. Leon took it upon himself to do so, and as *daed* some-times rattled out, sometimes a man just had to do what was best, regardless of what others thought. So, Leon had gone on instinct, and the bishop agreed that Eli's plan to build a farmer's market that could serve the community was a great idea that should not be swept under a rug and forgotten. Now to tell Hannah and Millie the news…

Today they were to start plucking apple blossoms from the last blooming field, considering she had plucked the rest already, he learned. It was a big farm, and he did rarely see her about. He knew nothing of apple farming but plucking blooms that would only grow more fruit made about as much sense as frying your last chicken for supper and ex-pecting eggs for breakfast come the morning.

Reaching the rise, heaven suddenly presented itself and Leon stopped abruptly in its deliverance. Waves of pink and white blossoms danced at the base of the hill as the light southern breeze carried their scent his way. While Hannah had him working to fix every forgotten and broken thing about, she was here, in the clouds, soaking up God's most perfect handiwork. Hiding among groves so vast one could be swallowed up. He had never seen anything so beautiful in all his life. So perfect and yet, untamed and pulling. God's hand never ceased to amaze him.

Careful of his footing, no need sparking another argu-ment between them because he stomped on a few dandelion weeds again, Leon stepped forward into another world.

A man could certainly breathe out here. Rows and rows of trees heavy in flowers welcomed him. He strolled with no intent to hurry. Here it seemed foolish to rush surrounded by so much calm. Scanning the landscape for her, light fil-tered through tree branches, playing shadows here and there. God made some mighty fine sights for eyes to see, this being by far a new favorite.

Had Hannah's *daed* walked this same path and sensed a similar calm? Living in a house filled to the rafters with women, Leon supposed so and chuckled. Eli Troyer had not been only blessed in *kinner*, he had been blessed for having an Eden for a backyard. Did the *schwesters* play and chase one another about under the trees? Leon tried to envision it, three little girls running about aimlessly. Barefoot with giggles floating on breezes and a man filling up on seeing his hard work enjoyed.

Perhaps *kinner* wasn't such a terrible thought, Leon measured with a smile. Little versions of himself seeing life's wonders firsthand and exploring its girth. Suddenly, twins didn't seem so unappealing but more like an adventure.

When his gaze finally drew on her, Leon felt the jolt standing under the fragrant shade. The orchard filled his hungry spirit, just as he reckoned it had the man before him, but Hannah, perched on a ladder gingerly plucking flowers and dropping them into a basket, stirred his heart. He had not forgotten the first girl who took his breath away and here she was, stealing it all over again.

Light strained in, catching her in its stream, highlighting the femininity she often disguised. His smile widened. She didn't look so troublesome right now. This was her world. Even at this distance, Leon could see that well enough. Unguarded, comfortably surrounded in a dream brought to life, and the very picture of everything he longed for. She was whispering, he noted and gravitated closer.

"A little strength today, Lord. That's all I ask, and I'll do the rest." Hannah spoke as if God was standing nearby, listening.

It warmed him to see this side of her and yet broke him by the confession of weariness on her tongue. She needed rest. That was plain to see. Leon added it to his mental list. It was growing where she was concerned, he mused.

This place, this orchard, and that house of women had many needs. That was for sure and certain. Leon could handle any one of them he figured. *Daed* sending him here no longer seemed like punishment.

"I get it, Lord. Little slow, but I get it." Leon chuckled heavenward before advancing toward his target.

"Millie said I could find you here." Hannah jerked at his voice. A high-pitched yelp escaped her before losing her balance, slipping from her foot hold. Her feet slid down the ladder rungs, raking her shins in her descent. Leon advanced quickly. His first thought was to grab hold of her, but that would be too bold and certainly improper. Instead, he put both arms at her sides, and gripped the ladder, walling her in. Then he placed a foot on the second ladder rung. Hannah all but latched hold of his forearms and sat on his knee. His noble intentions to keep her from sliding all the way to the ground didn't look too proper after all.

From this view, Leon had a sidelong look as she pulled in her bottom lip to harness the pain of whatever damage her shins had suffered. This close, he could hear her racing breaths. He was feeling everything but noble as she continued to cling to his arms. Every muscle in his body pulled taut as an unfamiliar rush thrummed through his veins. She smelled of the very blossoms she plucked, and he never had been this near to her before. Hannah gathered her wits way before him and let go of his arms, signaling Leon to move.

"Are you alright?" Leon took another step back as she peered up at him. Her face flushed again with that same strawberry tint that flushed her the day he arrived at her front door. Her green eyes glistened with dampness. Leon disliked tears, but he felt certain Hannah would stubbornly hold them, especially with him near. Her freckles not only drew you in but softened that hardness she worked so hard displaying. And those lips, plump, damp, and perfect, even when she scowled like that, tempted. How was a man supposed to ignore all of that? Leon wrestled with old thoughts of busted lips to keep his thoughts secure. She didn't need to know he was still completely and utterly smitten, and how bad he wanted to kiss her.

"You scared me." Her voice shook as she looked down

at her bare feet, no doubt wishing to examine her legs for signs of blood or bruising, but she wouldn't dare right now.

"I'm sorry. I didn't mean…." He shoved both hands in his pockets, willing them to behave when they ached to reach out to her again. "I can leave or turn around." She looked up curiosity wrinkling her brow at his remark. "So, you can check for *blut*. I know you hurt them."

"I'm fine." She sniffed and lifted her shoulders. "There is work to be done."

"Alright then." He would keep a close eye on her strides. If she limped, it was back to the house for her, even if he had to carry her the whole way. "I see that field has no blooms, but small fruit on them already. This one," he looked up and around, "looks to be heavy in them." In the distance, cicadas called. Birds darted from limb to limb in the background, but Leon's gaze settled on her. Hannah straightened her *kapp*, tucking in a few stray auburn strands that were knocked loose in the jarring. Anything to shift the sudden awkwardness between them he assumed.

"Those are the Lodi trees. I pulled their flowers over a month ago. They should be ready for harvesting by late July." Leon's eyes roamed over the landscape. He wanted to know more, see more, and hear her voice telling him. He quietly measured her strides. So far, so good, he noted.

"I'd like to know more if you're up for it." If her legs were aching or burning, she showed no signs of it. He should have figured she would muster the mishap as if nothing happened.

"I reckon I can give ya quick show of it." She tried to make it sound more burden than kindness and sighed heavily as she moved further into the orchard. Leon sidled alongside her, taking in the scents of woman and nature. Just moments ago, his arms had been wrapped around her and suddenly Leon wished he could hold her hand as they strolled under the canopy of trees. If it were any other woman, Leon would have simply reached out and guided her hand into his. Not Hannah. Such boldness earned you a bloody lip. No, Leon would have to do the work, for nothing worth having came easy. *Jah*, *daed* had outwitted him for sure and for certain, Leon mused.

"We have Gala, Jonathon, and Honey Crisp." She pointed left but kept walking. "The local grocery market is our biggest buyer of those." They reached a slight rise in the earth. Leon could see the water tower in Pleasants from here.

"Do they pick them up or do you deliver them?" He was impressed with her answers. Not just doing the hard labor, but Hannah apparently did books and deals too. He knew she had smarts, but he was impressed further.

"Mr. Spencer sees them picked up. He says too many get bruised when we haul them in the wagons." Hannah said.

"The game warden?" Leon asked. He had met Lewis Spencer first hand last year when Lester talked him into tagging along to a bonfire. The gathering was an equal mixture of Amish and *Englisch* youngies, and though Leon wasn't opposed to fun, his idea of it and Lester's weren't the same.

"*Nee*, his father," Hannah said. She lifted a hand, waving it toward the east. "Back there are another hundred or so trees. Red Delicious, Stellar, Fuji, and Granny Smiths. We harvest them from September all the way up until late October if the weather allows it."

"*We?*" Leon drew to a stop and pinned her with the question. "You and your *schwestern* have harvested all of this since…" Leon bit his tongue. Hannah was already sensitive after her near fall and now Leon had to go stick his foot in his mouth and mention her father. It was a sore subject, he figured.

"*Ich bin* sorry," he quickly said.

"It's *allrecht*," she said. "I don't mind speaking of him. He was a *gut* man. Taught me all I know, and *jah*, as much as it surprises, women can do what men can. We have tended this all since he passed." Her chin darted upward.

"I'm not surprised at all." He floated her a half-hearted smile. "I for one know you can do more than most and your aim is true enough." Looking ahead and not at him, Leon noted the grin tempting at the corner of her mouth.

"He taught me to aim true at volleyball too," she said with a shallow laugh. Leon kept his pace aligned with hers. He liked this Hannah, the one who shared her world with him and not the one who just as soon vanish him from it, but there was still the matter of why she disliked him so much.

"Hannah…" Her name came on a sigh. Leon placed a hand on her arm to stop her. "Is that why you hate me so? You think I don't respect you, or that woman do plenty enough as it is?" Leon thought the opposite. The way he saw it, women did a lot. They cared for their families, their husbands, and *kinner*. They nurtured and healed and guided young hearts to follow a faith, that when it was real, secured their very souls. *Nee*, women weren't less than. They were more than, and necessary.

Leon could see the doubt infused in her tight expression.

"Hate is a sin," she said, narrowing her eyes on him.

"But…" Leon prodded. How could he make right a wrong until he knew what he had done? "You dislike me like as not. Luke thinks it's because you are too busy to like me." Leon grinned hoping to coax a grin out of her. Hannah Troyer's smile was quite the sight. "Lewis thinks you'd be a fool to friend me because I don't like losing." She wasn't smiling, which meant she didn't find him funny either.

"Your *bruders* have more sense than you. You are prideful, *jah*. Wonderfully so." Her stance was teacher worthy.

He imagined she stood like that many a time when *kinner* got out of line.

"You think yourself the best at everything."

"I know nothing of apple blossom picking," he said.

"Mirim told everyone what you said to her."

Leon arched a brow. He told Mirim Stolfus a lot of

things.

"You said women had no business doing men's work. That we were too delicate and soft and should stick to the kitchen."

She yanked from his touch and shoved both hands on her hips. Despite Hannah's determination to prove she was anything but soft and delicate, Leon knew now first hand, she was.

"*Jah*, I said as such," he said. "She latched onto my heels, following me around. I was trying to shoe horses for her *daed*." His gaze pinched angrily. "I reckon you'd rather tend to a chore without someone underfoot too. Some people can't take a hint."

"*Ach*, I would, and yet here you are." Her lips curved at the comment. "You could've told her you just didn't like her. It's all games to you, Leon Milford. You like your games far too much. It's a wonder any woman wants to court you." Hannah huffed again.

There were plenty of *maedels* that would be happy to court him, but Leon didn't think it was best to mention it.

"I tried being honest." Leon had, but Mirim was a determined sort. "Then I got stuck taking her home one night when Lester stood her up and left a *singeon* with Kaynoshia Weaver. Mirim thought I had an interest and me telling her I didn't was useless after the fourth time." Hannah's eyes widen at his words. He knew she listened to gossip and yet not once thought to ask him outright. "I think she might have a hearing problem because repeating a thing to her doesn't work."

"It matters not. *Gott* knows your prideful heart and disturbing thoughts. Let's get to work before the day outruns us."

Hannah turned on a heel and aimed back to the tree she nearly fell out of. Perhaps her quick action was the cause, he wasn't sure, but for a blink, she stumbled, and he again found himself reaching out to save her from herself. The woman needed to slow down and quit letting her temper get the best of her.

"You better watch your sweet…" He started, one hand on her upper arm until she had gathered her balance again.

"Leon Milford, don't you dare."

"Step. I was gonna to say you best watch your sweet step." He couldn't hold back a bemused grin. He was tired of arguing with her, at least for today that was. Hannah really was cute all flustered, but he was of no mind to tolerate a lecture from someone who clearly had her facts all wrong. "Wouldn't want you to stumble," he said sarcastically.

"I don't stumble," she said. "Nor do I say what I don't mean."

The blisters she could wear on a man were many and Leon was getting weary.

"And yet, your ears are bent on the rumor mill. Bishop Schwartz would think that…stumbling."

She chortled.

"We have work to do." He tossed her words back at her. "I reckon if you can't hold the insults long enough to get it done, I could tape your mouth shut. Then you will be forced to listen to me sing all day."

"*Ach*, you." She was flustered and it had a way of turning her eyes greener. "If you weren't a man…"

"This wouldn't be half as fun," he said and finished by tapping her nose. Leon had many talents. Rendering Hannah Troyer speechless was now one of them too.

Propping a ladder nearby in the tree, Leon slowly climbed the close constructed rungs, feeling like a fish out of water among Hannah's giant well-kept pond. "I can see why you love this place but explain to me why we are pulling perfectly good flowers from trees you depend on for income." This was nothing like a few hundred dairy cows and smelled a lot sweeter. He could do this, he thought, a life different from all he thought he knew.

"We don't rob them bare. Just take a few, letting the rest

get bigger and healthier. Too many apples on one tree only damages the branches, weighing them down all summer."

Leon hadn't thought about that, but it made perfect sense. He had seen enough apple and peach trees to know, too much fruit did burden branches readily enough.

"We also pull some of the fruit too. It's called thinning. I will show you that after this field is done with those already with fruit."

He looked forward to it.

CHAPTER TEN

Hazel had to admit, Hank Fisher was a man of mystery and full of surprises. She had mentioned liking boats only once, and that had been years ago at a gathering. He had been speaking to Gaven Weaver if memory served her right. She reached their table and offered to refill their glasses. Hank had a regular hankering for Lydia's lemonade and fishing. So, when he looked up at her and asked if she liked fishing in a boat, Hazel had said yes.

How had he remembered that? How long had it taken him to build it? All thoughts that filled her mind as she floated through her regular day. John had taken her once, but he seldom had time for such things as boating and fishing with a farm to run. They had once owned the largest farm in the area, and without the blessings of *sohns*, a man had more than his share to tend to. Hazel bit back the ping of remembrance. Since selling the farm and moving her and Lydia into a new home, she had long put aside memories that tested her emotions. She had been blessed many years to be loved by a *gut* man. For that, she was thankful.

Yesterday, on the lake, had been different. Hazel had never had an off Sunday so well spent, she thought as she stirred the chocolate pudding mixture over the stove. Nothing sold faster than chocolate pie, so Hazel made sure there were also at least ten ready each morning.

The vessel Hank created with his own two hands was a beautiful work of craftsmanship. He had even carved out a slight dip in the seat to make the ride more comfortable, and now Hazel knew just how comfortable it was. The day had been perfect. Mallards hugged the shores, dipping their heads in and out for a meal. A few walkers strolled about on the concrete paths that encircled the lake, but none gave a care about two old folks venturing about as summer sprang forth.

Hank had only meant to show her how well it floated, but since he had his poles and Hazel had nowhere she needed to be, she hadn't seen no wrong in testing it out. They talked about Rose, her declining years, and Hazel shared more than a few tales of her *grosskinner*. Little Gideon was still the handful of the lot, but Hank did so enjoy hearing what trouble Silas and Lydia's *sohn* found himself into lately. Hank was very interested in matchmaking too. To think all this time, she thought he was pretending.

Hazel told him all about her calling to matchmaking. A woman who had known love as she had, had no business just forgetting there were so many young folks out there just wasting their days without it. Hank was quite the matchmaker himself. Hazel would have never thought to pair up Nelly Raber with anyone in the community after she posted that silly ad. However, Hank had just the right man for her. Hank's keen eye had seen what Hazel had missed.

The good Lord had seen fit to let the sun shine with the right amount of light and warmth to keep fish biting. Hank loved fishing and surprisingly Hazel was pretty good at fishing too. He had teased they would have starved if she depended on his skills and smiled when she wiggled on her own worms without much of a fuss. He was right about her skills. She caught ten of the eleven fish they cleaned and cooked over Hank's stove that evening.

Hazel absent-mindedly smiled as the pudding thickened. She removed the pan from the stove and poured its contents into the cooling crust. Hank was a humble man, much like her John. He thought his home to be just as humble, but that wasn't true. From the tall wooden clock in the sitting room, matching the same pattern as the mantle and the end tables, to the cabinets and the table in his kitchen, everything was made with a patient hand and a gifted eye.

Her favorite pieces were the little clocks and keepsake boxes spread along a wide shelf. Gifts he had made his late *fraa* in the years they had together, she reasoned. One, in particular, stirred her curiousness and Hank was more than pleased to explain how he got a wooden arrow through the wooden apple without using glue or some confounded trickery to do it. Yesterday had been a day of firsts, Hazel measured now as she looked back on it. She got plenty of lessons on softwood and hardwood, and the skill of soaking and persuading things to bend into unnatural states. Who knew what just a bit of water could do for a dried-out heart?

"I did as you said and told Tabor were to find Hannah, but it didn't work," Ivy said with a frustrated breath. Hazel sat aside her silly daydreaming, a horrid habit meant only for *kinner,* and turned to her young help.

"Not all comes to light in an instant," Hazel said. Some things took time. Love was not something to be persuaded nor rushed.

"Maybe Leon doesn't care Tabor is interested, and Hannah sure doesn't seem to care about either of them. She just stays out in the orchard all day."

Hazel began mixing the next pie. Some things couldn't be produced in bulk. Not if you wanted the best results. Hazel considered Ivy's intel. The Lord gave her a task and she needed to be doing it instead of thinking about the fisherman down the street.

Turning, she noted Ivy whipping egg whites, sugar, and

hopefully, a smidgen of almond extract considering she forgot it in the last batch. Hazel didn't fuss, she nurtured. As long as your arm held out, meringue wasn't something easily blundered. Ivy proved herself worthy in the kitchen, and all young folks made mistakes, she reasoned.

"The Lord does not work at our pace, but His own. You have to trust His plan," Hazel said assuredly.

"I just think we should focus on Addie more. Hannah is too stubborn for marriage."

The scowl on her face told Hazel that Ivy was flustered with the lack of progress.

"Her head is in the trees or she's barking about chores." Ivy shoved two pies into the oven, the mountain of meringue needing a light toasting. She wiped her brow and sighed again.

People tended to get used to things far too quickly these days. Routines could stand a little shaking up. Hazel thought of Hank again, and the look of gratitude on his face when she presented him with the lunch she had prepared in a hurry on their way to the lake. Why the man thought she didn't intend to feed him was beyond her. She fed everyone did she not? Her cheeks warmed recalling the way his eyes softened in appreciation. It felt good to be smiled at and appreciated. That's what Hannah needed. She needed smiles and appreciation.

"Well, I'm not giving up, so what do we do next?" Ivy huffed as she dunked a mixing bowl into the dishwater. "Should I run Tabor off the next time he comes callin', or maybe I can say more nice things about Leon, even if Hannah dislikes when I do that." Her face scrunched. "Oh, I got it. I could put some of Addie's bees in Tabor's buggy. That would sure fire send him running next time he shows up. Tabor hates those worse than Hannah does." Ivy gave a little giggle.

"*Ach*, Ivy. The Lord does not smile on bad behavior. We cannot hurt one to simply tip favor one way over another.

There is only one way to do *gut*, and that is with *gut*." Ivy shook her head but didn't look fully convinced. Hazel needed to find something that would open Hannah's eyes. Something to make her need Leon. It was prideful for one to think they didn't need anyone.

"Is there anything Hannah is fearful of? Say spiders, snakes, maybe dark corners." Nothing sent the heart racing faster than fear. "Fear is a good motivator." Hazel recalled her fear of snakes and how John had taken full care to see she'd never be scared again after that first encounter with a milk snake in her father's barn. John swooped in and captured the slithering beast and years later when they married, he purchased three guineas to ensure that all slithering things stayed away unless they wanted to become some squawking fowl's supper. Did Hank fear snakes? The thought announced itself unexpectedly. Her focus today was certainly squirrely.

"Hannah isn't afraid of nothing, but she sure hates those bugs buzzing outside her window."

"Cicadas?"

"*Jah*, those. I slept right through it, but you could see at breakfast this morning, she hadn't. She was up all night fussing over them Addie said." Ivy let out a sigh. "Wait. There is one thing, but it is a secret. Not a fear; just something she can't do and won't even try."

Hazel perked. Hannah Troyer didn't strike Hazel as one who feared trying anything either. That's what made her and Leon such good matches.

"Hannah can't swim. She thinks me and Addie can't either, but we taught each other how while she wasn't minding us. She isn't afraid of wading or skipping rocks, just swimming. I don't know why." Ivy jerked up. "You think Leon can swim?"

Hazel smiled greedily, "I am certain he can. Those boys grew up near a lake up there in Michigan. Irma talks about it all the time at the quilting bees." Hazel resumed stirring as she worked out a plan. "We will have to be smart on this one. *Gott* is depending on us."

CHAPTER ELEVEN

A slow-moving May vanished into a hot and humid June. The searing summer sun bore down on Leon's bare arms as he cut the tall grasses beneath the apple trees. An endless chore, he noted, but proving Hannah wrong willed his swings with the small, motored weed eater forward. After finishing out the row, he paused to wipe the sweat from his brow.

To his left, a worn path presented itself. It was heavily traveled by first appearances. Could that be a trail leading to the creek *mamm* spoke of this morning? Leon thought it strange *mamm* mentioned that Troyer's Orchard had a rolling creek with nice swimming holes. Now he was glad she did. Desperate for relief, Leon took to the trail leading over the earth's decline. He couldn't get any wetter but cooling off would be a welcomed recharge if he was going to get these last two groves done before having to do it all over again.

The trail wasn't long. No more than a few hundred feet through birch and oak and a couple well-aged sycamores. Two blue jays darted in and out of heavily clothed limbs, looking for a free meal. A red-headed woodpecker made his way into a crooked birch, his sound barely echoing over the creek bed and buzzing of summer trying to disturb the peace he could imagine the place capable of. Cicadas welcomed him to their breeding place with a buzzing hello but didn't stop their serenade as he drew nearer. All of Miller's Creek had been ravished overnight by the winged nuisances.

Cicadas screamed, not really buzzed like bees. They came about every few years or so doing their little summer dance. Lewis said this was the seventeenth-year time for them, meaning that despite already dealing with an angry redhead who didn't appreciate his help, a million bugs screaming all summer might try to finish him off.

Ignoring the ruckus, he shucked his damp shirt and kicked off his shoes. The water beckoned him to come. He made quick work of shedding his trousers and socks. Without a care, he hurried into the deepest part of the creek. Cold water sent immediate bumps over his flesh, but he didn't dare let them send him back to the shore. Hannah and her family were away today, and a quick swim wouldn't earn him any scolding.

His body adjusted to the temperature change quickly and Leon took in a gulp, cooling his tongue. He hadn't missed Michigan and the suffocating community that surrounded them…until now. The lakes and ponds were abundant there and had served his childhood well. When he had a place of his own someday, a creek or pond perhaps would certainly be part of it. He leaned back, went weightless, and let his imagination scratch out that home he would someday have.

God could be cruel when He wanted to. Plaguing women with monthly visits of pain and discomfort proved it. Hannah rolled over in her bed and moaned. Days like this she wished she wasn't born a woman or a redhead. The inherent trait had only made this natural thing completely unbearable. She had her share of missing Sunday services, family and youth gatherings, even work thanks to good ole Mother Nature.

Pumpkin rows needed hoeing, grass needed cut, and there was still the matter of a new milk cow she needed to remedy. Old Nell was finished and purchasing milk enough just for Ivy alone was becoming costly. For such a willowy thing, she could drink her share of it.

Hannah released another moan just thinking about where she would come up with seven hundred dollars to purchase a cow. Hank Byler was fair, a bit funny at times, but not cheap even when cattle prices were at their lowest. At least Ivy was happy. Nell was thriving now that she didn't have to carry the burden of supplying the family with milk. Hannah couldn't remember the last time she felt content or thriving.

Another sharp pain shot across her middle and she gritted her teeth until it passed. There was no time for this right now or being jealous of worn-out old cows pleasuring away the day. Too much needed to be done. If *daed* were here, he would tell her to walk it off. His remedy for everything and most times it worked well enough.

Somewhere, out there, Leon was messing up something, she could almost feel it. Cutting grass and weeds was an easy enough chore, but Hannah worried that without supervision that Milford would hack into a tree or chop down a few raspberry bushes still waiting for picking. She couldn't allow for one lost cent in what the farm provided. Seven hundred dollars wasn't growing on her trees and Hank wasn't taking apples in on trade.

Dragging herself from the bed, Hannah freshened up as much as possible feeling as miserable as she was and swallowed down two ibuprofens before heading outdoors. She should check on Leon. He would think no one was home today and catching him goofing off would reveal just how committed he was to his job. *Mamm* wouldn't pay a man who didn't work, and just what they spent on his wages alone would take no time to help with purchasing a cow and increase their income. She had to find a way to get him out of her hair once and for good. It was for the better of the family, after all. Handsome men were distracting and nuisances. Hannah had no time for nuisances.

As she climbed the hill behind her home, Hannah's thoughts drifted where they always did when she took to the rise overlooking the orchard. *Daed*. It was their standing place. The very spot *Daed* always paused, taking a breath, and admiring what God and generations had created. The way his eyes lit up each time he took her out here hadn't been forgotten.

Hannah could just close her eyes and see him. He loved the orchard, as much as he loved *mamm*. Lovebirds, if ever there were lovebirds. It was the reason *Mamm* took so long in her grieving. *Mamm* would never remarry, not after being loved so strongly. To be loved so fiercely as *mamm* had made a woman never want for anything less. Hannah understood, despite never knowing such throws of intimacy herself, she too could never accept anything less.

She strolled under the Stellars, small green fruits that would soon turn a sweet yellow, and wondered what it would feel like to be loved fervently by a man. Tabor was the most persistent, still coming by at least once a week to ask her to go riding or invite her to the next gathering. If not for Leon and the uncomfortable way he made her feel, she would have never let Tabor take her home in the first place, but now that she had, she thought about it.

Tabor held some appeal. He was chivalrous, helping her in and out of the buggy. He also told her more about framing small cabins than she cared to know. Who cared to live in a small house with barely enough room to move from one room to another without bumping into something? Apparently, working for Schwartz Sheds and Cabins suited him. She couldn't imagine working for anyone, but that was just her.

Maybe *mamm* was right and she should consider her future more. It wasn't far-fetched; she wanted a family, *kinner* that would one day learn how to tend to the orchard as *Daed* had taught her. Was Tabor the kind of man she could work alongside? A man worth submitting to? Hannah would have to trust him to make the right decisions for the orchard. The very idea of handing over reins had her stomach aching all over again. The orchard was her family's livelihood and choosing a husband meant placing their futures in another's hand.

She continued walking, a hot breeze at her back. Tabor was nice looking, turned heads easy enough, but could she see herself marrying him? The thought plagued her as she reached the next line of trees. She wiped her cheek with the back of her hand. June was certainly trying to put a whole summer inside of a short thirty days.

Along the Gala trees, the grass had been freshly cut. It was hard not to be impressed by just how far Leon had gotten in just four days. Addie said she was being unreasonable and that no man she knew of worked harder and faster. Hannah disagreed. *Daed* would never be matched in that area, or in any other as far as she was concerned, but it seemed Leon did have abilities she couldn't ignore altogether. He treated everything like a race to be won. The thought made her smile.

She could no longer deny that he had made a difference, but he need not know it. Feeding his ego would only spur another quarrel between them and Hannah was too tired for quarreling today. Two complete sections of the eastern lots were cleared to a shortened shade of green. The further she walked the more she felt a pang of guilt for partly hoping she would find him shirking duties when other parts of her, the weary ones, were happy someone else was tending the never-ending chore.

Leon really could work most men weary and still challenge them to a good game of basketball. She realized she was smiling again and then smiled wider because she was smiling in the first place. Weary minds were unpredictable, she mused.

It was all that endurance that caught her off guard. Leon had it and a good helping of determination. She shook her head, clearing out any tempting thoughts. Thinking a good thought about Leon Milford was as good an idea as befriending a bunch of bees. "So what if he has amazing blue eyes," she muttered. "He is stubborn and pigheaded." Leon was also amusing, or at least he thought he was, always trying to drive a laugh out of someone.

"He filled a buggy with manure," she informed the menacing bugs and the bees, and whatever else scurried about. "Just because he is strong and capable, doesn't mean he cares about what really matters." Hannah suspected he had a temper too. He had been rough when ripping and tearing away old metal and rotten boards, but it couldn't be ignored. Those arms of his could be gentle too. She wiped her forehead with her sleeve. Maybe walking this far was a bad idea. Leon seemed to know what he was doing.

When a low roar caught her attention again, she gazed about. *Cicadas.* Their constant racket had kept her up all night and now they were adding to her already achy head. Whatever caused a few cicadas to suddenly turn into thousands this summer, Hannah wished she could find it and give it a good talking to.

Sounds of splashing caught her ears. Curiosity courted her, and with little prodding, she followed the path leading to the creek. She and her sisters often cooled off on hazy summer days in the private watery vein that ran borderline of Troyer land. It was fairly secluded. No one ever dared catch them hiking their hems to the knees and wading in the cool spring-fed waters. The water was shallow, nothing like the lake everyone else frequented in summer, keeping their secret safe. No one needed to know they swam as good as any rock.

Through the tangle of trees, she followed the well-worn path. Deep paths of hoof and paw prints embedding the earth. The song of running water would've been calming if not for those pesky insects getting louder by the second. Another splash, followed by more buzzing. Perhaps an otter had strayed from the river, or deer were frolicking about. She hadn't a clue and curiously drove closer.

Stepping into the small clearing her gaze immediately noted a light brown shirt hanging on a tree limb. Panic filled her when she further spotted a pair of britches and suspenders on a neighboring branch, void of flesh and bone and swaying in the warm breeze. Frozen, her stomach twisted some foreign pocket of air that started rising up her throat. On the ground, a pair of black boots, dark socks half-tucked inside. Another splash and Hannah's gaze rifled upward, landing squarely on a set of long legs and bare feet sticking out of the water. The latest rains had refilled the creek, but even at its fullest, it was barely chest high.

Temporarily stunned and helpless, she watched the toes wiggle and then disappear. As if reprimand was required, Mother Nature chose right then to stab her for her curiousness. She tightened a fist against her mid-section, where pain radiated harshly.

Hannah sucked in a sharp breath when a head suddenly emerged out of the water. His careless sandy hair, the color of autumn fields, was lighter now that the sun had seen more than its share of it recently. Like that fountain in the town square, Leon spewed water out of his mouth and whipped his head like a dog drying off. His locks pounced back into the loose curls that often clung to him after a long day. He hadn't seen her, but she failed miserably at keeping silent even with all the cicadas screaming about. A surprised gasp escaped her.

Leon didn't even flinch when his eyes landed on hers. That cool calm way he had about him was utterly unnerving. He just studied her, closely, and she closed her mouth so not to look more a fool than she had already. A slow smile, starting with those breathtaking blue eyes, presented itself before reaching his lips, quirking readily. Adding salt to her already wounded state, he stood. Nothing in all her life had prepared Hannah for that. He was real; nothing exaggerated in his well-sculpted, broad chest. She suspected he could carry three apple crates full at one time with sturdy arms like that, spanning far enough to hug a tree and ending with strong hands she had noticed on an occasion or two. His body whittled down in ripples to a smaller, but no less healthy, set of hips barely covered in loose-fitting shorts.

The ringing in Hannah's ears grew louder than the insects had insulted already. Lightheaded, and contemplating sitting down, resting while she admired what God created, she fought for reasoning. It wasn't proper for her to be here with him, like this, and alone. She should run, but her two dependable feet weren't so dependable right now. Instead, they kissed the blistering summer stones aligning the creek bed and refused to budge.

"Wanna *kumm* in?"

He grinned, that same recklessness she saw in his eyes the first time they met, part exciting, part terrifying. The very thought of joining him made her palms sweat.

"I… I saw the britches hanging…and shoes. I heard…" she was rambling, tongue tied tight against any rational words that better served the moment. For someone who never ran out of words, she sure couldn't grapple enough for a complete sentence right now.

"I didn't want to get them wet," he said in a voice he had no right using.

Not at a time like this. She wiped one hand down her dress and fiddled nervously with her *kapp* strings with her other. Those blue eyes were studying her so closely one might think he had a test on it later. Hannah hated feeling intimidated and worse, vulnerable. Sensing her discomfort Leon lowered his gaze and glided his wide hands over the water, causing small waves that looked much like how her insides were feeling right now. Churning and swishing.

"I have little time for fooling off." She went on the defensive. It was never a good idea to let your guard down around Leon. Crossing her arms to protect herself, she squared her shoulders.

"It's hot." His tone was sharper than a few pesky bugs.

Absent-mindedly, she wrapped a fist around one finger, the single digit she had jabbed in his chest over a month ago still ached, but it was a distraction to keep her from simply standing there and admiring him like a picture book.

"Why do you dislike me, Hannah Troyer?"

It was a fair question, but completely unexpected and his timing needed help. She didn't answer.

"Your family appreciates my help, yet you look at me like a wasp on your shoulder. Why?"

What could she say? She had hated him for two years and suddenly as she stood frozen to the banks staring at his half-naked body and tempered face, she couldn't remember why.

"Hannah." He shook his head in reprimand.

So, he doesn't like raising his voice to women. "I'm sorry." Rising out of the water again, Leon took a few steps toward her. She would walk away now, but then she would miss what he had to say. *Mamm* would insist on walking away while another is talking, rude.

"I don't dislike you." She admitted it carelessly, but it was truth. She wanted to hate him. To hate men like him who thought themselves stronger, better, and put women in a dainty box. Did they not see women bear *kinner* and hard work in their own *mamms*? She didn't like how he made her feel unsure when she had heard him plain enough that first day. Leon claimed he could court any maedel he wanted, boasting to his *bruders*. Little did he know his words were heard by others who found it not so funny.

"Then join me." He offered a hand and a genuine smile. Both felt like a truce. Her eyes went from his offered hand back to his eyes. She couldn't let those eyes, that handsome smile, affect her. She took a step back.

"You know I won't," she said. He must be suffering from sunstroke. Hannah had read plenty about it when she was still a teacher.

"It's just water," he said, looking about him and coming up with a grin. "Just step in a little. It's like a hundred degrees out here. Might cool you off."

He quirked a grin. He probably used that grin on every woman to get what he wanted but it wasn't going to work on her.

"My temper isn't the issue, and you know it. It's not proper, and unlike those you often give your attention to, I don't risk breaking rules for spontaneous adventures." There, that would put him in his place, she reasoned.

"Your temper is always an issue and spontaneous or not, I was only offering you a respite."

Something in the way he said that, weakened her knees.

"I cannot."

He lowered his hand, and his shoulders went heavy.

"Because of Tabor?"

He almost sounded wounded. She could use Tabor to keep Leon a good distance for the rest of the summer. But it would be a lie. Two buggy rides weren't courting, and she wouldn't lie. Disappointment marred Leon's handsome features. Had no woman ever said no to him before?

"*Nee*. I don't swim." She regretted her honesty, revealing her secret the second she said it, but words out couldn't be shoved back in, now, could they? It was one truth or the other she had to give and didn't dare mention her womanly time did not allow her to tempt such a reckless idea as swimming with a half-naked man who was clearly awakening her rusty-latched heart. The ibuprofen hadn't done its job and a sharp pain fleeted across her middle again. She closed her eyes and hugged her center, causing her head to spin. To her surprise, Leon cleared his throat.

"I know you're the teacher but let me teach you."

Her eyes burst open in surprise. Was he serious? Maybe she was hallucinating. The loss of blood was taking its toll. Why would he dare waste time teaching her anything?

"It's not deep enough to fail, and just the right amount to learn," he said convincingly. "I can't imagine you not swimming. You do everything else."

If he was trying to compliment, it simply fell into insult.

"My sisters would like that; none of us swim. *Daed* was afraid of water and never taught us." She was telling him too much and yet Leon still didn't laugh. Not even a grin tugged that left corner of his mouth as it so often did. How long could she stand here before she needed to sit down?

"Our *mamm* cannot swim either. She nearly stopped breathing all the times us *bruders* went to the lake where we grew up." His head tilted, showing him in a different light. Leon's eyes twinkled, mentioning his mother. Did he even know he did that?

"But even she said learning to do things that scare us helps us face life without fear. I can have you swimming by summer's end if you will let me. You are teaching me about apple farming after all," he said.

Maybe it was the heat, maybe something warmer, but either way his offer was dangerous. Hannah stepped back to retreat and stumbled into the dark.

CHAPTER TWELVE

"Hannah, its *mudder*. Wake *mei liebling*."

Hannah stirred from the dream. Why was she dreaming of Leon, bare-chested? She winced as she felt a warm hand touch her shoulder. Opening her eyes, she met her mother's staring back at her. Surely, she hadn't slept the whole afternoon. She sat up into a sitting position and rubbed her eyes. Good thing mothers couldn't read dreams as easily as they did mischief.

"I must have been weaker than I thought. Have I slept all day?" Her head was pounding nails and she reached up to where her *kapp* normally sat and touched her head. The raw sensation stung. She winced again. "Ouch."

"It's okay now dear. You hit your head, but Martha promises you will be fine. It's just a bump."

Mamm assured her as if that cleared all questions in her aching head.

She eyed her room, searching for the culprit of her headache. *Martha?* "Did you say Martha was here?"

Mudder nodded her head. "You had a spell, like before. Just get some rest," *Mamm* said.

The pounding was messing with her brain. Confused she

touched her head again, trying to recall.

"A spell?"

"You fainted dear. This is what happens when you skip suppers," Mamm said in a motherly tone. "Leon found you and carried you to the house and fetched the midwife nurse. I'm glad he thought of Martha before fetching me. It could have been worse. I would not have known what to do for a head injury." Tenderness glinted in *mamm*'s eyes as she brushed Hannah's cheek affectionately.

"Found me!" It wasn't a dream. Horrification sank its teeth in. *Not a dream.* Hannah had been at the creek staring at a half-naked, soaking wet Leon Milford. *Mudder* fussed over the covers, smoothing them out. Her lips pursed into a fine line.

"I admit it troubles my thoughts to know our Leon carried you to the right room." Millie swallowed hard "Come yet, we are grateful for his help, once again. *Gott* seen you were cared for in my absence." Millie stood and brushed her hands down her apron front.

"Let me fetch you something to eat and you will be right as rain. Martha wants you to start taking your iron again and you know how it troubles your stomach when you don't eat."

Before Hannah could say a word, *mudder* slipped from the room.

Hannah gave her head a mental slap. What was more disturbing than having your mother think Leon knew what bed was yours? *Finding out he carried you from the creek to the house.* He looked strong, but she was no dainty. She dropped her face in her hands, utterly mortified.

For days, Hannah managed to elude the orchard's hired man. Today that would be impossible. Harvesting the Lodi trees, all ninety-two of them, would require any help she could get to meet her quota for the local market. Anything beyond the agreed numbers would be sold at the roadside stand to passersby or made into applesauce for purchasing. Ivy was helping the Millers at the bakery again today and Addie was working the roadside stand at the end of the drive. Hannah suspected Addie wasn't alone either. Levi Milford was not so subtle parking his buggy under a grove of walnuts. Did he really think no one would notice since he had the only white buggy horse in the area?

It would be just her and Leon harvesting. Swallowing back her impending embarrassment for fainting, Hannah marched toward the eastern orchard. "Maybe he didn't notice the root of my troubles," she muttered. She could blame the heat for fainting. Yep, that's what she would do.

Two ladders were already leaned into thick fruited limbs where Leon was surprisingly already filling baskets and placing them in the wagon. It bruised her to think he had beaten her to work. The man really had no stop button.

"You look to be feeling better." He greeted her; his focus buried in picking apples.

She didn't smile. Smiling was not a good idea.

"I bounce back fairly quickly," she said.

"So, the old adage, an apple a day...must be true." He winked.

Hannah collected a basket and ignored his flirtations. She owed him a thank you and it nearly took all she could muster to offer one.

"I reckon I owe you, so *danki* for saying you found me." It didn't sting as bad as she expected, thanking Leon Milford, that was. Her mother hadn't asked for further details on how Leon came to find her, and Hannah wasn't offering any, but the truth of it was Leon had helped her.

"Couldn't have your sweet *mamm* thinking you were watching half-dressed men as a hobby. It might give her a heart attack."

"You're impossible." She groaned and pulled an empty

basket from the wagon and got to work. Leon climbed the ladder opposite her as Hannah leaned into her own propped securely to the same tree. She tested its sturdiness just in case but found it sound.

"*Mamm* fretted over you knowing which room was mine," she said after a long silence wafted between them. Truth was, Hannah too wanted to know.

"Only bed unmade. I figured since you were home and not feeling well, it had to be the one."

That made sense. He was so calm. Why was he always so calm? Setting her unease aside, Hannah continued filling her basket and perched it on the ladder rung in front of her. She loved the smell of ripe apples as much as she loved the spring blooms.

Hannah looked forward to all the tried-and-true recipes her family would make again this year. Pie, applesauce, apple butter, and fry pies. And one couldn't forget *mamm*'s vinegar. Crocks filled the cellar floors as it worked its magic. *Daed* claimed that a few teaspoons a day was the reason for all his family's healthy success. Rarely did a Troyer fall ill to even a summer cold and all lived to ripe old ages. Her sinuses pricked her. *All but daed*, her heart spoke.

If not for the disaster, he would have been on that ladder across from her, and not Leon. She glanced through the foliage and limbs. Leon looked to be in his own world, jaw clenched and brows furrowed as they were. She wondered what troubled his thoughts currently. Was he thinking of his brother, or perhaps some *maedel* awaiting him to steal by her bedroom window and beg her to sneak out for a ride under the stars? She shook the care aside. Whatever had him so deep in thought was none of her concern. She scurried down the ladder, emptied her basket in the wagon below, and climbed up the ladder again.

As the breeze flirted with day, they both worked, minds stuck in their own worlds. She loved this time out here where a person could think uninterrupted and was surprised

Leon seemed to feel the same.

She would always be grateful for this life her *daed* had given her. She cherished the simple life and all the wonder of ordinary days over the temptations elsewhere. She was born here, and in her heart, knew she would die here. Problem was, what did she do about that pesky middle?

Would Tabor ever find himself farming over building tiny houses and cabins? She hadn't a clue but thought not. Maybe she should ask if he even thought to ask her for another buggy ride that was. Could he have carried Hannah that far? As the cusp of her womanhood merged into newness, many such fanciful thoughts flirted with her these days.

"Does that sort of thing happen often?"

Hannah's head snapped up and she peered through the full, drooping branches. Leon wasn't looking at her but focused on the chore at hand. He was filling three baskets to her one. *The show off.*

"Or is that just what happens to you when you see me without a shirt?"

She rolled her eyes and eased her basket down the ladder. The man was impossible.

"Unlike Tina or Mirim, I assure you I'm not one to go soft in your presence." This close to the woods, the buzzing of cicadas grew louder. *How many weeks would they be here?* Hannah tried to ignore them, but between Leon's teasing and that ruckus, her nerves were growing taunt.

"Figured as much," he said and clamped his lips tight.

She preferred the quiet, which was a bit scarce at the moment.

He did get help for you.

Hannah let out a sigh. She of all people appreciated a good deed. "Those things are going to be a bother."

"Cicadas?" He lifted a brow, still unwilling to set those blue eyes her way. "Bass love them," Leon said quickly and casually as they both climbed down with their full baskets to add to the wagon.

When Hannah's foot touched the ground, she felt his arms come at her from both sides.

"Let me get that. You filled it too full."

"I have been doing this since I could walk." Ignoring her, Leon lifted the basket over her head as if it weighed but a feather and deposited it with the others. He took up two more empty baskets and brought her a fresh one.

"You didn't answer my question. You think because I have no sisters that I don't understand the hardships of women?"

His clear insight of her fainting surprised her as much as his forward-speaking tongue. His face warmed considerably as she searched for a proper reply. He offered her a basket. No embarrassment could ever be this full.

"Once you're up to the chore, we'll start those swimming lessons." He looked down at her as if he had not affected her. "Your *schwestern* seem eager for it."

"I didn't agree," she said as he skirted around the small tree and moved her ladder between two fresh limbs.

"Afraid?" He cocked his head and lifted a sharp brow. Without his hat, one could see every emotion he wore.

"I'm not afraid." A lie if ever she told one. God would surely be unhappy with her now. *Daed* had schooled her on all the dangers of water, and after finding Leon standing in the center of it, she could add one more danger to the list.

"Then learn," he said sharply. "You're never too old to learn something new, are you?" The wisdom was sound, and she hadn't a sarcasm to deflate it. Leon painted horses, pranked bishops, and winked at *maedels* more often than not. A sinner, who showed no signs of repenting of his ways. She shouldn't be so drawn to a man with so few admirable traits.

However, there was more, a goodness about him too. That couldn't be swept aside. For so long she thought of Leon in a dark light, but he was more sunshine than night. If what he said was true about Mirim, Leon had done noth-ing wrong, not really. He carried her home and offered to teach her how to swim. Her head was spinning. He was making it awfully hard to keep up defenses.

"What say ya?" He lifted a daring brow, challenging her.

Could she trust herself to spend more time with him than necessary? Her sisters had already agreed to his stupid idea. Could she trust him with her sisters? With that excuse in mind, she surrendered, for now.

"Only if you wear a shirt," she said. Leon's deep chuckle echoed through the orchard raising the hairs on her arms.

"Only if you wear a bathing suit."

He quirked a smile, meeting her demands with his own.

"Can you be serious, ever?"

"I'm very serious when talking to you."

She took a deep inhale, tired of quarreling. "Leon Milford, I think I do dislike you," Hannah said on a worn-out fluster.

"*Gut*. It's a start."

A start to what?

"And you'll be swimming by the time those cicadas stop screaming."

Chapter Thirteen

Hazel cracked a smile as she listened to Ivy and Rose mutter behind her. It seemed everything was going just as it should. *Swimming lessons.* She'd have to give Leon credit for that one.

"I never would have thought it, but Leon is much smarter than we thought," Ivy said tying her apron on. Hazel's daughter Lydia thought matching aprons was a sweet idea and great for business. Hazel didn't dare discourage her. Folks didn't mind what aprons looked like as long as the sweets were fulfilling.

She ran her hand over her own stiff apron, her fingers brushing across the Miller's Bakery logo that Lydia must have spent hours embroidering, and smiled.

"I thought you said you could swim," Rose said before stepping away.

"*Jah*, and really *gut* too. But remember Rose, that part's the secret."

"I think we underestimated that one too, rightly so," Hazel said as she cracked an egg over a bowl of flour.

"You, I mean *Gott*," Ivy said with a bit of unnecessary amusement, "still has His work cut out for Him."

Ivy worked, beating the buttercream frosting until it was

smooth. Pumpkin cookies were a good seller no matter the season. Hazel added a splash of vinegar and a quarter cup of water and began working the dough with her hands for pie crusts. "Hannah is a hard egg to crack." All three women agreed.

"She had been dealt a hardship, losing Eli and having to stop teaching all in a week," Rose said.

Ivy's face sobered, and Hazel could see she too felt the loss of her father. But like many things Ivy did, her attention to one thing quickly shifted to another.

Ivy let out a timid laugh, catching both women off guard.

"Yesterday she laughed out loud. I tell ya I ain't heard Hannah laugh like that...well...since, you know." Ivy shrugged.

"You have all been through a painful thing Ivy, but *jah*, laughter is good medicine for a broken heart." Hazel hoped the old wisdom helped.

"If he were here, he would smile at me and give me a pat on the back. He'd be happy that I found work and I'm doing my part. He did that you know." Ivy bit her lip, perhaps not meaning to be so open with her thoughts.

"Eli never looked at the lot of you that he wasn't wearing a smile. It was no secret the man carried stars in his eyes for the love he had for each of you." Hazel wrapped an arm around her when a tear slipped from Ivy's eyes. Hazel was only one woman, could only help heal one heart at a time, but it was clear, Ivy might need a little extra helping of her attention.

"I miss how he used to tease *mamm*, testing her mixtures and kissing her cheek while she baked," she said on a sob. "He would poke a finger in her mixing bowl and say something kind." Ivy smiled speaking on the memory.

Hazel recalled such loving moments with Joseph over the years. He too liked poking a finger in a sweetened batter and groaning with delight at whatever ingredients she had thrown together. She sunk her bare hands into the dough and let the memories wrap her like a warm blanket.

"He would carry me on one shoulder, making me dizzy with laughter."

"And now laughter has returned to your family. This is a blessed thing, Ivy." Ivy wiped her face and quickly stiffened, not meaning to let her melancholy interfere with a most perfect day. With each of her own children happily married, Hazel's whole purpose in life now was to help promote healing for everyone affected by the disaster two years ago. Watching the slow change from chaos to a near-normal again warmed her heart in ways others couldn't understand.

"And Hannah was laughing at Leon of all the things." Ivy cocked a grin, getting back to the topic at hand. "He tried petting Tom. My cat doesn't like being touched." Ivy wrinkled her nose."

Poor Leon. No one said falling in love didn't prevent a few scrapes and bruises. Hazel restrained a grin.

"He suffered two deep scratches for that mistake. *Mamm* gave him an extra slice of her blueberry crumble for his troubles. He eats a lot."

Before Hazel could add to that, the bell overhead jingled. It had been a slow morning so far. Just the regulars and one older man who left unhappy because he had a hankering for cherry tarts, but they had sold all out of them yesterday.

Luke and Levi Milford smiled as they made their way to the counter, which was a good indication they were bringing good news. Hazel rubbed her hands together, dispersing the sticky dough from her fingers. There was only one reason Luke was here and not home with Penny who has already been in bed for three days. Martha, the local midwife, was certain new life would be born soon.

Luke removed his hat and ran his fingers through his sandy hair. Despite anticipation thickening the air, Luke took his time to speak. His overly calm demeanor was principled, except right now. Right now, Luke's slow turn to speak was stoic, bordering on nerve-racking.

"Well," she blurted out.

"*Gut morgen*, Hazel, Rose, and Ivy." Luke greeted them with a wide smile. "Fine weather we are having, *jah*?"

"Not a cloud in the sky," Levi added. "We have been sent to ask if you have a few extra sweet rolls."

"For my dear *fraa*."

Hazel's mouth fell open as both *menner* pinned her with a bemused grin.

"That's it? You came for sweet rolls?" Hazel's voice squeaked. She didn't like that smirk on Luke's face any better than she did when Hank did that. Handsome men tended to think smirks and grins were great distractions.

"And to see if you would like to come meet my *sohn* this day," Luke added, the beam in his eyes as wide as the Licking River.

If not for the joy pumping through her heart, Hazel would've given the two a lesson on how not to tease your elders. Penny was like her own *dochder* and this day her happiness had Hazel's heart swelling.

"A *sohn*." Hazel and Rose said in unison.

"They thought it was a girl." Ivy shrugged.

Maedel was still too young to know what was spoken in the bakery need not be repeated.

"The Lord has blessed you both," Rose said.

"He has indeed," Luke said smiling and accepting her hug of congratulations.

"We will put together a few of Penny's favorites." Hazel went straight to selecting the biggest sweet rolls on the tray. "And if she is up for company then nothing short of *Gott* Himself will keep me from coming after I close the bakery today." Hazel dropped a half dozen peanut butter chocolate cookies, and an equal share of chocolate walnut fudge in the box before closing the lid shut. She slid a box of four sweet rolls toward Luke. She felt absolutely giddy with this news. New life always made her feel young and eager and hopeful. And new life was just what Miller's Creek needed. Nothing promoted healing better than family. Penny was a perfect example to others that joy did cometh in the morning.

"We missed seeing Lester at the last gathering," Rose said, giving both her most sorrowful expression. "We continue to pray your *bruder* joins us again soon." Rose was not one to elude from the obvious. Hazel nodded. Her prayers each night and morning were filled with many, and Lester Milford was one of the many. She bent an ear for his answer. Luke's expression matched Levi's as both brothers passed a glance between them.

"As do we. Lewis spoke with him two days ago. I think Leon paid him a visit too, but one cannot know the plans or thinking of another." Levi said with a look of disappointment.

The quiet one, as Hazel always referred to him. Yet, as she took a closer look, she reckoned he wasn't so much just quiet. He, like Luke, just didn't waste a word unnecessarily. It was an admirable trait, worthy of only the perfect *maedel*. Once he and Addie were done dancing around the fact God only intended them to be friends, Hazel would see to it that one found his match too. Hank was right about that.

"Lewis will get through to him. He has a knack for such."

Lewis Milford, the eldest of the lot, had more than a knack for persuasion.

"But Leon has his hands full with helping the Troyers and should be focused on learning about apple growing, not running about when there is so much work to be had," Hazel said, ignoring the beady look from her mother-in-law.

"Lewis knows how easy one is to be pulled into the world, *jah*," Luke said.

It was no secret the eldest son of John and Irma Milford had run off for a spell during his own Rumspringa years long before the family called Miller's Creek home. He had dated an *Englischer* and had wandered so far from the straight and narrow it had landed him in jail. But Hazel wasn't one to judge, that was the Lord's business and truth be it, she could see Lewis had a pure heart. Like her, he had a good eye for seeing inside others. Mistakes earned wisdom and when a rebellious one learns hard lessons, more often than not they returned with a greater value to their community. Who better to help a brother back home than one who had seen two sides of the fence and chose the plainer side?

"Leon will do his part as we all will," Luke said.

Hazel nodded, but she couldn't have Leon so consumed he would forget he was supposed to be winning Hannah Troyer's heart. "Your Leon has been *gut* help for Millie and her family."

Luke lifted a brow. "He is giving that farm a whole new face, and spilling life into it," Hazel said.

"He doesn't shuck a chore, *jah*," Luke said, narrowing one eye as if to see her better.

"He's a blessing for sure and certain," Rose said. "He can't be spared there with so much yet to do." Hazel could always rely on her mother-in-law to help make a point.

Luke stared between the two women, calculating them. "I hope you two ain't match meddling."

Hazel tightened her lips.

"Should I warn *mei bruder* he has caught your attention?" A grin tugged the corners of Luke's mouth.

"You'll do no such, Luke Milford. *Gott* don't like us meddling in His plans," Hazel said firmly.

"His plans are a mystery, some days." Luke pinned her with a knowing smile and then cleared his throat. "I did not know you were one who enjoyed the water."

Hazel stiffened.

"Did you enjoy your boat ride last Sunday?"

Hazel couldn't believe he just called her out, and in front of others too. Her face went hot.

"I hear the fishing was *gut*." He dared grin.

"Now, Luke Milford, you know better than to ask a woman such things. You best be minding your own and get back to that *fraa* of yours," Hazel said urging his leave.

"Boat ride?" Rose asked. "You went on a boat ride?"

Hazel shot Luke a glare, but he simply tipped his hat to her, smiled, and strolled away as if he had not just caused her a heap of trouble. It was her duty to see the rumor mills didn't spin out of control, not be the center of it. Those Half Dozen really needed a lesson in how to treat their elders, she thought before turning back to find Rose and Ivy both staring at her.

"Now what kind of Christian lets an old man go out on the lake alone. Gott frowns on those who don't look after others," Hazel said and quickly strolled off into the store room.

CHAPTER FOURTEEN

Leon rolled his shoulders and let up on his grip on the reins. His legs were sore, his arms heavy, and everything connected was equally spent. Who knew picking apples was such work? Hannah surprised him again. Leon already knew she was a hard worker, but she could literally outwork most men he knew too. He was glad he was helping, lessening her burdens working there. He would do anything to help take that wearied look from her.

He did well to hold back the surprise she gave him by agreeing on swimming lessons. The idea had been birthed out of the air. Just the thought of being near her more pleased him. Despite telling himself to keep a good arm's length away, he found himself drawn more to her as days lingered from one to the next. She hadn't a clue how much she amazed him. Few her age would dare take on such a task as she had, and it was plain to see she had put her future on hold.

He shook his head and let out an amused chuckle. He still couldn't understand it. Out of all the *maedels* out there, the one who found nothing about him pleasing was the one he couldn't stop thinking about. Leon was a smart man, he figured. He knew that some forces couldn't be ignored.

The sun inched away over the hills behind him. He shouldn't have left the Troyer's so early today, but he needed to talk to Lester. His brother's continued absence was hurting their parents. That worried look in *mudder*'s eyes, the stern frown on his *daed*'s face when they gathered at the table for supper each evening, was wearing on the lot of them. Even Lovis, the youngest, seemed not himself these days. Tonight, Bishop Schwartz would be joining them for supper. Lester needed to be present, or Leon feared the church elders might take to hand to search him out themselves.

"Can't be riding two horses with one hind end," he repeated the old adage Bishop Brennon used to spat. The man said a lot, but Leon found this wisdom a good one. A man had to choose the life he wanted to live and dodging between worlds only showed his lack of faith, responsibility, and ability to make a decision. The way Leon saw it, his wandering *bruder* had had his fun and needed to come home. Leon feared if he didn't act now, try to talk some sense into him, Lester might never return. That would break their poor *mudder*'s heart for sure and for certain. It was time to herd his brother back to this side of the fence.

Leon veered Marva down the long stretch of street and found a safe place behind the three-story building in town. The dark alley held a sense of eerie demise, a stench of garbage punished the air. He climbed down and tethered Marva to an iron gate, perched in welcome with no fence connected to it. Just deserted, standing there alone. He walked to the front of the building. Even at this late hour, muggy air clung like a wet shirt.

If ever a place needed burned to the ground instead of fixin', this apartment house was one. Paint peeled into tattered sheets and hung loosely, exposing rotted wood that even termites deemed unhealthy. Windows covered in foil or black drapes hid the goings-on inside. Leon hoped he never found out all the goings on inside where his *bruder* frequented so often.

All Leon knew for certain, was that Faith had spent a spell living here with her *bruder* and since neither she nor Lester was at her house, this was the next place to look. He had never met Faith's *bruder* and from what little Lester had spoken, that was a good thing. Then again, before having the door slammed in his face, meeting Faith's parents was an experience Leon hoped never to repeat.

When he stepped inside the building, he was met with the overpowering musky scent of damp walls and forgotten corners. It smelled as bad in here as it looked out there. Leon knocked on the first door, unsure which apartment Faith's *bruder* occupied and he hadn't a name considering their father refused to offer one.

The door swung open so quickly Leon reacted by taking a quick step back. A bare-chested man with a healthy appetite growled at the sight of him. *Please let this not be the bruder.*

"What do you want?" The words came out with a rancid breath. Even three feet away Leon thought he would be nauseous.

"I'm looking for Lester Milford or Faith but wasn't sure which apartment they stayed in when they are here." Leon towered over the man who smelled of alcohol, cigarettes, and upon closer study, was quite possibly allergic to soap and water.

"They aren't here." The stranger said flatly. Leon shifted, glanced up the stairs to his right. Surely someone here knew where he could find his brother.

"You Leon?"

Leon jerked to attention at the mentioning of his name and nodded that he was. Talking required opening your mouth and he had no desire to taste that air again if it could be helped.

"Hold on. Les told me to give you something if you stopped by. I think they were heading to Ohio, but Les doesn't like sharing much." *Les.* So, this *was* the *bruder*.

Leon waited uncomfortably as the man disappeared, not willing himself inside where foul odors only grew stronger. When Faith's *bruder* returned he handed Leon an envelope and without another word, slammed the door shut. The impact knocked Leon's straw hat from his head. He collected the hat, fisted the letter, and marched back out into the creepy street where at least there was fresh air.

After climbing into the buggy, Leon studied the envelope. He could wait until he got home to read it. It was addressed to him and that only told him Lester knew he would be coming for him. A sense of gloom overshadowed his hopes of bringing his brother back to the flock. "Might as well," he said to himself. Fear and concern were good fuels to killing patience. Leon tore the envelope open.

Leon,

Naet coming home. I'm sorry. Faith needs to get away from here and I am taking her far. I will write once we have settled. I am sorry to put this on you to tell the family, but there was no time. I promise to explain one day. I love and will miss all of you, but this has to be done. Please forgive me.

Always Your faithful brother

Lester.

Leon's hands shook as he stared down at the words in front of him. "That's it?" he flipped the letter over, blank, before searching the envelope for more. *Nothing.* Panic filled his lungs and emptied out in heavy breaths. What could have possibly happened for Lester to need to get Faith out of here so quickly? Leon thought to go back inside, inquire more of the man, but decided against it. It wasn't their way to be physical and Leon knew himself well enough. If he didn't get the answers he needed, he might find himself tempted.

His brother was gone, leaving behind no clue of his destination and no promise of his return. How did he even explain such mystery to his family? He sat in the buggy, staring at the letter with mixed emotions.

After a few minutes, Leon wiped his face, tucked the crinkled-up letter into his pocket, and aimed for home. Bishop Schwartz was coming to supper tonight, which Leon felt was on account of his concern for Lester. He would wait to speak to Lewis and Luke before sharing the letter with his family. *Mamm* needed to cling onto hope a little longer and Leon didn't like the idea of being the bearer of bad news. No man had it in him to break their mother's heart.

He shifted his thoughts, hoping for a reprieve from his achy heart. He had plenty to speak to Bishop Schwartz about concerning Hannah's family and if talk guided towards Lester's whereabouts, Leon was prepared. The orchard had potential, and it was a shame to see it not reach it. That should keep everyone's attention for now. Hannah might get angry if he meddled, but Leon wanted to remedy some of her hardships, and she wasn't exactly one who accepted charity.

Leon closed his eyes and whispered a prayer for his brother. Surely, God would bring him to his senses. If not, Lewis would know what to do.

An hour later Leon looked up from his plate at the bishop. Joshua Schwartz was a small man, but his voice had a way of filling a room like no other. His pointy grey beard was slightly distracting and *mamm* had already prodded Lovis under the table to wipe that smile off his face.

"So, you haven't heard from him," the bishop asked.

"*Nee.*" John pushed his half-eaten plate forward. Leon had only nibbled at his supper but *mamm*'s scalloped potatoes were fermenting in his gut right now.

"We have lost many of our youth over the years. *Kinner* without a father to guide them, tend to seek attentions elsewhere." The bishop's frown deepened. "I for one know the hurt of it, having lost a nephew myself to the world. As bishop, I feel none too far lost that cannot be saved."

"I agree," *Mamm* said. "Lewis has been a great example to his *bruders* that no distance is too far to return from."

Truer words had never been spoken. Leon always accredited his unwavering faith to Lewis. When their family moved here, so much was new and exciting. The community of Miller's Creek had its rules but none so harsh as the community they were raised in. It was easy for him, like Lester, to take such freedoms and indulge in them. Leon wouldn't. Lewis had been his big brother, the apple of his eye growing up. He'd seen firsthand how hard Lewis struggled with alcohol, with a broken heart, and leaving the girl he loved behind. But he also saw him take those bruises and aches and sinful indulgences and convert them into a steadfast faith.

A faith so sturdy even the strongest storm held no temptation. Lewis even managed to marry a woman most found annoying. The Jenny they all knew two years ago was nothing like the Jenny they knew now. That, Leon knew, was just how influential his eldest brother was.

"That brings me to the true reason I came to join you tonight." Bishop Schwartz sat back in his chair and stroked his wiry beard. "Our community has found itself without a deacon."

"Thomas Miller is stepping down?" John lifted a brow.

"*Jah*, and with John Schwartz still suffering with his health, he too feels the need to step aside as minister." The hairs on the back of Leon's neck bristled. Was the bishop here to ask *daed* to step up?

"Sorry to hear this," *Daed* said coolly. "Though John has had a time of it we all know." No doubt he was thinking just as Leon was. Leon glanced across the kitchen where *mamm* was cutting a pie for dessert. Her stiff shoulders and trembling hands couldn't be ignored. No man was eager to be placed in the *Der Los*, in the lot, any more than they wanted to be chosen by Gott as the one to fill a minister or deacon's shoes. Being chosen was a great responsibility. It was life changing. Surely, the bishop wasn't going to ask *daed* to accept being added to the chosen few.

Thankfully, Bishop Schwartz only wanted to ask questions about how *daed* felt about the community, if his married *sohns* were comfortable living in Kentucky, or did they think to move back to Michigan where the family came from. Leon knew the bishop was simply fishing and relaxed a little. It was standard to query eligible men when the need for drawing lots was near.

As the bishop readied to leave, Leon followed him out the door. "Got something on your mind *sohn*?"

"*Jah*, a lot actually."

"Well then," Joshua motioned Leon outside where they both found a seat.

"You know I have been helping with Troyers, and I noticed that since the passing of Eli Troyer a lot was left undone."

"You're speaking of the marketplace he hoped to finish. I have told ya, if you can find a way, I'm not against it. But Millie can't afford to finance such an undertaking."

"*Nee*, but the community could, and with so many looking to prosper from it, they should."

Bishop Schwartz stroked his beard. Leon felt as if he was not only going against Hannah's approval but crossing a line by being so forward speaking. To his surprise, the bishop didn't appear to be offended.

"I'm listening."

CHAPTER FIFTEEN

Sunday morning, rumors were spreading like wildfire and the whole community was abuzz. A new deacon would be chosen today. Leon was just glad it took all the attention away from Lester, buying him more time to find his whereabouts. After a sleepless night of contemplating, Leon knew he had to switch tactics if he wanted to locate his brother. So far, the clues were scarce. All Leon knew was Faith's brother suspected the pair traveled to Ohio. Leon had only one connection there, a cousin. Thankfully Markus answered his call and agreed to do some digging around to see if he could locate him. It was a long shot, so Leon spent half the night on his knees hoping the Lord would show some of that mercy he had seen before.

With Penny still not fully recovered after bringing baby Daniel into the world, Jenny decided to stay with her this Sunday and help where she could. Leon rode alongside Lewis and Luke in the buggy to church this morning.

"Miller's Creek will be absent of a second minister too I heard," Lewis said.

Lewis had always been more laid back. He looked different this morning, more focused. "*Jah*, the bishop said there would be more than one lot chosen today." Leon couldn't understand God's plans when it came to those who already suffered. John, the soon-to-be-former minister, had survived the disaster two years ago, and since he was still mending damage that day had put on his leg, crumbling the bones to dust under concrete, now cancer snuck in and decided he had not endured enough. In the blink of an eye, life changed. Leon was beginning see just how quick a blink truly was. Life was vulnerable, limited, and precious. Another reason for setting aside his boyish ways and giving into many of the thoughts he had been courting with of late.

"Why does *Gott* allow for such things?" Leon asked. Hannah rushed his thoughts. Her family struggled in the absence of their father. They weren't the only family who suffered, and yet, many had found themselves out of the darkness. Some re-married and combined families. A few moved to other communities where they felt a fresh start was their answer.

Not Hannah. She gave up teaching and took full responsibility for her family's future. Leon crossed his arms and sat back in the buggy seat, his eyes on the passing fields and farms. God surely didn't want that kind of life for her, he reckoned.

"*Gott* didn't do this. He is not responsible for bad things happening, He just promises to be there for us when they do." Luke put in.

"*Jah*," Lewis said. "It is man that makes mistakes. We are given free will and many will it freely about as if it carries no consequences, but the Lord is always there, always present to see us through what follows."

"If they are choosing a minister and a deacon, then do you two worry you might be chosen to accept the call?" All married men were expected to be ready to be called upon as *Gott* saw fit. *A gut reason to never marry.* Yet, these days his thoughts lingered more toward than against.

Luke put both reins in one hand to scratch his leg. He

looked tired, weary even. Was this what it was like to be a new parent? Leon had been so consumed over Lester of late he had failed to notice his brothers had their own lives.

"*Gott*'s will should not be feared." Lewis looked over one shoulder and sported Leon a dry grin. "No worries little *bruder. Gott* would never let one like me serve more than leading a song." Lewis chuckled amusedly.

"You are no longer that man you were before, *bruder*," Luke said in a serious tone.

Leon admired them both. For the things they said, the lives they led, and for all the years of bringing fun and adventure into his life. They were a band of brothers like no other, close and supportive. That's why they couldn't simply give up on Lester.

Leon wrestled with sharing Lester's letter. He could use their advice right now, but was now a good time? Were his brothers concerned that today their lives might change entirely?

"We don't know if either of us will be chosen as possibilities, then if we are, who's to say we pick the lot," Luke said.

Leon and Lewis agreed.

"I heard Thomas Miller left without a word. I must say, *Gott*'s will never cease to amaze me." Luke grinned.

Thomas Miller was a hard sort to figure out.

"That man got under my skin more than any other," Luke said.

He had been bruised personally by how the local deacon treated so many in the community small, especially Penny when she was at her lowest. Leon never regretted removing his buggy wheel after the way he heard Thomas speak to her years back. No man should talk to a woman the way Thomas had.

Pulling up to the bishop's house, buggies filled the front yard and Leon found himself searching out an old gelding that looked to be on its last leg. Hannah would sit with the other baptized women, but Penny would not be at her side today. Young Aiden Graber took the horse's reins and led him around back where other young boys charged with pasturing horses were.

In matching dark trousers and short waistcoats, the three brothers strode across the yard and entered the three-story house where services would be held today. Lewis looked a pinch nervous as he aimed for the large sitting room toward the east side of the house. Leon followed, saying a few hellos as they moved through the crowd. *Jah*, his brother was nervous, Leon measured.

The very thought that one of them or his *daed* might be called upon, nearly made Leon ill. The pressures and responsibility that came with such a gift, as the bishop called it, would no doubt change the lives of his family. Leon shot a glance toward Luke, always confident, always ready for what life tossed at him.

Luke would do well as a minister or deacon of the community. He had a sound faith, never wavering or bending the rules to his will. He exuded calm and freely gave. Luke's whole life was the epitome of a faithful Amish man. If one of his family members had to be selected to step up and do his duty, it would be Luke. Surely, God knew this to be best. Just in case, Leon silently shot upward a quick prayer as they filled the room.

"Find a seat, men, they already started," Abner Fisher said as he escorted the three further inside the room already filling with the echoes of song. Leon took a seat toward the back of the men's side, nearest the door. It gave a better view without many noticing where his eyes had been wandering more often of late. Hannah sat with Addie on one side and Kay Reihl on the other. A cardinal among wrens. She really hadn't a clue how beautiful she was. That too was an admirable trait, and another reason Leon couldn't stop thinking about her, worrying over her.

More than once her comment had come back and stung him fresh. She had assumed the worst of him, thinking him a flirt as she had. A wry grin tugged at the corner of his lips. What would she do if he planted a kiss on her? It wasn't proper to be thinking such thoughts here, but as his gaze landed across the room, he could think of little else when she was near.

Two and a half hours of staring at Hannah Troyer was no hardship. At the finish of the final hymn, Bishop Schwartz came forward and cleared his throat. Leon pulled his attention away and stiffened to what came next.

"I know many of you in the community have heard much talk about the situation we have come to find ourselves in. Let me put truth to the rumors." The bishop winked and a few chuckles lifted. Joshua Schwartz was nothing like their old bishop at all. The man could drag a smile from the grumpiest face with that wink.

"It is time to draw from the *der los*. John Schwartz, our minister for the last twelve years, has felt called to step aside and face the battle put in front of him. Most of you know his condition and I ask we keep him and his family in our daily prayers." Bishop Schwartz shifted to fan his gaze over the other side of the room. "I will not take your day by long talk. Each of you knows we need to draw the lot for a minister." Bishop Schwartz cleared his throat again and Leon felt himself do the same.

"We must also choose a new deacon as well." Murmurs filled the room, but the bishop didn't dare speak about what had caused Thomas Miller to step down and move off so suddenly. Two men's lives would be forever changed today, and Leon felt his throat tighten, seeing the odds that one of his family members might be chosen after all.

"Now, I will call the names and you will come and stand to my right. Then I will call three more, and those men will stand at my left." Was the bishop nervous? He wiped his brow then pulled a folded piece of paper from inside his jacket pocket. Three women, their *kapps* catching his eye, peered around the kitchen doorway. No one would miss this.

"Jacob Lewis, Hank Fisher, and Lewis Milford."

Leon's breath hitched as did the rest of the room. He could just hear what everyone's mind was struggling to keep silent when Lewis made his way to the center of the room.

"*Kumm* to my right men."

Lewis followed Jacob and Hank to the right of the bishop, his face blank and unreadable. Was his stomach twisting as tight as Leon's? From his seat, he couldn't see *Daed*'s face, read his expression, but *mamm* was holding her breath, Leon was certain of it.

"Luke Milford, Gavin Weaver, and Matthew Reihl." Bishop Schwartz looked up. "To my left."

Leon was going to be sick, acidic bile rising fast into his throat. In a room of more than a hundred and twenty crammed souls, his brothers were both standing among those selected. Luke met his eyes, sensing Leon's thoughts, and gave him a subtle smile. Luke always did that. Knew when one needed a calm, but it wasn't working, not this time. He glanced at *mamm* across the room again, biting her lip as she often did when any of her *sohns* faced something new like riding a horse, climbing a tree, or learning to swim. Yeah, she was that worried and her worry only fueled Leon's more.

Edith Schwartz and Hazel Miller stepped from the kitchen carrying three Bibles. Solemnly they placed them all on the small table center of the room. Hazel paused and Hank gave her a slight shrug. Luke had mentioned that the two had been seen fishing on the lake in town recently. Perhaps the local matchmaker was finding herself a second love. The thought nearly brought a smile out of him. Everyone deserved love, especially those who had it and lost it. *Like Hannah*.

"*Menner*," the bishop looked to his left and urged each man forward.

Leon wrung his sweaty fingers as Luke sidled at the end

of the three. *Please, Lord, choose wisely.* Leon prayed silently. If Luke selected the Bible with scripture written inside, Leon would rejoice. Luke would do well as a deacon to Miller's Creek, far better than Thomas Miller ever had, and no one would dare touch a buggy wheel if he did. Gavin Weaver, driven by something akin to anxiousness opened his Bible first. A sigh of relief flittered across the room when he displayed the bare inside.

Luke went next, always one to take whatever life threw him with confidence. Leon held his breath when his *bruder* stared blankly at the open book. It was only when Matthew Reihl went wide-eyed and hurriedly flipped his Bible open, that Leon realized *Gott* had spared Luke from a life of serving a community as a deacon. However, one brother safe didn't mean the day was over.

Chances were thinning that a Milford would serve, but there was still a chance. Leon whispered the same prayer as three more men awaited their future. Lewis didn't hesitate, stepping forward and opening his Bible. Lewis wasn't afraid of anything since he had already done about everything and survived it. His impatience didn't surprise Leon one bit, but that frozen look on his eldest brother's face did. Jacob Lewis stared down at the Bible sitting before Lewis and placed a hand on Lewis's shoulder. Lewis didn't even flinch. He simply stared at the page.

"What *Gott* has decided shall not be hindered." The bishop spoke. "Men, I will speak with you two at supper tomorrow. We will discuss your duties over some of my Edith's best roast. Let us all pray for these men and the life they have been chosen to take up from this day forward."

All heads bowed, except for Leon. His head was still spinning. Lester was gone, Luke had a new *bobbli*, Levi was always off somewhere when he should be at home, and now Lewis, former wayward who once spent three days locked in a cell, had just become Miller's Creek's newest minister.

Everything was changing so fast he couldn't grasp it. He

glanced across the room again and felt a surprising warmth bathe him fully when his eyes locked with Hannah's. With the other heads bowed and *kapps* lowered, they were the only two people in the room.

CHAPTER SIXTEEN

Leon sat in the back of the buggy in a state of shock as his *bruders* chatted ahead of him about the weather of all things. Weren't they both aware that Lewis had just been chosen Miller's Creek new minister?

"How can you be so calm?" Leon finally interrupted. The annoying clip-clop of Marva on asphalt, mingled with the look on Hannah's face when his brother was chosen, was enough to drive him mad today. She would have an opinion he reckoned, and Leon couldn't wait to hear just what that was.

"It was *Gott*'s will. Not right to question it," Lewis said staring forward. "Even if there were a dozen better choices." Lewis shrugged.

There was no undoing what the Lord had gone and done. God didn't make mistakes. Leon wanted to believe that with his whole heart.

"You'll do well with it, as you do most things," Luke said, always the encourager.

"You would have been a *gut* choice." Lewis returned to looking out from under the brim of his black felt hat. "I'm no pillar. Heck, I'm not even a cornerstone," Lewis said between clenched teeth.

"You are to your *bruders*. The first is always the cornerstone." Leon added his ounce of wisdom.

"With a crack in it." Lewis countered, a slight lift of a teasing smile tugging at one corner of his lips.

"*Nee*. We are all sinners, even I," Luke said. "But who better to minister to the youth than one who has seen two sides of the one world. Your decision to accept the faith and be baptized after everything is why *Gott* chose you. You can give direction and clarity, mostly to those who found themselves fatherless. He chose you because you know temptation and how to offer a *bruder* good advice when he needs it." Lewis glanced over to Luke, temporarily awestruck.

"And that…" Lewis pointed, "is why you would have been a better minister." Lewis shook his head and smiled. "I will do my best, that is all I can do," Lewis said.

"Starting with our *bruder*," Luke said.

He had a secret to share but hadn't been sure how to approach telling his brothers about Lester, until now. "He won't be back." Leon blurted out before he changed his mind.

"And you know this how?" Luke asked. Both brothers turned and shot him a curious look.

Leaning back, letting the wind bully him as they rode under a relentless sky, Leon cleared his throat and began telling them about the apartment building and Faith's brother. "He says they're heading to Ohio. The letter only said he was sorry but would call when he got settled." Leon removed his hat and ran his fingers through his hair.

"Letter? He wrote you a letter, or left a letter behind?" Luke asked keeping his eyes forward.

"Does it matter?" Neither brother commented on that.

"One of us must talk some sense into him, or her, doesn't matter," Lewis said. "This is going to break *mamm*'s heart if we don't convince him to let go of that girl."

The brothers all agreed.

"We could call our cousin," Luke said.

Leon could tell Luke's lips were pursed into a tight line without seeing him. He always did that when he was upset but holding his frustration in check.

"Did that," Leon said. "He will be getting back to me in a day or so." Both brothers turned and looked him over again.

"Well. Glad to see you joining the crusade." Lewis mocked. "So, we are agreed, one of us needs to go after him?"

They did.

"I wouldn't have come home if not for Luke hunting me down and pestering me."

"Tough love," Luke said with a laugh. "Besides, you weren't hard to find."

No, Lewis was in the county jail for public drinking. Lester could be anywhere from there to Ohio.

"I can take a few days off and…"

"You have Penny to tend to. We all know she needs her rest, and I can't leave now that I have just been made minister," Lewis said as they turned on Penny Patch Lane. "He did leave you the letter, little *bruder*." Lewis looked over one shoulder and grinned.

Leon had every intention of seeking Lester out, without Lewis's mentioning it, but realizing Luke and Lewis couldn't go because of the responsibilities they had, he suddenly thought of Hannah. Leon now had someone depending on him too. How could he leave, possibly for days, in the middle of her early harvest?

The thought plundered him just as a buggy in the distance drew near. It seemed the Milford brothers weren't the only ones skipping out on the fellowship meal today. Leon stiffened as the buggy drew nearer. He recognized that shape, and that lifted chin pointing in his direction.

As the buggies grew closer, Tabor smiled a crooked, toothy grin. If bruising Leon was the point, he accomplished that. The buggies passed one another and against his better judgment, Leon glance around and surprised even himself when he locked onto emerald-green eyes, looking at him. The woman made his heart stop, again. It would have been better if he hadn't turned around at all. Leon had seen her at her best, and more so, at her worst, and neither changed the way his heart kicked up.

"Looks to me Tabor finally found someone who likes him back." Luke chuckled.

"Hannah won't settle for the likes of him," Leon muttered. "She has standards." He smirked with an eye roll. The Lewis brothers all had reputations that mothers warned their *kinner* about. Hannah would see clear soon enough, Leon reasoned.

"And yet she speaks to you," Luke said sarcastically. "Our *bruder* sounds jealous."

"Of Tabor?" Leon scoffed. "I courted two girls," Leon clarified shoving two fingers toward him. "Same two I figured most around here stole a kiss from." Three if you counted kissing Maria Raber on the cheek.

"Tabor never painted a whole horse," Luke said in a sharp jab.

"Or filled a buggy with manure," Lewis said.

"Or prodded his youngest *bruder* into helping him."

Okay, so Leon had conned Lovis into helping shovel all that manure.

"*Jah*, but he left Penny alone after I did, ain't so?" Leon asked. "You're welcome by the way." Leon slumped back in his seat, folding both arms across his chest. He would not be compared to the likes of Tabor Lewis.

"He never removed buggy wheels I don't 'spect either," Lewis lifted a brow and shot a cunning grin to Luke.

"Scared, *bruder*?" Leon teased, not backing down from their games. They forgot he was carved from the same tree as they were. "*Gut* thing you aren't deacon, but let's hope you're a *gut* minister."

Lewis chuckled off the threat. Leon was known for his pranks, his courting habits, not his hard work, and faith. The thought disturbed him now that he gave it a second thought.

"He is afraid." They veered Marva into the drive where Lewis and Jenny lived.

"What do I have to be afraid of?" Leon straightened, yanking off his hat.

"You're afraid to grow up. Hannah Troyer needs a *gut* man who will help her and love her as *Gott* calls us to do. She is no Plain woman in the traditional way. She owns a farm and works it. She is out there in the sun, laboring to see her family farm doesn't fail."

"I know that better than you," Leon said. "I have been alongside her doing it, and I'll have you know I'm blown away by how hard she works." She did amaze him by her fortitude.

"She has no time for boys who want to play pranks and steal kisses," Lewis said coldly as he climbed down from the buggy.

Leon was speechless. Hannah needed a partner, in all things, and Leon had never been much of a team player. He liked winning and controlling the outcome.

Jenny rushed out of the house and Lewis opened his arms wide and took her in, leaving all talk about pranks and kisses and growing up behind. For all the things Jenny wasn't, she was Lewis's *fraa* and loved him. The look of admiration in her eyes said more than enough. Who would have thought such a sassy woman could look so smitten. His brother was a blessed man.

"What be it?" She lifted a firm brow.

Lewis swallowed hard, looking down on her in a slightly deflated stance. "I was chosen minister. Luke and *daed* came out of it unscathed."

Jenny's eyes filled with immediate tears, but she lifted her gaze to Lewis and forged a smile.

"I prayed *Gott* would appoint the right man to minister

to our community." She placed a hand on each side of Lewis's face. "I see he has chosen wisely because you, Lewis Milford, will make a *wunderbaar* minister to our community." Her confidence floated to Lewis, straightening him taller, ready.

Leon had never thought of it before but right now he wished he had a Jenny in his life, chicken casserole and all, someone to look at him the way Jenny was looking at Lewis. Someone who believed in him and stood beside him no matter what life tossed in his path.

Lewis bent down and kissed her affectionately.

"We're leaving now." Luke chuckled and took up the reins to begin making his way toward home.

"Those two will never cease to surprise me," Luke said.

Leon agreed. No two people could be more opposite, and yet, they fit the other perfect. Clouds overhead sat low and full beneath a baby blue sky. Leon took a breath until his lungs were full, and then let it out slowly. His mind drifted to Hannah. Always to Hannah, he collected. Those beautiful green eyes, her strong determination, and wondered what life with a woman like her would give him. Did he really want a woman who cooked and cleaned all day? Or did he want a partner, beside him, encouraging him, and kissing him without a care of who was watching? She drove him mad, and she amazed him. She was a challenge, for sure and certain, and he never buckled at a good challenge.

"Cicadas," Leon said. He let out a spontaneous laugh.

"What about them?" Luke asked, a grin tugging at the corner of his lips.

"She hates them. For an apple farmer, she sure has a thing for bugs." Leon grinned recalling just how many times each day she groaned at their racket. Suddenly, the sight of Hannah and Tabor camped out in his thoughts. Tabor was not the best choice for a woman like Hannah Troyer. Matter a fact, not too many men could handle a woman with that many brains and an overload of determination. She required something special, as Lewis suggested. A man who could deflect ill moods and tolerate her bossy nature. He imagined few could see inside that sharp glare and find a heart that just needed someone with a careful hand to hold it. There wasn't anything he couldn't do, and do better, when he put his mind to it.

"Bass like them," Luke said.

"She can't swim either."

"An easy fix." They reached Luke's small two-story house behind their *onkel's* farm.

"She hates me," Leon said.

"Another easy fix. She doesn't really know you like we do."

Luke stopped the buggy but didn't budge to get out. He always had a good sense about him, knowing when someone just needed to share his thoughts.

"She's as easy to see through as a board fence," Leon said.

"And what do you see?"

"She's hurting, misses her *daed*."

Luke nodded but didn't say a word.

"She works so hard like she is trying to…well…impress him. I don't know how to help her with that."

"Be her friend first. Pray for her, with her. *Gott* knows what He is doing, Leon. Penny was so broken when I met her. She lost a *daed* too. Her mother suffered depression something terrible. She too worked hard, barely slept, but I didn't give up and neither will *Gott*." Luke patted his leg. "And I am glad you took off that buggy wheel," Luke said.

"Had to happen," Leon said, no shame in his voice. He would do it again, given the chance. Leon was never one to sit by and watch another being treated poorly. All of his *bruders* were like that in reality. Yeah, Lewis becoming minister would bring a lot of hope and comfort to those still suffering here.

"She was with Tabor. You saw it." Leon added.

"I see both get a rise out of you."

"Exactly. I spoke with the bishop. Once we work out a few more details, would you be willing to do some work with me?"

"Doing?"

"Building a marketplace on the Troyer property. Hannah's father was building one when…you know." Leon shrugged under his brother's surprised look.

"And how will we pay for such a place?"

"I have more than any two men need I reckon," Leon said. Hopefully, Luke wouldn't find it a dumb idea. A man didn't wisely invest all his savings in endeavors of others, but Leon felt called to do it, with help from the community of course. When his brother studied him more closely, Leon readied for a lecture. To his surprise, none came.

"I see we have underestimated you. Count me and our *bruders* in."

"Give me a few days to get things in order at the Troyer's. I'm still hoping Markus will call with some news on Lester. I can find him and see if I can get him to return before anyone knows he left the state."

"I'll say nothing of it, for now." Luke patted his back before stepping down from the buggy.

"There's more wearing at you," Luke said.

It wasn't a question, but an observation. Luke was good at reading people's thoughts.

"You're worried about going to find Lewis and leaving Hannah behind to harvest alone, aren't you?"

"Ivy works at the bakery and Addie isn't much help even if she's present. Millie limps plenty enough and spends a lot of her days visiting other widows and offering them help. I can't leave Hannah to see to it alone."

"If we all need to help out with the harvest so you can do this, just say so."

Leon's heart warmed at the offer.

"What changed Lewis? I mean what made him decide to

come home and take his baptism and marry after being out there where there are no rules to follow?"

Luke ran a hand over his beard as considered his next words.

"The Lord speaks to every man differently. All we need to do is listen and heed his word. Lewis thought to be in love, but he still yet didn't know what true love was. He grew up *bruder*, felt *Gott's* love for him"

Luke turned and walked away without another word. Yes, Luke would serve well if ever chosen, of that Leon was certain.

Leon slapped the reins and urged Marva forward. "*Danki*, Lord, for loving me."

CHAPTER SEVENTEEN

As heavy rains moved in, stealing away any chance to harvest today, Hannah decided to join her family at Penny's for a summer canning frolic. She seldom took the time for such anymore, but she had also been itching to see the newest addition to Miller's Creek. Had it not just been yesterday that she, Penny, and Lydia were *kinner* talking about marriage and *bopplin*? Like her, both her dear friends lived through dark days, felt the sting of doubts that God was merciful leaving them all fatherless, and each of them had endured more responsibility than most *maedels*. Now Lydia was married to Silas, mothered his three *kinner,* and become a mother naturally too. Penny had married Luke, and she too had become a mother.

Hannah remained, no further ahead nor behind. *Stuck.*

"He is so…perfect, Penny." Hannah cooed as Daniel's dark hair, feather-soft, floated between her fingers. "But if I don't put him down now and help with the beans you will think I came to swoon over Daniel and not help with the canning." Hannah handed the small round bundle of dark eyes and rosy cheeks back to Penny. That sweet unfamiliar smell of his recent bath was immediately missed. A sense of longing swept over her, a natural ache for something created by her. What would it be like to have a *boppli* of her own? She had thought about it, years ago. Four being the perfect number she had in mind. Boys and girls, and none with her unruly red hair.

"You could probably do both at the same time. You always could tend two things at once," Penny said.

Hannah hadn't missed teaching, though there were a few little faces that had grown close to her heart. Regret was something she never considered when she traded one purpose for another. Yet, she did long for the same things others did. Her life was different, of that she knew well enough. What man would willingly take up the helm, fill boots her *daed* once filled, and let a woman work by his side instead of tucking her away indoors?

"I can see you one day strapping a *boppli* to your side and picking apples, whereas I can't even can all these beans without help." Penny praised.

"You had a hard time bringing that big fella into the world. Martha insists you rest and build your strength back," Irma Milford said. "I know the hardships of bringing a Milford into the world."

Hannah had met Leon's *mamm* on a few occasions, but they had hardly shared a word in passing. Today, Hannah would be working alongside Irma. She wasn't one who let nerves in the way of a chore, but currently, she felt them down to her toes. Irma was no different than any other woman Hannah worked alongside in the past. However, the unease that crept over her couldn't be ignored.

"Women have been having *bopplin* for centuries. That's no excuse for me needing help," Penny said.

Her pale complexion was all the evidence Irma needed to insist Penny sit and hold her *sohn* and enjoy a day among friends.

"Luke would not want you overdoing it, my dear. All of my *sohns* are attentive like that," Irma said, glancing in

Hannah's direction before fetching another five-gallon bucket of beans and hoisting it onto Penny's kitchen table.

Something about the way Irma pinned her with that look set the hairs on the back of Hannah's neck upward. Did she think Hannah disagreed? In truth, Hannah admired the fact that even Lester knew how to be chivalrous.

"Ivy, why don't you break, and Hannah can help prep jars. Irma can have some *mammi* time with little Daniel," Millie said as she dunked more jars into the sudsy sink water.

"So how is Lewis?" *Mamm* asked, referring to Miller's Creek's newest minister.

Hannah went to the sink and took over washing jars as *mamm* spread a fresh towel across the table and began breaking another run of beans. She still couldn't believe it. The choosing of the lot was no simple task and yet, God had placed the community in the hands of Lewis Milford to be their minister.

"He would never admit worry. My *sohns* are all like such," Irma said. Hannah figured they were all prideful, Luke being the exception. Penny indeed got the pick of the litter there. "He is asking John many questions about verses of late. The two sat long into the night last night reading scripture. I must say I worry he is concerned when his time to preach comes."

"Bishop Schwartz won't expect him to preach his first Sunday right after being chosen, but I think Lewis will do *wunderbaar*," Millie said. "All your *sohns* have proven to be *gut* additions to our community."

Hannah's hands froze mid-washing. *Good additions?* Two waywards and one ego-fed flirt. *Mudder* was shelling out too much kindness today. Remaining tight-lipped, Hannah continued washing dishes and not let the comment trouble her. *Mamm* always had a nice word to hand out. It was simply her way.

"Luke says that because of all his wandering, he feels Lewis will do well," Penny said.

Hannah didn't agree. If a man could so easily be

persuaded to leave his family and his faith for an infatuation, he would always sit on the edge of tittering, but she would never mention such and upset Irma. It had to be hard to raise *kinner* who didn't heed good lessons.

"And what of Lester? Any word yet?" Millie asked more carefully.

Hannah stilled again and bent an ear hoping to hear Irma's answer. Had he really run off with an *Englischer* as it was rumored? Hannah's heart went out to Irma Milford. On all accounts, she seemed a good person, a dutiful *fraa* and *mudder*, but to have one bring shame upon the family, as Lester had been of late, had to be terrible to endure.

"*Nee*. I think our *sohns* know more than they are telling." Irma gazed down at Daniel a smitten look reflecting in her blue eyes. "But I know them well and they will bring him home, where ever he is."

Irma sounded certain. She obviously had a lot of confidence in her sons. Hannah paused, taking in the woman who bore six *kinner*, moved across the country, and fit like a glove in Penny's house. Her pale blue dress matched her eyes and that little scar across her jaw enhanced her, instead of taking away from her fine features. Not all strong women lifted apple crates, some just endured and overcame.

"So, Hannah, has Leon been doing a *gut* job helping with your orchard?" Irma asked.

Hannah felt her throat tighten.

"Leon has lightened the load, *jah*," Millie said while Hannah worked the sandpaper in her throat down.

Irma's brows knitted together. "He has always been *gut* at learning new things. A quick learner John says." She fingered a hair on Daniel's head. "Of all me *sohns,* he is the most capable of accepting change and trying on any chore."

Hannah couldn't disagree with that. Leon did take to a task quickly and one only had to instruct him once before he knew what he was doing.

"He   wasn't   built   for   routine.   Leon   likes things…unpredictable." Orchard life was unpredictable for sure and certain. If the weather wasn't trying to kill, maim, or spoil all your labors, then it was insects boring in for a season to make your life miserable.

"He has a soft heart for helping others too. But don't tell him I told you that. He would fear his *bruders* teasing." Irma winked and then laughed softly.

"He is the reason we are permitted to wear pants while tending the bees again. He talked to the bishop and made it so." Addie chimed in as she stepped in the door with another bucket of green beans ready for breaking. Hannah pivoted at the sink and turned to her sister. This was news to her. Since when had the bishop agreed to britches on a woman? Of course, they often wore them, but no one knew they did being as the hives were so well back from the sight of passersby. *Until Leon told, that was.* Hannah blinked back her surprise. She hadn't asked Leon to go to the bishop on their behalf. *How rude.* What right did he have speaking for her family? She was eldest and so it was her job to handle such affairs.

"He thinks of others before himself."

Or perhaps trying to get on the good side of the bishop, Hannah mused. Irma began to rock back and forth with Daniel slumbering in her arms.

"Little Daniel here is blessed with *onkels*. A child cannot have enough love surrounding him, *jah*?"

"'Tis true," Millie replied and then poured her full bowl into a tub of cold water to soak and clean. "He does things like that, you know?"

Hannah looked at her just as Irma did.

"Leon thought to finish Eli's plans of building an auction house," Millie said.

She took up another handful of beans into her apron before sitting back in her chair. Penny reached out and scooped up another handful herself, saying nothing to this new bit of information.

"I did not tell him to do that," Hannah said. *What nerve.* How dare he think to barge into her life and take over? She set the jar she was washing down harder than she should have. Luckily, little Daniel was too comfy to care about the sudden noise.

"I did. Your *daed*'s hope for our family and the community was a *gut* one."

That was true, but none of Leon's concern. Why was he intruding in her life when he had no right to?

"Leon does not need your approval to help where he sees a need."

Mamm shot her a knowing glare. Hannah turned back to washing jars, pricked by the news and worse that her mother had fallen for Leon's smooth tongue and charms.

"A marketplace will be *gut* for many. In Michigan, we had two. It made a big difference for the community to put everything in one place. The *Englisch* love coming and buying all our homemades." Irma delivered Daniel back to his *mamm* and strolled up to Hannah.

"I know Leon takes some getting used to my dear but know this. Once you see his heart, it grows on you."

That's what Hannah was afraid of and didn't dare agreed with.

"*Jah*, I know. I was just surprised by these things. No one shared them with me before today." Hannah admitted, hoping Irma saw the reasoning behind her earlier outburst. As eldest, the orchard had solely been her responsibility and a small part of her was surprised her mother had gone around her to do something Hannah didn't approve of.

"You know, Sister, it is okay to accept help. Leon isn't foolish, and he is learning about my bees and your apples and overseeing finishing the marketplace *daed* always wanted. I can't tell you how much not sitting at the end of the road for days tending to our vegetable stand means to me."

Addie was right, which Hannah discovered she didn't like

one bit either.

Noticing now that everyone was focusing on her, Hannah's face warmed in the unexpected attention. All but Penny at the far end of the room nuzzling Daniel and smirking. They had been friends long enough Hannah knew she had a thought or two of her own on the matter.

"I assume you want to add to this," Hannah said boldly. She wasn't naive. She had in fact become the subject of the day just because she didn't like Leon Milford.

"It is time for you to enjoy life. Look just how beautiful it can be," Penny said in a mothering softness.

There was no arguing that. Hannah let out a sigh.

"Fine." She surrendered, completely outnumbered as she was. "Maybe I have been a little hard," Hannah said. Addie coughed fake and loudly.

"A little. I can't see why he bothers to return each day," Ivy said, causing Hannah to wince. "He surely doesn't get paid enough."

Had she been so unreasonable that everyone saw it but her? Well, maybe tomorrow at their first, and hopefully last, swimming lesson, Hannah could try a little harder to be kinder to Leon Milford, the thorn in her side.

Chapter Eighteen

Leon didn't break promises, and he had no intention of doing so now. Rain had left the earth soft beneath him as he strolled down the short path through birch and brambles with three shadows trailing behind him. He had been looking forward to this all week.

When he reached the clearing, he sought out the old log nearby, sat down, and began removing his boots. He needed to wipe the stupid grin off his face, but when the women stepped into the clearing, eyes wide with mixes of excitement and dread, Leon couldn't tap it down even a notch. Nothing was more amusing than three red-headed women looking at forty-eight inches of running water like it had the ability to strike out and bite.

"It's going to be cold, like as not," Addie said to no one in particular.

She kicked off her black-soled shoes, and without prodding slipped off her socks. Ivy followed suit, but Leon gave neither any mind, his gaze focused solely on the eldest Troyer in a thin, brown chore dress, barefoot as the day she was born, and wearing a look of utter undoing.

She was trembling at the sight of a mere puddle. Leon's

heart wanted to reach out to her to offer assurances considering he had grown up with a lake for a backyard. She was in good hands. However long it took, how many ever pounds of patience it required, he would help her move past this little hiccup in her life.

Suddenly, an unbidden image intrigued his imaginative nature. One of Hannah standing on the rocky shores, facing the vast waters of the Coldwater, or perhaps Lake Michigan, her dark autumn mane catching a cold northern wind. One day, he would show her his birthplace, the vast waters of his youth where his best memories were made. He could show her the little school house that was so small it could sit inside the very one she had schooled *kinner* in herself. First, trust had to be established before old memories could be replaced with fresh new ones.

"Eldest goes first," Leon said. "I don't make the rules." Leon shrugged playfully and moved closer to her. Hannah tossed him a sharp emerald glare. "Those looks don't work on me like you think," he muttered against her weak threat.

"I can't believe I let you talk me into this," Hannah said with her fist gripped tightly to the sides of her dress.

If she thought she would back out now, she was sorely mistaken. "And I can't believe you agreed," he said taking a slow step into the water. "But you did, and what's done is done." Addie and Ivy giggled, but Hannah didn't even break the barbed stare locked onto him. "Don't fret, I won't let anything happen. It's not deep enough to worry and you wade here all the time, rightly so," he offered a hand. Barefoot and trembling she took it and slowly stepped into the water.

It wasn't the touch, the feel of her smaller, calloused hands sliding into his that had Leon's heart humming a slow pulsating beat. It was that trust, a rare gift she was giving, and it spoke volumes. He had maintained a clear head from the moment he escorted the three women down here, and now all his good sense floated downstream as water quickly wicked up her brown dress. Leon would keep earning that trust too, even if it was one drop at a time.

"I hate you," she muttered before turning and instructing Addie and Ivy to follow.

Leon noted neither wore the fierce expression of their elder sister, but three fraidy-cats were two too many.

"First try to relax. Move around and get comfortable. It is important to be comfortable." Leon instructed. Addie dipped down and glided her hands over the water, a little smile tugging at her lips. Ivy followed her movements and tossed him a grin. If Leon didn't know better, those two weren't so much afraid as they let on when they jumped at the idea of him teaching them to swim.

Hannah was momentarily distracted, searching the rolling waters for threats. Too distracted to even notice her sisters had pulled the wool over her eyes.

"How about you help Addie, and I will help Ivy with floating." Hannah did better when she was busy, so giving her something to do he imagined would calm her frayed nerves.

"What do I do?" Hannah asked.

"Just don't let her sink," Leon said. They practiced floating and when Ivy swallowed a mouthful of creek water, they all laughed. Leon's toes were freezing, and he reckoned theirs were too.

"Now your turn." She didn't lower her displeasure in his prodding, but true to her word, Hannah slowly waded his way. What a strange feeling. He was Leon Milford, strong under pressure. He never once flinched at the punching game. However, anticipating Hannah in his arms, he was mush.

"Relax. It's just floating, and I won't let you go under." She cringed despite his promise.

"*Ich kann naett* do this, Leon," she confessed with a whisper.

"After all, I have seen you do, this will be easy."

Cautiously, Leon placed a firm hand on her back. She gave a slight shudder under his palm but as cold as the water was, he didn't think too hard on it. Ivy and Addie tossed stones nearby, chatting about whatever sisters chatted about. Leon heard nothing but the cicadas starting another round of screeching.

"Trust me, Hannah, this is nothing compared to all you have done so far." Her eyes widened. She wasn't one accustomed to regular compliments.

"I guess I have no choice. Trusting you that is," she said. She took a quivering breath, lowered into the water, and let go. "Don't you dare let me drown," she said before laying back as Leon lifted her to float on the surface. He kept her weightless body from sinking, his hands cradling her lower back and neck.

For a moment, Leon knew what it felt like to hold the world in his hands. Something inside woke a protectiveness. It may have been a fool's errand, but her trust was becoming his greatest deepest longing. Leon lifted his eyes to the heavens where they should be and not on Hannah floating in his arms.

"That one looks like your Tom," Leon said to distract her, or himself. At this point, he wasn't sure which of them needed it most.

"Ivy's Tom." Hannah corrected, squinting to see what he saw. "She's the cat rescuer. I'm not fond of them at all." She confessed just as her teeth began to chatter. Blinking to adjust, she studied the cottony puffs above and pinned her eyes on the one that was a perfect likeness to the mangy feline. "It even has one ear," she said, slightly amused. In this position, Hannah had a perfect view of Leon. She noted the strong jawline and wide neck as he studied the heavens. She had to give him credit; he had a way about him to ignore her stubbornness and still find the words to coax her into trying something she swore she would never do. His patience was impressive and unnerving. He probably thought those charms could talk her into about anything.

The cold water lapped at her skirts, but currently, being this near Leon was doing plenty to her to keep her warm. *Leon Milford stares at clouds.* She mocked before closing her eyes and simply let herself forget he was the kind of man who liked dainty women who giggled at nonsense. She let herself float, drifting on a strange wave of trust and relaxation. *This was good medicine.* Feeling even more at ease with herself, Hannah let her arms slowly move in long glides just below the surface. Maybe it was the day, the fact he was not as horrible as she once thought, or perhaps creeks had powers she hadn't noticed yet, but Hannah felt light and content and safe.

"And stars," he said. "Does that surprise you?"

She opened her eyes as he lowered his gaze to her. Those blue eyes had her heart racing again. She quickly closed her eyes just as Ivy used to do when playing childish games of Hide and Seek. It wasn't fair that eyes could do that to a person.

"*Nee.* Just did not see you as one who enjoyed *Gott's* little gifts is all."

"I'm His biggest fan," he said in a voice that sent shivers over her.

She could only hope he wasn't gawking and kept her eyes tightly shut. Letting her head fall back, Hannah let the water have her. She longed to hear its whispers, stories of each raindrop's journey. How far did a raindrop travel before dying a dry death and birthing fresh out of the clouds? She could disappear here, under the surface, at least for a while, listening to all of the nothingness.

"Huh," she said, hearing Leon's faint voice.

"Autumn leaves," he muttered above her.

"What about them?" she muttered back.

"Your hair is the same color. Like a rug of autumn leaves laid out."

She stiffened and her eyes burst open. He was indeed watching her.

"Just stating a fact."

"I prefer you didn't." She countered as they both held gazes.

"Then I shouldn't mention that you have a full parade of freckles too. From one cheek," his eyes roamed from cheek to cheek, "over the bridge of your nose, to the other cheek."

She tensed when her ears went deeper in the water and one hand swung up and gripped his arm.

"Relax," he whispered encouragingly, floating her higher.

"Your ears are crooked." He laughed at her appraisal of him. "And you have one brow thicker than the other." He lifted the thinner one but made no remark. Hannah studied him, then, searching for more unbalanced traits. She closed her eyes again and said, "And you tend to clench your jaw, a lot. That's a horrid habit and you will spend lots of time at a dentist for it."

"They are rarely still, but you have delicate fingers but strong hands." To this, she smiled. "It's an odd mix but suits you."

"You are strong too, you just aren't all that smart," she smiled wider. His laugh sounded muffled under the water.

"True, you are far smarter than me, but I fuss less."

Without warning, her body jerked and went down. He grappled to hold her, but she had already managed to collect and right herself. Coughing, she made her way to the bank, and he quickly followed. That's what she got for letting her guard down.

"Hannah, wait," Leon called out.

"This is ridiculous. We have chores. This was such a silly idea."

"Wait, Hannah. You were doing fine. Don't just give up."

He begged as she stormed through the brush, barefoot

and soaked. Give up on what, she suddenly wondered.

"Guess we should go too," Ivy said collecting their things. Addie stood, giving him a hard look.

"You know, we put this out there all nice and easy for ya. Try not to keep messing it up." She turned on a heel and marched off too.

Once alone again, Leon tried to drown himself, but it proved much harder than he thought.

Chiding herself, Hannah marched home and went straight to her room. She should have known better, kept a safe distance. Angrily, she shucked out of the damp dress she might as well burn now. She had let her guard down, played his stupid game, and now look what it got her. A case of fresh embarrassment, tied with a thick ribbon of confusion.

"Swimming lessons." She harrumphed. "Thinks he's so smart does he," she said between chattering teeth. Leon Milford liked attention, that's what that was. Well, she wouldn't make this mistake again, she balked silently, and she shoved her blue orchard dress over her damp head.

Leon's smile was becoming too distracting. Those charms he naturally possessed getting harder to ignore. She tossed her soaked brown dress toward the door with an angry arm. It wasn't solely her fault. The way he looked at her would have made any *maedel* shiver with delight. She wasn't just any *maedel*. And she was in trouble. She liked him. Like other girls liked him. Wasn't that just foolishness?

"What is the matter with you? You stormed off acting *narrisch*."

Addie stomped into the room. She picked up the wet dress and shut the door behind her, her own dress leaving a puddle at her bare feet. Hannah unpinned her damp hair and shook it free.

"Did he say something mean to you?" Addie asked, her

breath labored.

The bedroom felt smaller than usual, stuffy without a bit of good air in it. "I'm fat and dumb and I want that man gone." Hannah could always be honest with her sisters but maybe that was too honest. She went to the window and gave it a hard shove upward. Musky damp air rushed over her immediately.

"What?" Addie said in a shocked tone.

Hannah regretted saying anything, an outburst that now would require further explanation. A tear slipped down her cheek as she stared out the window. Addie's small footsteps crossed the room and the familiar creak said she sat on the bed.

"I can't believe he said that to you?"

He might as well have.

"He didn't say it." Hannah huffed. "He was thinking it." Hannah turned. "And you're getting *my* bed wet."

Addie stood. "And how do you know what he thinks? Are you a mind reader now?" Addie cocked her head and lifted a sharp brow.

Hannah ignored her questioning tone. She didn't need Addie's reproach right now.

"Look at you, Sister."

Addie took her arm and forced Hannah to face her.

"You are beautiful and far smarter than any other in this *haus*."

Addie leaned in and smiled, trying to urge her out of her mood.

"I'm *griddlich*, all the time," Hannah admitted.

"*Jah*, but only because you do so much and never rest up after," Addie said. "And it might be sinful, but every *maedel* I know in Miller's Creek wants to be you, even I."

Hannah's gaze collided with Addie's.

"Of all the stuff and nonsense to spill out of your mouth." Hannah rolled her eyes. Addie was being far too kind saying such untrue things.

"It's true. Many look at you because you're *schee* and others look *up* to you because you are a *gut* example to many. You don't see how *wunderbaar* you are. I could never earn the respect of so many as you. You are Hannah Troyer the school teacher, the woman who runs her family's orchard." Addie took her hands. "*Gott* made you strong and brave because He knew we all would depend on you. He knew this farm would not stand without you holding it up."

Hannah felt the pricks of tears sting her cheeks.

"You take care of all of us and see that we have the things we need. You let *mamm* have the time she needed to grieve, without pushing. You let Ivy bring home strays even though it's more mouths to feed. You let me complain and get out of chores." Addie chuckled. "You keep going even when you're so tired you want to stop. And you look like this while you're doing it." Addie stepped back, their hands still connected, and looked Hannah up and down. "Trust me, Leon Milford does not think you're fat or stupid," Addie insisted. "Now tell me what is going through that head of yours to think otherwise."

"He looked at me like…and then said things…" Hannah sucked back a sob. She had tangled herself into a mess alright. It wasn't supposed to be like this. She wasn't supposed to let Leon Milford make her feel anything. "I'm so confused." Hannah dropped her face into her hands. In the water, she had let herself forget. Forget she had responsibilities. Forget she was with a man she detested. She forgot everything until those soft blue eyes saw into her heart, exposing every blemish, every shortcoming. Panic ravaged her like a storm and her only option was to run. Leon was looking at her like he did *mamm*'s apple pie. Hannah knew better. His talents were well-honed, but how it made her heart skip, her breath rapid. She had no idea how to deal with it.

"So, he looked at you and said some things. Well, that explains everything."

"He made me feel like he cared. Like he liked what he saw. I just…"

"Don't know how to deal with it after thinking him a scoundrel so long." Addie grinned.

Hannah nodded.

"He is smitten with you. We all see it, and he always has been. It wonders me how you feel. Do you like him?"

It was undeniable and utterly disturbing because she did. "It matters not. I'm not like Tina or Mirim. There isn't a delicate bone in my body, Addie. I'm bulky and big." She ran a hand down her hips then up toward a healthy chest. "I have thighs and these things get in the way more often than not." Hannah sighed heavily.

"Oh, I can see your problem now." Addie laughed.

"I'm serious, Addie," Hannah said. She knotted her fists.

"What you see as flaws are blessings. Me and Ivy can only hope to have half your blessings one day." Addie laughed and rolled her eyes playfully. "You are a *gut* person, with a big heart, and not the kind of person who worries over such things. *Gott* knows this, we know this, and so does he."

Addie pointed out the window as Leon crossed the yard and slipped into the barn. After hitching up his horse, he left. The unease she had felt didn't leave with him.

"I need some air." She informed her sister.

"I agree. One of your walks in the orchard might help. I know you go out there to pray and feel close to *daed*."

Hannah turned to her sister and gave a half-hearted smile. "It's where I feel him most. Out there I can think and breathe."

"I feel him at the kitchen table," Addie said in a more somber voice. "I miss his laugh. It rattled the floors, the windows. He was so big, you know. So safe."

Hannah pulled Addie into a hug, surprised how wonderful the contact felt. They held on for a time. Hugs were good medicine too when the heart was ailing.

As she stepped out of her room, Hannah nearly tumbled

over Ivy leaning on the doorway. "Eavesdropping, little sister?" Ivy shrugged, caught red-handed. Just for good measure, Hannah pulled Ivy into a quick hug and then aimed for her orchard.

CHAPTER NINETEEN

Hannah hadn't a clue how long she strolled about the orchard, but it had, as always, brought a measure of calm. When she reached the eastern field, she noted the empty wagon waiting to be filled. There was a lot to do, but right now work was furthest from her thoughts.

It was the cicadas that drew her to the tree line with their annoying buzz and relentless need to annoy the whole state. They clung thick as sap on nearby cedars. Some were louder than others. Some rubbed their wings together while others scooted about doing something else. There were hollowed-out shells, shedding remains hanging about the bark. She leaned in for a look, poking at a crisp empty shell before plucking one up for a closer inspection. "A small thing for such a big noise," she mused, noting two very eerie black eyes.

Cicadas screamed, not really buzzed at all, but either way, their penetrating noise was deafening. It was enough to make one aim to hunt down every last one. Putting the cicada back where she found it, unharmed, she slipped into the foliage. She reached the small clearing. Damp earth and fresh water were faithful companions of what always soothed her inner hardships. Mud squished between her toes as she followed the trail. Rushing water welcomed her, where just an hour before it had sent her running.

For a moment her head was quiet, her hands empty. She stepped gingerly over a fallen branch lying before her. Life had been just fine before Leon came in and ruined it with his penetrating blue eyes and flirting smiles.

The water called to her, and her feet knew what she was about to do, even before her mind reasoned with it. Her sisters could help with supper, and she, well, she could settle one problem today. Tomorrow would come soon enough. She crossed over the stony landing and cautiously waded in. Sticking to the shallows, she hiked her dry dress as cool water lapped at her shins.

Life had sure grown complicated. She always thought herself of practical mind and sensible, but that was changing too.

"Trust in the Lord with all your heart, and do not lean on your own understanding." The Psalm burst out of her. "Well, I don't understand. I don't understand why You would take healthy men, with families, and leave us all here alone." She rebuked. "I don't understand why You would give us a minister who has sinned to help those who have been forgotten. I don't understand why you are making me feel things we both know I have no to time to feel!" Her fury cried out.

Her only response was the gurgling water and pesky bugs. Hannah's gaze shot heavenward, where sheets of blue and puffy white clouds formed a backdrop to full willows and oaks aligning on the other side of the creek.

Commit thy way unto the Lord; Trust also in Him, and He shall bring it to pass. More scripture her father once offered to a seventeen-year-old Hannah, who was straddling a fence of liberty and traditionalism.

"A merry heart doeth good like medicine, but a broken spirit, drieth the bones."

Hannah jerked around to find the root of her current woes, standing in the shadows. "You left," she said in a small voice. "Were you spying on me, Leon Milford?"

He took three cautious steps forward. "*Nee*, I just didn't like how things were left. I wanted to make sure you were okay."

"What do you care?" She turned from him and heard his steps unsettle rock behind her.

"I don't know why, but I do," Leon said with a hint of humor in his tone.

"What are you doing?" she asked when his boots hit the water.

"I'm coming to you."

She couldn't read his blank expression and wondered what idiot walked into the creek with his boots on.

"Why?" Her voice shuddered; her breath quickened.

"Because we both know you wouldn't come to me." He offered a hand. "Hannah."

Her name came out in exasperation, stalling her from leaving. "Must we spend another two years pretending we don't like each other?"

Hannah's heart wanted his words to be true, but her head didn't agree. Her mouth opened; a ready reply was usually there. Right now, she couldn't find one. She hadn't dreamed up those feelings he gave her.

"I don't pretend. Save your charms for Tina or Mirim."

"Lewis is more the charmer," Leon said, quirking a grin.

"Or Lester? It seems such runs thick in some families. I still cannot believe Lewis is our new minister." She lifted a finger and waved it in his face. No more jabbing it into that hard chest. Lesson learned. "I know what you did to Tabor's horse, and that trick with the bishop was foolish. Did our new minister help?"

Anger burned in his ice-blue glare. She had never seen that look before and almost regretted putting there. When would she ever learn to just keep her mouth shut? But how else would she rid herself of this man who was all wrong for her? He would never care for her the way she was beginning to care for him. A man like Leon could never be content with apples. Hannah was only being sensible. She turned to find a clear path out of the water and away from him, but Leon took her arm.

"Because of Lewis's choices, my *bruder* will show love and compassion for those who struggle. He is a faithful servant of *Gott*. He knows what it is like to be judged by others too."

Leon let his eyes take her in. This time with disgust and she now knew the difference.

"I will find Lester and talk some sense into him, because sometimes, Hannah, people make mistakes. Sometimes they say and do things they shouldn't."

He leaned in closer, stealing what air she needed to keep breathing as her heart pounded so hard, she felt she might faint.

"Like agreeing to let you work here," she said. "*Jah*, we all make mistakes."

"Like hurling insults about without a care."

His voice held a hint of caution and she gasped beneath his truth.

He stepped back, pulled his hat from his head, and raked his fingers through his hair. "Like you, I care for my family and will look out for them no matter what."

"You did those things for your family?" She mustered a defiant laugh. "You painted Tabor's horse for the sake of family?"

"Luke loved Penny and between Tabor thinking to court her and Thomas Miller sharpening his bitterness on her, they were making her life miserable. She grew ill, Hannah. Luke told me everything."

Hannah remembered well all Penny had endured. If she hadn't had her own family to deal with, Hannah would have been a better friend and helped her too.

"The bishop wouldn't put an end to their hounding.

Someone had to see it dealt with," he said matter of factly.

He was breathing awfully hard for a man standing in one place. Hannah considered herself fairly smart, born with enough good sense to see things done well, but right now she felt as brainless as a rock. Leon's pranks weren't just un-supervised childishness. They were still wrong, she con-cluded, but his acts had ended the hounding Penny suffered.

"You miss him, I understand that. All say your *daed* was a *gut* man, but you cannot blame *Gott* or me, or anyone else that catches you off guard. And it's time to stop thinking you can do it all. We all need help, Hannah. At some point, we all will."

Hannah's eyes blurred as Leon's words broadsided her. "You don't know…" She tried to quarrel back, but her throat thickened.

"I know more than you think." He held her gaze and took another sharp breath.

She did miss her *daed* and was worn to the bone. And Leon was right, about all of it. Eating crow, as *daed* used to call it when one had to admit failure, tastes awful.

"You're right. Penny needed those two to leave her alone. It was a very hard time for her." Hannah's shoulders low-ered. "I'm sorry," she muttered staring up at him.

"Then tell me what I did wrong," Leon said on a worried breath.

He was serious. That Hannah could see plain enough. And he hadn't a clue. "I'm just not…made like other…" She pulled from her strengths to continue. Eating crow was aw-ful but humble pie was even worse. "I know now it wasn't on purpose you let me sink under the water, and I just over-reacted." Leon's mouth lifted slowly. Here she was being honest, and he was smiling. He continued holding her hand and made soft circles with his thumb over hers.

"You know, if a man stands still long enough, he can hear and see everything. You are thinking foolish thoughts now."

His eyes smiled as the failing light of day reflected on the water and shimmered in his eyes.

"I'm sorry for letting you sink. It wasn't you. I was…"
He swallowed. "…admiring the beauty about and wasn't
paying attention." His lips hiked to one corner. "I did carry
you all the way to the house. Well, I did drop you once."

"You dropped me!"

"I'm just teasing. You are way too serious, woman." He
belted out a laugh.

His focus returned to her eyes. She opened her mouth
but not a word came out.

"I reckon you just don't know how *schee* you are and perfectly made by *Gott*."

Did Leon Milford truly think her pretty and not bulky at
all? Hannah was certain her knees just might buckle. What
Addie said was true.

"So, stop fretting so much, and let's practice kicking. The
water, not me, alright?" he quickly added, cracking another
devilish smile and tapping the tip of her freckled nose.

"How about we just sit? I don't think my toes can handle
getting any colder."

"And we wouldn't want to put any smudges on your reputation," he said before waving off her need to add to that.

"And that." she managed a smile. Were they becoming…friends? He offered her a hand, and Hannah accepted
it. He never flinched or commented about the callouses she
bore or how long her fingers were. Leon simply helped her
to the fallen log, and they sat as the cicadas thought it too
quiet about and decided to all remedy that at once.

"They really are noisy. I don't know how we are going to
get through a whole summer without going crazy listening
to that."

"Don't deny them their chance. All life gets it."

Leon stretched out his long legs and crossed them at the
ankles. Hannah felt a bit guilty when she noted the water line
on his trouser legs and figured his boots were soaked clean
through. She let herself watch him as he faced the heavens,

taking in all the parts of him she merely sneaked peeks at on a regular day.

"Their chance at what?"

"That racket is their mating call. They waited seventeen years for this one summer. It's their season."

He held up one finger and looked down at her with a smile. A warm liquid traveled through her veins. No man ever looked at her like he did, and certainly not while explaining the mating rituals of bugs.

"Well, I'm glad I wasn't born a pesky bug," she said, holding his gaze. All that noise just so they could bear fresh life. It was crazy. Leon placed a hand over her own.

"I guess some things just need to make a little more noise to get noticed."

The calm that often drove her furious now melted her like ice cream in August. His hand was so warm, comforting to her cold fingers. He was being fresh, flirting like that, and this time, Hannah didn't mind at all.

"Hannah!"

Ivy's high-pitched voice broke through the evening and even quieted the cicadas. Hannah wasn't surprised. After all, Ivy did have the best lungs for it.

She groaned. "I never told anyone I was here." They got to their feet before Ivy reached them.

"Tabor is here, again," Ivy said bursting into the clearing wearing a fresh dress and a clean *kapp*.

She came to an abrupt halt at the sight of Hannah and Leon alone at the creek. It wasn't proper and was against the rules.

"Oh, I'll tell him you will be up to the house in a few."

Ivy giggled, covering her mouth with her hand before running away again. Hannah rolled her eyes and let out another groan.

Jaw clenched so tight two bulging muscles appeared, Leon looked at her with narrowed blue eyes.

"Until tomorrow night," he said in a casual tone.

Hannah nodded. She couldn't explain to him, not now, how fast her heart was pounding because he wanted to continue what they started. Hannah just wasn't sure Leon meant swimming anymore.

"I'll go this way," he pulled on his boots and nodded up the creek a way. "I wouldn't want to upset your boyfriend." Without looking back, he slipped into the brush and was gone before she could say otherwise.

"Tomorrow night," she whispered under the noise of a cicada summer, just starting.

Chapter Twenty

Hannah slowed her approach as she reached the porch, the hem of her dress still damp from the creek. Tabor stood at the top, his eyes probing, and wearing a frown. Then again, Tabor often wore a frown, so she ignored it. No one could be happy all the time.

"Hannah enjoys her walks," *Mamm* said.

Hannah wondered just how long Tabor had been there but noted it had to be a while by the look on *Mamm*'s face.

"So, you mentioned," Tabor said. "Hiya, Hannah."

"Tabor," she greeted. "Sorry, I had no idea we had a visitor."

"I like to think I'm not just any visitor." He smiled.

Hannah said nothing. She wasn't sure she cared at all what Tabor thought currently. Leon Milford just told her she was pretty. Surely, that would take a few days to sink in.

"If you're not too tired from your…walking, I'd be happy if you would take a short ride with me this evening."

Tabor seldom gave a person time to answer and already began descending the porch steps and offering an arm. Hannah peered at her mother and couldn't ignore the look of hope in her eyes. Tabor was a fine man, he knew what it was like to lose a parent, and as eldest of his lot, he understood the pressures of being responsible for his siblings. They had many things in common. So why wasn't the prospect of courting Tabor stirring bees in her belly?

Tabor was only a few inches taller than she, and like *daed*, he bore wide shoulders and a mountainous frame. He had a long chin that ran parallel perfectly with his sharp nose. Most girls thought him handsome. Hannah wasn't as convinced. Her idea of handsome was slowly coming into view and looked nothing like Tabor at all. He was too perfectly symmetrical. What one hair did on the left, the right one mirrored. Those ears, she noted giving them a quick glance, were way too perfectly aligned, and big enough to hold his hat a little higher on his head.

Leon's left ear sat down a tad lower than his right. And if she wasn't mistaken, he had one shy dimple, not two. *Nothing symmetrical about him*. Shaking off the urge to suddenly compare them, she opened her mouth to decline his offer. It wasn't right to let Tabor assume she had an interest.

"Oh, that would be just lovely." *Mamm* urged, most likely to be free from hearing all about his latest build.

"*Mamm*, it has been a wonderfully long day. I think…" Hannah began to protest.

"The fresh evening air will do you some *gut*," *Mamm* said with a wide grin that was completely unnecessary. Her unsubtle coaxing wasn't appreciated, and Hannah shot her a pleading look. *Mamm* had spent two years mourning the death of her husband and now decided Leon could build the marketplace building and Tabor could court her daughter. Whatever had gotten into her of late, Hannah hoped she lost it, and soon.

"I'll have her back safe and sound" Tabor said before turning to Hannah and shooting her a wink. Tabor touched her elbow and thanked Millie with a curt nod. "I won't keep you out long. It really is a nice evening and I have never been one to waste a *gut* evening."

How could she say no now without upsetting her mother and Tabor? Hannah had no good excuse currently. *Like missing supper*, Hannah bit back. *Mamm* would feel bad for being so pushy if Hannah starved, now, wouldn't she?

A warm summer breeze stirred as gravel crushed beneath his heavy soles. Hannah followed Tabor to his buggy but kept her focus on her footing and the man beside her who was making her uneasy again.

"Millie says you finished the first harvest."

Hannah nodded.

"I hate knowing you have to work out here all day instead of doing what other women enjoy."

"But I do enjoy it, as a woman," Hannah said sharply. The front screen door slammed shut, sending an uncomfortable jolt through her.

"My job ends at four each day."

Tabor reached out a hand when they reached his buggy. Hannah didn't need help into a buggy. She had been doing it alone since she was five and learned climbing was a thrill in itself.

"I could spare a few hours each evening to help if that is something you would like for me to do."

What she would like is to go back home and curl up in her bed. The day had drained her body and flooded her head. Sleep was a good remedy for both. Instead, she climbed into the buggy and hoped they could get this ride over with quickly.

Saying nothing to her standoffishness, Tabor rounded the buggy and climbed in as well.

"Millie thought it was a good idea. I just wonder if you do too." He gave her a sidelong look. "She thinks we would work well together."

Was *mamm* trying to marry her off? Would that not solve all of their problems? As eldest, she felt the burden of it. Many married for security and safety just as they did for love. Hannah's love was the orchard. She was bound to it by blood and oath. Flirting with fanciful ideas about Leon was only making things harder. And Tabor, poor Tabor, Hannah needed to be honest with him. She did not want a future with him, or to take buggy rides with him any more than she wanted to think about summer ending and Leon leaving. Though both men had many qualities worthy of her, none came close to the man who tended this ground all his life.

"That's kind of you Tabor, but I have been seeing this over all my life. I need no help with it," she said mildly. He veered left, following the road running parallel with Troyer land. The sweet scent of freshly mown alfalfa drifted through the warm evening air. The cicadas weren't as loud out here along neighboring pastures as they were near the woods and water veins, but she could still hear them stirring up a ruckus in the distance. She would pray for cicada-eating birds to flock to Miller's Creek for the summer if not for that seventeen year wait Leon had mentioned. Imagine waiting so long for a moment's love.

"Yet, you aren't doing it alone. You've hired help."

Hannah couldn't ignore the change in Tabor's tone when he drew the buggy to a stop at the crossroads.

"*Mamm* hired him. It's his job," she said flatly as a car sped by.

"It troubles me that he is here so often. You should know that." Tabor said and gave the reins a slap. The buggy jerked forward.

"*Mamm* did that," she said. "I didn't like it at first either, but he has proven useful. I think we should head back. I have an early morning." Tomorrow they would be harvesting all day, making up for a few damp days, and staying out late only made her tired just thinking about it.

"Hannah, do you truly not understand how it troubles me to know that one is here, with you, every day?" Tabor made no motion to veer into the wide drive at their right. Perhaps his hearing wasn't so good.

"There is another wide area just there." She pointed to a

dirt lot where many long-haul truckers parked their long trucks. Tabor clenched his jaw and made the turnaround. In an unexpected move, he reached out and placed one hand over hers. Hannah peered down to where their hands connected. His touch didn't seem to have the same effect on her as Leon's had. It didn't take a smart woman to know the difference.

Lord help her. Leon was the only man who made her want to feel things she had no time for feeling.

Looking at Tabor, all could she do was think of Leon. Irma was right. Leon was a better man than she thought him to be. He exhibited a decency she had never taken time to notice before *mudder* hired him. He had a profound patience, especially in dealing with her. And that impulsive nature she once thought reckless and sinful was no more than bottled energy and eagerness to do something instead of standing idle. Hannah had based her whole opinion of a man solely on the gossip of others. *And I busted his nose plenty for it.* She grimaced.

"I don't understand, but I'm sorry you're troubled by it."

She tried pulling her hand away, but his grip held firm. He pulled the buggy over and drew in a long breath. Whatever he was about to say, Hannah was already working up the words to let him know she wouldn't be riding in any more buggies with him.

"Hannah…"

Her name came out as if spoken by another. It didn't sound like Tabor at all. Then he leaned toward her, lowering his head to hers, and those eyes told her just where his next thoughts were heading.

"Tabor." Hannah immediately hugged the edge of the buggy.

"I can offer you more than some hired help," he said with no hidden motive.

"Tabor, we are not courting." Hannah stiffened.

"We could start."

Hannah was certain that before his father left the world, Tabor Lewis's *daed* must have dropped him on his head. She had always preferred those who got to the point but right now, she wished he was slow and awkward. She had no more interest in what Tabor thought than she did in eating mud.

"I know Addie told you about Carrie Deinner," he said.

Hannah flinched. Addie had told her nothing about Carrie Deinner.

"We aren't courting. I just took her home the other day because her *bruder* forgot to pick her up. I am interested in you, only you."

"Tabor, I'm sorry, but I'm not of a mind to court anyone." Her stomach twisted in the half-truth.

Tabor straightened and his frown returned. "I'm ready for marriage, a family. No hiding my intentions."

"Tabor, I'm sorry, but I'm not ready for that." She expected a bit of fury and promised herself she would take a few hurtful words if necessary. She owed him that much, but Hannah had her limits.

Tabor took up her hand again. "You know I care for you and can provide for you. You won't have to spend your days laboring in the fields any longer."

"I love what I do," she quickly said. "I don't need provided for." Hannah climbed out of the buggy. Who did he think he was? She was no damsel in distress and didn't need saving.

"For a teacher, you aren't very *schmaert*," he said. "Your place is not laboring in fields. I am only thinking of you. People are starting to talk, Hannah. You and Leon shouldn't be working together, unchaperoned. It doesn't look proper. It wonders me if the bishop is already considering paying you both a visit."

"The bishop knows our days are spent working and would never think me one to ignore our *ordnung*." Then again, the bishop might not approve of swimming lessons, she held back. "I will not give up this orchard for anyone.

Not you or Leon Milford or any other who comes around seeking a *fraa*." The longer she thought on it, the angrier she got. Hannah started marching across the nearest field. It would be much faster than walking the road all the way home.

"What are you doing?" Tabor called out.

Hannah could hear him chasing after her.

"Walking home, alone," she said angrily.

"It's getting dark. We should stick to the road." His words were breathless. "Hannah you are acting like a *boppli*. You have to see it from my point."

"Then perhaps you should seek out someone more mature," she said. "Your opinion of me matters none and you should not leave your buggy on the side of the road."

"You are as stubborn as a stick."

Hannah halted and turned swiftly.

"You sweeten my *mamm* so I would ride with you and then try to make me think two people can't work together without being the talk of all the local gossipers."

"Hannah, you haven't shown me interest regardless how many times I try. I'm not getting younger and I'm ready to marry and start a family. I didn't know what else to say to get you to see some sense."

"Well, let me help you know what not to say *if* we ever speak again." She halted and shoved both hands onto her hips. "You don't tell a woman she belongs in a house. It's rude to think something she loves and works hard for is wrong. Even *Gott* tells us to labor for our fruits." Tabor opened his mouth to reply but Hannah threw up a hand as if still teaching a room full of *kinner*. "And just because *you* have an interest in someone, doesn't mean they have to return it. Life is too short for making lifelong mistakes."

"I won't leave you to walk home in the dark. Let's get back to the road."

"*Nee.* I don't need to be escorted through a field." She rolled her eyes as she moved further from him.

"You stubborn woman," he yelled. "You are being un-reasonable. You can't possibly spend the rest of your life ig-noring the one person who cares for you. I am willing to offer you a future. He will not do that."

Could his arrogance grow any dafter? She harrumphed sarcastically.

"He has nothing to do with this," she motioned a hand between them. "I am the only one," she quipped, temper flaring to new peaks.

"Caleb was right. You have never been the same since," Tabor left off the words, but Hannah knew what they were. *Since your* daed *died.*

"*Danki*, Hannah Troyer. Perhaps you just helped me see more clearly. A lifetime with *you* would indeed be a mistake." The words cut as intended, but her thick skin barely felt it. Tabor turned and marched back toward the road.

She watched him turn into a shadow and then vanish be-fore she let out a shuddering breath. She couldn't decide be-tween fuming and crying, but crying was for *kinner,* and she hadn't been a child for a very long time. With tears in check and teeth clenched, she gripped her dress and aimed for home.

"*Daed* would have never liked him anyway," she said into the night. She didn't need anyone, just a full moon to stay visual until she was safely home.

CHAPTER TWENTY-ONE

"They seem to be getting along better of late. At least Hannah ain't run him off or drowned him yet." Ivy set the stack of boxes on the bakery counter. It had been a busy morning already, but right now, patrons were winding down. "And they were laughing about Luke changing diapers."

Hazel reached for a box and began shaping it.

"Look at that." Ivy set down the misshapen cardboard and went to the large bakery window. Hazel followed; a towel flung over one shoulder, a common look for her.

"It wonders me if Hannah knows about that," Ivy said with a sigh.

Outside the window, just across the street, was Tabor Lewis, walking Carrie Deinner into the Cozy Nook book store. "Do you think we did the right thing?" Ivy glanced over to Hazel. "I mean meddling like we have."

"Don't fret," Hazel said. "The Lord knows what He's doing. You told Leon she was down by the creek. You didn't tell her to like talking to him. Hannah just needed to know she has options. For a *maedel* who has many gut talents, she surely does not see her own worth," Hazel said. "And Leon needed a little competition. Nothing urges a man forward faster than thinking he might be looked over." Hazel grinned as the Cozy Nook bookstore door closed behind them.

"What if Leon gets tired of her fickleness?" Ivy nibbled at her bottom lip.

"A man in love tends to bring out the best all about him."

Ivy lifted a doubtful brow.

"Hannah has been doing much alone, and now she will see how much more can be accomplished with two. Be patient, Ivy." Hazel patted her shoulder. "*Gut* things are happening even if we don't see them yet."

"I hope you're right." Ivy let out a sigh.

Hazel went back to cutting fudge. Each perfectly sliced square needed boxed and there were still pies to make before the day got away from them. Being a servant to the Lord was hard work. Work that was never ending. Still, Hazel loved the duty pressed on her. Seeing others happy, was her life's purpose.

"Tomorrow night, see your family joins us for supper." Hazel couldn't help but smile when Ivy's eyes lit up. "At Luke and Penny's," she said. "Nothing encourages a young heart more than *bopplin* and fellowship." Hazel smiled as she placed another slice of white chocolate and cherry fudge in a blue box. *A woman's work is never done.*

Hannah climbed out of the buggy, a warm apple pie balanced carefully in her right palm, as Addie collected the cobbler and climbed down behind her. "I hope Levi will be here," Addie muttered in an excited breath.

"You two seem to be spending a lot of time together," Hannah said with a grin.

"We are *freinden*. Levi tells the most interesting stories about growing up in Michigan. Did you know they could swim before they could ride a horse?"

Hannah didn't. No wonder Leon thought it strange they couldn't swim. To him, it was second nature.

Hannah glanced about. If one twin was here, the other surely might be there too, and Hannah wasn't prepared to see Leon right now. They had managed just fine, working at a distance lately, but since the night at the creek, she didn't trust herself to see him as the hired help any longer.

There were only four buggies parked about. None looked to be Marva, Leon's horse. Her shoulders slumped.

"Irma says she had a sibling drown when she was but a *kind*. I reckon that would be reason enough to start them early," Mamm said.

Hannah didn't know that, and it saddened her to know now. She couldn't imagine losing one of her sisters, even if they were pests.

As they neared the house, Hannah gave her decision to wear her best Sunday dress a second thought. Far too often she was dressed in drab chore clothes. Spending an afternoon with one of her closest friends warranted something special. She hadn't worn it for any other reason than that, she told herself.

Hazel Miller met them at the door with a wide smile. Hannah always felt Hazel looked like a woman hiding secrets. Those gray eyes of hers twinkled no matter the time of day.

"Millie, how *wunderbaar* you all could make it. I worried the harvest would keep you."

Hazel looped an arm around *mamm*'s and herded her inside. *Mudder* had been spending more time in the company of others of late. It was good to see her healing and beginning to feel like her old self again. But, Hannah scrutinized, it was clear her new found friendships had been what had prompted her of late to be so bold as to interfere with Hannah's future.

Stepping inside, it didn't go unnoticed how the old farm looked reborn under the care of Luke. Hannah particularly liked the wood-stained railing leading upstairs, as well as the scents of warm beef and bread from the kitchen to the left. She and her sisters crowded the foyer until *mudder* moved on to where the women were all seeing to the meal.

"Hiya."

Hannah turned to find Leon walking her way from the sitting room.

"I didn't know you were coming," Leon said.

Hannah choked back a panicky breath. "Penny and I are dear friends." Looking around her for support, Hannah realized her sisters had disappeared into the kitchen. "I didn't know this was a gathering."

"It's not." He chuckled, taking the pie from her hands. "It's just a few of the best folks spending time together." He winked

July heat brushed through the open windows. Dipping her head, Hannah followed Leon into the kitchen.

"Apple pie," Penny called out as Leon sat Hannah's pie down on the counter. "Yours is my favorite. When are you going to tell me that secret ingredient?" Penny cocked her head playfully.

"You have a secret ingredient?" Leon mumbled and eyed the pie more closely.

"I'll never tell. Promised *mammi* only to pass it to a *dochder* of my own someday." She had no idea why she even said so much, but Hannah's legs grew unsteady when Leon's eyes sparked at her comment. Amish kitchens in July were hot enough, without being looked at like that.

"I'm sure she will be just a *schee* too. When do you find time to bake?" Leon's voice lifted beyond a whisper.

"Hannah makes time for everything that is important," Millie said. "She is much like my Eli in that way, and just as hardworking."

Hannah felt a blush ride over her cheeks.

"So, I am learning," Leon said, pinning her with another signature grin.

When the room fell suddenly silent, Hannah quickly retrieved her pie from the counter.

"This needs cut," she said in a shaky breath, needing something to do with her hands.

"Are you going to stay in here with the women or *kumm* help me," Luke stepped into the kitchen and slapped Leon on the back, breaking his stare. "Let's see to the horses. It's too hot to leave them all out front."

Leon gave Hannah a curt nod before shuffling his hands into his pockets and following Luke out the side kitchen door.

"I think Leon really wants to know your secret ingredient," Penny whispered.

Hannah blinked a couple times before regaining her composure. She probably looked like a silly *maedel* staring after Leon as she had been.

It was no use in pretending, not with Penny. Hannah leaned closer. "I don't think I'm going to give it to him." Penny wrapped an arm around her.

"You might want to change your mind on that," Penny, her usually shy friend, said.

Hannah's mouth fell open. Motherhood, and marriage, changed a woman. Hannah wasn't sure that was a good thing or not.

"Let's sneak upstairs and check on Daniel. I want a few seconds alone with my friend." Penny led the way. "Though by the looks of things, a few seconds might not be nearly enough to tell me what's going on with you two."

"I'll get the Troyer's. You can get Hazel's." Luke said.

Leon knew what his brother was thinking and wasn't sure he liked it. He had meant to be subtle when he discovered Hannah was coming. Unfortunately, the moment she walked through the door, Leon's heart jolted. He never knew he could need to be near another so much.

"You can stop grinning now."

"Not yet. I'm still amused by the way you two were gawking at each other," Luke said.

"Poor old fellow." Leon unhitched Hannah's horse, ignoring Luke altogether, and gave the horse's ears a scratch. "I think they could use a younger horse. This one is worn down to nubbins," Leon said as the brothers led the two horses toward the pasture gate.

"Can't have that now, can we?" Luke winked.

"*Nee*, we cannot." Leon floated a grin his brother's way. With brothers, words weren't always necessary. With Luke especially, there was never a need to share what was on your mind. He had *mudder*'s knack and a third eye for scooping out thoughts.

Luke offered a softer pat on his shoulder and his low, "Well then. That's settled," was all Leon needed to follow his natural instincts straight into the unknown. "I know just where to find what you need *bruder*." Leon perked.

"Silas Graber had a lot of new horses freshly broke. We can go see him tomorrow and see which suits."

Leon nodded appreciatively.

When they finished seeing all the horses were freshly watered and fed, the brothers stepped back inside. Leon noted immediately Hannah was nowhere to be found. He should have told her how nice she looked in her dress. She seldom wore anything besides her chore dress or her Sunday blue dress. He wanted to think she had done that for him, and yet, she had been surprised he was here when she arrived. *A man could hope.* He silently groaned. The dress was a darker shade, complimenting her warm olive complexion. That deep blue had always made him think of the lake he spent his boyhood exploring.

Penny's mother, a stern-looking woman with a pair of eyes that could cut a man in two, urged everyone to the table before the food caught a chill. Leon took a seat near one empty chair, Luke the other, and ignored the look Addie shot him when he purposely assured Hannah would be sitting next to him. He hated being so transparent, yet again, he needed to be near her.

The meal of roast beef, vegetables, and coleslaw had his stomach growling. He was famished and no matter how much he ate these days, it seemed he was hungrier afterward. At Luke's urging, everyone lowered their heads for prayer. Leon had a lot to pray for this evening. A brother missing, another, the community's new minister, and a woman with red hair that proved more interesting than anything Leon had ever encountered before.

Luke cleared his throat and all heads lifted. As food began being passed about, footfalls descended the stairs in the next room. Leon figured this was what a blind man witnessing his first sunset felt when the subject of all his recent thoughts moved into the room holding his new nephew cradled in her arms.

Luke stood, offering Penny a seat. Leon followed his gesture and was awestruck when Hannah accepted a seat beside him without a single glare or comment. She was obviously distracted, too smitten with the dark-haired bundle nestled against her. He didn't blame her. Daniel was a fine-looking collaboration of his parents.

It was mighty hard to focus on food with Hannah beside him. She teased the bottle in and out of Daniel's mouth, swooning at every expression he made. She was a natural, but Leon had already suspected as much. Behind her weary head and quick tongue was a woman born to be a mother.

"He has a mighty appetite," Hannah said with a laugh.

"He gets it from Luke. Few could clean a plate faster," Leon said playfully.

"You being the few," Luke lifted his fork, a chunk of potato dripping with gravy attached, and winked. Hannah set the empty bottle aside and lifted Daniel to her shoulder. Leon, knowing now from firsthand experience just what babies did who finished a bottle in three seconds flat, fetched a towel and draped it over Hannah's shoulder.

"He might ruin that pretty dress." He winked. But Hannah's heart was stolen by the boy in her arms, and unaffected by the bigger one beside her. As she patted his little back, encouraging a burp, her cheek brushed against his nephew's affectionately.

"You are *gut* at this too. Should have figured," he whispered her way as chatter rose up around them. It was those short sporadic moments, when she stilled long enough that she wasn't simply a blur, that Hannah's tenderness was revealed.

"I helped with *mei schwestern* plenty so." Hannah started to hand Daniel over. "But you are his *onkel*." She giggled at him. "I hear you need the practice."

"He is too tiny, Hannah, don't," Leon said. "He just throws up on me every time I even look at him." He should have expected a laugh, but not the full table.

"You will do fine and I'm hungry."

She smiled knowing she had put him on the spot. Leon wanted nothing more than to play and snuggle his nephew, when he was big enough he didn't fit in a boot. Handling a newborn, so fragile and new, was not something he was practiced in.

"What's wrong, can't handle holding something so sweet and innocent?" She whispered before lifting that sharp challenging brow.

Unable to resist, Leon took the bait.

"*Jah*," he leaned closer to her ear. "But I reckon he is more breakable than you are." When her flesh warmed and a gasp of air slowly expelled from her well placed lips, Leon felt like he had won another round.

"Hand him here."

Hannah gingerly placed Daniel in his arms and Leon went rigid. "He weighs nothing, nothing at all."

Hannah adjusted his little head and gave his blanket a

tuck. "Oh, that will change soon enough." She said softly brushing a finger over the *boppli's* fine hair.

"I'm afraid to even blink," Leon muttered. Their gazes collided and held one another. She was smiling, over his weakness perhaps, but sitting here, holding Daniel and being smiled at like that by Hannah Troyer made a man want a whole houseful of twins. He was glad when a knock at the door broke the rare moment between them before he did something stupid like tell her just what was on his mind currently.

Hannah focused on her plate, not the man beside her. Seeing Leon, with little Daniel cradled in his arms, was not an image she would easily forget.

"Hannah, have you talked to Hank yet?" Penny sipped at her water.

She barely ate enough to keep a bird alive. Hannah gave her friend a narrowed look to shush her. It was no one's business what her family's needs were, and Penny of all people knew that.

"Levi told us just the other day he has a cow he is willing to sell at a decent price. She isn't too old, just doesn't give as much milk as the others."

"*Jah*, we spoke," Hannah squirmed in her seat. "I will tend to such after the harvest." Why had she told Penny their old cow dried up? In the next room, she could hear Luke greet another visitor.

"*Jah*, our Hannah puts nothing before the harvest," Millie said.

"Budgets can be stretched," Hazel said, always the optimist and always one to discuss matters she shouldn't at supper.

"It's not a fitted sheet. We are fine," Hannah said, soundly hoping the subject would drop. "I told you the harvest needs tended to first."

"Aww, someone has a need."

Hannah gripped her fork tightly and swallowed her mouthful as Luke ushered a visitor into the kitchen.

"We all know the church has special funds for widows. And in times like these, no one questions your family's need of a cow," Tina Raber said in a sweet tone, but everyone heard the meanness implied.

Hannah's shoulders stiffened. Her family had no needs that required the community's help, or Tina's opinion. Her mousy voice always gave Hannah a shiver. She dared a sideways glance. Leon forced his attention away from the babe in his arms to shoot her a 'not a bad idea' look.

"Though we are never too proud to accept it, we could never press on the community for such when there are far more needs among us." Hannah shoved back her chair and stood. "Excuse me. I need some air." Hannah slid from the room but not before she heard Tina address Leon.

"You look to be a natural with him. Ben dropped me off and *daed* said you had permission to take me home."

The front door slammed, causing Daniel to cry out immediately. Instinctually, Penny stood, walked around the table, and scooped him up. She mouthed the words "I'm sorry." Leon wasn't sure if she meant for her child's sudden outburst, or the fact Tina was here and in three seconds flat had turned a perfectly good day into a miserable one.

"I can wait for you on the porch," Tina said. "I wouldn't want to disrupt your meal."

Leon bit back his first response, considering she had interrupted everyone's meal.

"I never offered." Leon wished Hannah had heard his reply, but she was already gone, the door already shut, but hopefully not for good.

"Now, Leon, we can't have Tina walking all the way from here." Hazel grinned from the end of the table.

"And *daed* says you have permission," Tina said.

Luke's smirk wasn't helping matters. Leon stood and retrieved his hat.

"Fine. Let's go," he said his voice gruff and edgy.

"But your supper…"

"Is already forgotten."

CHAPTER TWENTY-TWO

Hannah stared at the cob-webby corner of the barn loft. Life had a way of spinning in and out like that. Arms achy from working so hard of late, she leaned back on the straw bale, sneaking in a moment's peace for herself. For over a week, she managed to avoid Leon. She divvied up chores, so they were always at opposite ends of the orchard. Last thing Hannah wanted to talk about was supper at Penny's or if he enjoyed giving Tina a ride home.

Mamm dared mention that Leon no longer whistled when he worked, and Ivy said she heard through the rumor mill was Lester had jumped the fence. Hannah had been tempted to inquire about his brother, Lester. Had he heard from him? But every time she felt tempted, she remembered he drove Tina home without so much as seeking her out first. Proof she was right about Leon all along and was the biggest fool in all of Miller's Creek.

Hannah jabbed a stalk of straw into the bale, thinking of the two taking long rides down by the ponds other couples frequented. He hadn't even once mentioned swimming lessons since. Hiding in the loft every afternoon at this hour was being a big chicken for sure and certain and yet, Hannah couldn't think of anything better.

The sound of a truck engine pierced her brooding. Hannah got to her feet and ventured over to the loft opening. The blue truck pulled a small horse trailer. Curiously, she watched as two men wandered around the back of the trailer and swung open the door. Tilting her head for a clearer view, the driver appeared, leading a cow toward the barn.

Hannah jerked upright. Leon appeared from the right, coming from where he had been dallying at fixing the back porch steps *mamm* had been fussing over. A big grin was on his face, and he accepted the animal and began leading her the rest of the way to the barn. Hannah clutched her apron front as she watched the men get back into their truck, turn around, and leave.

"He bought a cow." Her voice hitched. From the sounds of things below, she knew he was putting the young Guernsey in the stall Nell once used. Had *mudder* given him money and permission to purchase the cow? Well, that wasn't his place.

Leon led the Guernsey through the barn and got her settled in the freshly prepared stall. "She's going to love you," he whispered. Those big doe eyes smiled at him appreciatively as he offered her a pat and a healthy scoop of grain. Pleased with himself, he made his way out of the barn and hurried to the creek. Hannah hadn't shown for days though her sisters had. After four days, Leon learned that neither needed a lesson in anything but truth telling. He was fairly certain his own *mamm* and Hannah's had something to do with Tina showing up the other day too. Leon liked games. He was good at them. Though he had never before played it with a gaggle of women.

He wanted to tell Hannah how he rushed Tina home and set her straight. He would have told her he came back, hoping to take her home that night. He would have told her more if she would have talked to him. He gave her four days, and he bought a cow. Still, she kept hiding away or claiming she had some chore, always farthest from whatever duty he was doing, and she was skipping suppers again. Proof she was bothered by Tina's interruption at supper and proof she cared more than she wanted to admit.

He sat on the familiar log for what had to be more than an hour, waiting. "This is ridiculous," he finally said, tossing aside a brittle stick that he had snagged on his walk down here. Waiting on a woman to appreciate you was a waste of time. Here he mended the rundown farm, harvested wagon loads of apples, and carted them to the markets and stores in town. He had worked with Lewis, drawing up plans for Eli's marketplace, and now spent his hard-earned money buying a cow for milk that he would probably never be permitted to drink. "She'll certainly give that ugly cat my share." He fumed. *How dare she not show again.*

Cicadas mocked him, screaming out their mating calls to one another, strangling his last nerve. "Keep it up and I'll be eating bass all winter," he threatened the helpless insects. He wasn't sitting here another minute feeling like a fool. He shook his head and stalked back to the Troyer's house.

Knocking, Leon tried to tap down his temper. Between Lester and Hannah, he was muddle-minded and gravitating toward a good fluster. Addie answered the door, and her cheeks went immediately flush.

"Hi, Leon. Do you need some water?"

"*Nee*, I need your *schwester*." He pinned her with a knowing look and Addie crossed both arms over her chest cunningly.

"You'll have to take a turn then. I'm not sure if she is here or out with Tabor."

She had none of her sister's pluck, but he felt just as humored watching her lift that chin. Leon knew Tabor was courting another and no longer had an interest in Hannah.

He nearly had to pull that information out of Sam Lewis at the last Sunday gathering. Addie was just another woman to add to the gaggle of meddlers.

"You right eye jerks when you aren't being honest," Leon said bluntly. Addie let out a huff. Just as Leon suspected. "I could care less what you meddlers are up to. Where's Hannah? She promised to meet me for lessons again."

"She's hiding in the loft of the barn pretending to be working just as she does every time she is supposed to be meeting you for swimming lessons." His eyes narrowed and he felt another sting in his jaw, so he let up a little before he cracked a few good teeth.

"She wants to avoid me?" He was speaking to himself, but Addie replied.

"Needs to, I think is the better way of putting it." Addie smiled. "She's moving hay and straw from one end to another."

His brow lifted quizzically.

"She does that when she's upset about something. *Mamm* calls it thinking," Addie rolled her eyes.

Without another word, Leon tipped his straw hat with two fingers and aimed for the barn. Leon crossed over the yard of newly mown grass, past the new chicken coop and the once brown shed now painted grey.

"Thinking huh," he muttered angrily. Leon would have to give her more to think about. He had transformed their life and though he knew it was not Christian to want a pat on the back for it, a little appreciation would be nice. He would not be ignored.

Late evening sunset spilled between barn slats, giving the open barn a slightly warmer feel. He had mucked those stalls for days when he first came here and now fresh straw was laid daily, filling the air with sweet aromas compared to the gut-wrenching ones he first encountered. He stomped past new gates hung straightly on new hinges. A whiff of leather filled the air. The tack hung to his left, rubbed down and displayed in rich earthy browns. Not one centimeter of this farm had been neglected by him.

Millie had delivered a thousand thank-yous in these few short months. Addie appreciated any help he offered with her bees or toting heavy produce to the stands in the mornings, and Ivy complimented him plenty for seeing the horse and buggy readied when she aimed for work four mornings a week, but Hannah, Leon hadn't earned a single spit of gratitude.

Tom sat on a feed bucket, eyeing a corner with a hungry lust. He would give the beastly critter credit. Since his first week, Leon hadn't seen one mouse thanks to the ugly barn keeper. "Keep up the good work. I'm sure there will be cake or something at least for you," he said and marched past the tailless feline.

Hay floated down, bringing Leon to a halt. Addie said she was up there, rearranging straw and hay as if it was something needing doing. *And thinking.*

He took to the ladder two rungs at a time until he reached the wooden second story floor. He might lose his job after today, but no longer would he allow her to keep skirting around him as if he was contagious. If he had a pet peeve, that was it. People stuffing troubles and hurts under a basket, thinking they didn't exist or would simply disappear. How could you fix a thing hidden?

Dim light reflected dust. Each particle danced, flickering in the streams of light pushed through cracks and crevasses of wood and timber. Overhead hung a battery-operated lamp. He would compliment her for spending the extra on batteries, keeping the barn safe from flicker and flame up here where threats were more obvious. Leon got to his feet at the top, his gaze landing straight on his mark.

Hannah grunted, lifted a bale of hay, and turned, freezing in mid-step when her gaze collided with his. Her body tensed and all his intentions evaporated. Her face was flush, blotted with red patches from the heat of summer and strain of labor. Her hair was not tidy under her kerchief, auburn strands sticking to her delicate neck and cheek, some floating curiously about. Her shoulders remained forward, and she looked to be holding back a thousand tears. He could see it all now. The burdens she thought solely her own. In that quick collection, Leon knew he was going to only add to her burdens, and yet, knew he had to. Hannah would never heal, never find happiness, unless she dealt with every cut and sore she had.

"You worked all day; shouldn't you be resting? I mean since you weren't up to swimming." She dropped a bale of hay as Leon crossed the floor. He wasn't the only one who liked working off his frustrations, that much was clear. How many times had he chopped a full winter's wood when plenty was stacked and dried already?

Lamplight swayed, playing tricks on the eyes between shadows and figures. "I thought you stood me up to ride around with Tabor." Frowning, he waved an arm over the room. "Not sure this makes me feel better." She was a strange creature donned in drab grey and frowning again. He lifted the bale she dropped between them and carried it across the room. They were perfectly fine where they were stacked. And right now, it was just the two of them Leon wasn't letting anything come in between.

"I'm not responsible for how you feel about anything," Hannah said. Wasn't it enough he made her think she was worthy of affection? Now he had to barge into her time alone? "And…" she folded her arms and gave her chin a defiant lift. "I would think you would be happy enough I didn't. If I'm here doing all the work, that gives you more time for courting." Two could play this game.

He looked mad, the tight jaw a clear indicator. Well, he wasn't the only one. Wasn't it enough she had responsibilities to shoulder and people depending on her, then he would come around her with his charming smile and smooth words, only to run off with the likes of Tina?

"Tina doesn't take kindly to fellows being late. It's a nice evening. You best not waste it."

"I don't care about her and I'm not courting anyone." He shifted, planting both feet apart and folding his arms across his chest as if to mimic her. "And if I did, not sure that should matter to you."

She studied his eyes; they rarely hid secrets or lies and measured he must have perfected his talents. He looked serious, and yet she knew better. Tina's brother dropped her off just so Leon could take her out. And he did.

"None of my business." Hannah shrugged, pretending not to care, and then turned, grabbing a hold of two more baling strings, and lifted the next bale.

"Not sure why, I might be catching a rare disease or something, but I'd rather be here." He lowered his arms and looped both thumbs around his suspenders.

"You are for sure ill," Hannah said with a sneer. She pivoted, dropping the straw. "You can go for the day. You are not needed any longer." His features sharpened just as stone-sharpened steel.

"I'm not ready to go. We have some things to sort out."

"You work here. Your job is to do as you're told." His long legs licked up the distance between them in a blink.

"I work for your *mudder*, not you. I'm not just a hired hand to be pushed about and you know it.

"You *are* a hired hand," she said. Leon reached out and gripped her hand. "Hey." Hannah tried yanking away, but his grip was too firm.

"Hold on. I saw blut." His eyes narrowed, turning her hand for a better view.

Hannah tried to release herself again, his hold so perfect that pulling away didn't work.

"This is no time to be proud. Hold still."

"I'm not being proud. Pride is a sin," she said.

"*Jah*, it is. Like declaring your family doesn't need charity because *you* can handle everything." He locked gazes with her briefly, cold anger in his blue eyes. "Now let me look."

Hannah did. Only heaven knew why.

"You have a thread of twine stuck in there."

Hannah looked down and sure enough under the leaking lifeblood was a thread of twine embedded well. Now it did hurt, and she winced. Looking up again, he was staring at her, that trademark smirk that made *maedels* melt.

"What?" She asked. "The twine is in my hand, not my eye." He lowered his gaze, but humor replaced his earlier scowl.

"You drive me hard, Hannah Troyer."

Between two perfectly trim nails, Leon attempted to pull the thread free. Failing, and sensing he was causing her pain, he brought her hand to his mouth.

It happened so fast she had no time to react when his warm lips touched her fingertip. Using his teeth he removed the invader in her flesh, his eyes never leaving hers. She froze and so did her lungs and liver and heart. Leon was practically kissing her hand.

His larger fingers wrapped around her smaller ones, he pulled back and revealed the twine between rows of perfect teeth.

"You should go put something on this, so it doesn't get infected."

His voice rusted over, sending chills over her. She couldn't breathe, couldn't think. His eyes traveled to her lips, and the awareness of where his thoughts had traveled jerked her back to attention.

"I need my hand back to do that." He hesitated before letting go. She must have lost more blood than she realized because Leon was about to kiss her, and she was going to let him.

"I just yelled at you." She looked up, bewildered by the

man looking down on her.

"Perhaps I'm immune at this point. Perhaps I understand sometimes yelling is better than dealing with what's in front of us."

He grinned wickedly sending more alarm through her. Leon had delivered some mighty tempting looks her way, but never one so arrowed.

"You're Leon Milford," she stuttered out in shuddering, quick breaths. "That is who you are." Her words were barely a mutter. Not the normalcy with which she wished they were delivered.

"You say it as if it is a bad thing." He grew rigid and that jaw worked tight again.

"It is a bad thing. This is silly, stupid." Crossing two arms defensively she hoped he didn't hear the flutter of her words.

"Tell me and I'll let you know if it's stupid."

He cracked a grin, challenging her.

"Why were you leading a cow into our barn?"

"It's your cow. Where else does it need to go?"

Why did he have to be so...so...annoying?

"I didn't buy a cow. We don't have the funds for such."

"I am just the delivery guy, or the hired hand, remember. Her name is Marla."

Saying nothing more, he took two steps back, turned, and left the barn loft he rudely entered. Hannah let out a long breath.

CHAPTER TWENTY-THREE

Leon wasn't sure why he was so restless. He wasn't even the one put on the spot today. Still, it built up inside him like a terrible ache. The Zook barn had been swept clean, barely a hayseed littered the floor where fifty backless benches formed two sides to an open center. He watched Lewis, the bishop, and the other minister slip out of the room as the community began raising their voices in song. So far Lewis hadn't done more than lead a prayer.

Across the barn, Hannah sat. A light breeze played with her hair, sending a few auburn strands dancing. She was as blunt as a hammer, stricken with grief, and the most beautiful creature he had ever known. Leon hadn't misread her. Hannah might have feelings for him that went beyond drowning him.

She couldn't hide the true softness of her heart from him all the time. The thought made him smile. He liked her openness, no flattery forged in batting eyelashes. A man knew just what he had with that one. Perhaps getting things moving along with Eli's marketplace would help her in her healing and give her something of her father she had lost when he died.

As voices wound down from the opening hymn, the door leading to the Zook's tack room opened. Lewis, Bishop Schwartz, and the newly chosen deacon stepped back into the barn. Lewis's eyes fell right on Jenny. She nodded assuredly. With that, his brother grew taller. Lewis and Jenny were a team, supportive of one another as it should be. Leon wanted that, a partner who understood him and one he understood. He was sure he had Hannah figured out, but suddenly Leon realized, she knew nothing of him. He had never shared what ate at him or what drove him to be better all the time. She had no clue where his mind wandered on rainy days or that he preferred bananas over jelly on his peanut butter sandwiches. He had made things between them one-sided.

Leon noted the bishop and deacon take a seat and a shiver ran up Leon's back as confirmation hit him. His *bruder* was going to preach today. Only a few church Sundays since being declared minister and he was given the task.

Lewis cleared his throat and Leon mimicked the sound across the room in support. He wished he could stand by his side as Lewis and Luke often had for him, but Lewis was on his own up there, center of the community with all eyes on him. He whispered a silent prayer and when their gazes collided a second time, something in his brother's brown eyes flickered, changed from mischievous boy who once put roaches in their old bishop's feed barrels, to all-knowing and wise.

The prodigal. His brother was like the prodigal son.

"When I was a child, I spoke as a child," Lewis began, his eyes evenly roaming over the room. "I understood as a child, I thought as a child," his *bruder* began in a mixture of Swedish and German dialect, his voice clear, precise, and commanding.

Lewis had chosen perfectly the words today, personal, and yet aimed for the many who doubted his being chosen. Leon scanned the room for snarky looks. Some would not want to hear a message from a former sinner. However, all eyes were on him, and every ear was bent. Leon returned his gaze to his *bruder*.

Lewis was serving. His fate sealed by the flip of a Bible and now eyes looked upon him as if he was the wisest man in the room. It was personal, his chosen words, Leon believed. Lewis had behaved childishly, but a child he was no more. Leon felt a grin sneak up in one corner of his mouth unbidden. Lewis spoke straight to him in a barn full of everyone, without a care too.

The rascal.

"But when I became a man, I put away childish things." Lewis nodded his way and that all too familiar grin tugged at the corner of his lips. The jolt of the message hit its target. Lewis was not speaking only of himself, about himself, but to Leon too.

The room grew brighter, clearer, so clear he thought air held its own shape. Light danced over surfaces, along walls, and around bodies, until it touched everything. He was the child, his pranks and games and competitive nature. Time had passed for fun and games, though this summer has sure been short of them, Leon mused. He gave his brother a nod and with a subtle grin of recognition, Lewis continued to deliver his message, seeing that he had hit at least one of his marks for the day.

If only Lester was here to bear witness too. It was time to stop waiting for his brother to come home. Leon knew where he was now, and he knew what he had to do. He glanced across the barn again, his eyes locking with Hannah's. She had been watching the exchange, but Leon wondered if she understood what passed between brothers just then. He hoped she did. Because Leon had to go after his brother no matter the harvest. *Gott* was pulling him to do the right thing, and right now, Leon felt that was steering Lester back to the flock. He prayed she would understand.

Turning his attention back to the service, Leon watched

a man accept his calling and do well with it. *Gott* made no mistakes. Leon listened to a full service with new ears and drank in every word.

That evening, Leon stood on the porch with his duffle draped over one shoulder. "Here is some extra money." Luke handed Leon a few extra bills as a blue car raced up the drive.

"Just remember," Lewis wrapped an arm around Leon's shoulders. "Lester may not listen. Do your best but don't let it trouble you if he doesn't return with you. He must choose so on his own. All you can do is your best. The rest is up to him. *Gott's* will, *bruder.*"

"I'll convince him," Leon assured his brother. He never lost a battle he didn't want to. Lester was coming home.

"*Nee.* Lewis is right. We know you, *bruder.* This is not win or lose. This is giving your all and accepting the outcome."

Leon nodded. Did they think him unprepared?

"Marcus will put you up while you're up there and he said he found a driver to take you both over to where Lester has been staying."

"He has work and this isn't really his problem." Leon shrugged. "I can't let him miss work with another *boppli* on the way because our *bruder* can't sit still."

"You can't sit still." Lewis chuckled. "Marcus is family. Family does what it has to for family."

It was what neighbors and community did too, he reminded them.

"You two just remember what we discussed." Leon pinned them both tightly. He had their word, which was plenty, but had to say it again, for his own guilty heart.

"Don't worry. Those trees will be picked clean before you return."

"Not all of them, I hope. I told you, just the Lodi apples

and Galas. She's fussy, but I know you two can find a way to convince her," he said. "The Jonathons have a few weeks and the rest won't be ready until September." Both brothers stared at him in awe. "What?"

"Who would have thought," Luke wrapped an arm around Leon's shoulder and squeezed, "our Leon an apple farmer."

"*Daed, mamm*, and perhaps the local bakers." Lewis belted out a laugh. "Your driver is here."

Lewis held out a hand and Leon took it. Luke repeated the gesture but pulled him into a hug.

"You surprised me *bruder*." Luke pinned him with a grin. "You might be worthy of her after all."

"I'm not sure about that," Leon muttered. "But we all know I don't do simple and plain so well either. I think arguing with her for the rest of my life might be more fun than it should be." The three laughed as Leon gathered his bag.

"This is serious." Lewis lifted a brow.

"He's met his match. *Gott* has readied the perfect helpmate for you bruder." Luke chuckled stepping down from the porch. "*Mamm* always said it would take a hard egg to crack you."

"*Jah*. It's one of her more admirable traits. Her aim is pretty good too." Leon chuckled before opening the car door. Luke spoke to the driver and handed him a wad of cash.

"I will pray for you and Lester. Safe travels," Lewis said. It was no secret a lot rode on Leon's ability to convince Lester to come home. He was good at persuasion, unless you counted redheads, but even he knew it would take the Lord's intervention to see his hopes granted.

After three hours with the chain-smoking man named Johnson, the car pulled up his cousin's driveway. Leon got out and retrieved his bags. "I'll only be here two days," Johnson said. "If you linger longer than that, you'll have to hitch another ride home. I hate Ohio."

With that, Johnson left in a rise of gravel dust.

"Nice fella," Leon murmured as Marcus, Sybil, and their two small children stepped out of the one-story gray house.

"*Willkumm* cousin. I see you made it unscathed."

Marcus offered a hand.

"Barely. I was lucky not to die in a fiery crash, but I'm thinking lung cancer is still pending." Leon followed his family inside. He hadn't seen Marcus in years. Four to be exact when they had come to stay in Michigan for a few weeks during his mother's illness.

Sybil served a pasta dish Leon found just hit the spot for his nervous stomach. The strong, pungent, garlic bread smothered in butter had been even better. He played a few rounds of catch with Emery and Marcus Jr. before following Marcus to the barn to help with evening chores.

"I have a driver taking us early in the morning, but I should warn you," Marcus said as he scooped out feed from a barrel and delivered it to two squealing piglets. "Place isn't much. The bishop from that end of Berlin found out who he was, that's how I knew where to find him. From what I gather, the ministers had paid him a couple visits. I think they are even planning on penning your folks a letter."

That's how it was among each Amish community. If there was a fear you might be swayed from the faith, intervention was required. Sometimes it was cordial visits, words, and verses to support the cause. Other times, Leon remembered from his younger years, it was brutally harsh with fierce ultimatums. Marcus seemed to feel this particular bishop was simply trying to coax a young man into making the right decision without applying too much pressure.

Leon shoved a sleeve of hay into a stall nearby. The young mare attacked it as if she hadn't eaten in days, but by the look of her, Leon could see she was eating for two. "I wish they wouldn't do that. *Mamm* and *Daed* blame themselves plenty enough." That's why Leon was here, after all, to convince Lester to return home before they were even aware how far he had gone.

"It was his choice," Marcus said. "And still is."

Leon nodded. Like his brothers said, the choice was Lester's in the end. Each man had a choice of which path he took. Though it would be easier, the way Leon looked at it, if he just boxed his ears and forced him into a car home.

"So…" Marcus glanced over. "Lewis and Luke found *fraa*s."

They both laughed. Lewis's past had many thinking the opposite and to most Luke was shy. Though Leon knew he wasn't really. Luke just didn't like to waste his words.

"Is there someone special for you?" Marcus's rich brows wiggled playfully.

"Perhaps, if I can find a way to measure up to her tall order of things." Leon chuckled.

"Well, now. Nothing worth having isn't worth working for."

Leon had said somewhat the same.

"All will come out right," Marcus added. "Tell me about her."

Leon's lips tugged into a grin. He could talk about her green eyes of emerald, her autumn locks, or her strong determination. He could talk about her love of family or the way her eyes widened when threatened with a kiss. He could talk about how she trembled, facing new things, but how she dove into them, refusing to be defeated. Leon could talk about Hannah all day, and still not run out of things to say. He settled for simple.

"She breaks the mold of conformity," Leon said flatly.

"Sounds like your match." Marcus chuckled, his belly moving jollily as he did.

Married life had certainly improved his lanky state in four years.

"If memory serves me, Lester wasn't the only one always getting his fingers whacked for mischief. I think I was more afraid you *mamm*'s wooden spoon than daed's whoopings."

"She is nothing like I imagined I wanted before, but I can't see anything else but her," he said.

"I remember that feeling." Marcus leaned on a gate and slowly gave his dark beard a couple of strokes. "You think yourself invincible, able to handle about anything and suddenly something fragile and sweet steps in and has you fighting for air, for reasoning, for a lick of common sense."

"Sounds about right." It was exactly that, Leon measured. "She has a lot of responsibilities. She takes everything she does head-on." Leon shifted and gave the old mare's nose a few strokes of his hand. "She acts so strong and capable, and yet, she is self-conscious, fragile, breakable."

"All hearts are." Marcus winked.

Leon had never had such a deep conversation about a woman before. It was strange to be having it with Marcus, instead of one of his brothers. Yet maybe that was why it was so easy.

CHAPTER TWENTY-FOUR

The next morning after a hearty breakfast, Leon climbed into the car next to Marcus as they drove the thirty minutes to the nearest town. The tall gray building looked better than his last apartment, but not by much Leon observed. Ivy snaked over and swallowed the southern end as sunlight burned away at another. Long water-stained trails spilled over gutters barely clinging to flashing, rusted with time.

"You sure this is it?" Leon looked up out the window to the endless height. More than a dozen windows blinked into the morning sun. Two were decorated with iron enclosures, not big enough for a chair.

"It's the address alright. You want me to wait for ya or tag along? I don't want me being there to make things more uncomfortable for him, though having two of us might force him to listen to some reason."

"He will feel we have ganged up on him, *jah*. I will go alone. He's my *bruder*."

"We'll wait here then. Take your time."

Leon climbed out of the car, adjusted his hat, and aimed for the doors marking an entrance. After two attempts, for one door was obviously not budging, he made his way inside and was greeted immediately by an elevator. The moody gray walls offered no welcome, but he hadn't expected one here.

He pushed the elevator button and felt like a kid again when the doors opened. Once when Levi fell out of a tree and broke his arm, he had to have a special cast at the local hospital in Michigan. It had three floors, unnecessary for elevators, but he and Lester played on them all day. Could he really convince Lester to come home, join the church, and forget all about the *Englisch* girl who seemed to have stolen his heart? It seemed so easy before. Now, Leon knew his own heart much better and knew the task before him might be harder than it looked.

Outside the plain metal door, the number thirty-two was in black, center and eye level. He took a deep breath, formed a fist, and knocked. Footsteps sounded inside, and he stepped back and removed his hat as the door opened.

"Leon." Lester pulled him into an immediate hug. "I can't believe you're here *bruder*. Please, *kumm*."

His pinned-up breath released, seeing as Lester was surprised and pleased to see him. *So far so good.*

Inside the bland apartment, Leon studied the room. A long, worn couch, flowery and not something he imagined his rough and tough elder brother to have chosen, sat in the center of the room. A table with two mismatched chairs sat in an open kitchen that looked less than useful. Dishes filled one side of the sink, drying, and a small coffee maker to its left.

"What brings you to Ohio?"

Leon shot him a queer look, his earlier delight vanished. "You did. We haven't heard from you, not one word in weeks." Leon moved further into the room. "I had to sneak around behind *mamm* and *daed*'s back just to find you."

Lester sat on the couch. "They don't know you're here, do they?"

Blue eyes widened with concern. No matter how old a man was, he always feared upsetting his parents.

"*Nee.*" Leon took another study of the sparse living quarters. "Why are you here and not home with us, your family and community?"

"Let me get you something to drink. Faith made a cake. She isn't the best cook, but it's edible." Lester bounced into the kitchen, pulling two small plates from a single rusted cabinet.

Leon followed him to the kitchen. "Where is…Faith?" Leon tried not to sound angry saying her name.

"She's next door. A friend of a friend," Lester said in short, not willing to say more. "How is everyone? I heard Levi took over *Onkel* Hank's dairy."

Which would have been yours if you hadn't left, Leon wished to add.

"*Jah.* And Lewis is Miller's Creek's new minister." Leon smiled offering that bit of news.

"Are you pulling wool?" Lester chuckled and it slowly died down. "You know," Lester cut two healthy slabs of what looked like chocolate cake onto the plates. "He would make a great servant. Who better to help guide the wicked home?"

Leon's thoughts exactly. Perhaps Lewis should have been the one to come here. "Should I have let him come in my place?"

Lester didn't belong here, in this rusty old crumbling place.

"*Nee.* You think me wicked *bruder*?" Lester met his glare, hands suspended in the air holding plates.

Leon let out a sigh. He didn't come to fight but to reason and reached out to accept the offering. He had no desire to eat Faith's cake, but if it kept him here and not kicked out onto the street, he would. It wasn't the first time he ate something he rather not for one of his own.

"I'm glad you have *kumm*," Lester said, "and I know why you did. I cannot give you what you want. I told you in the letter, I would get in touch." Lester sat his plate down; he too, had no appetite apparently.

Leon closed the distance, setting his plate on the counter harder than he should have. Lester was his brother, stubborn, but they could always talk forwardly. Neither skirting around a topic.

"That letter is nearly two months old. What about your faith, your family? I cannot let you give those up."

They squared up, nose to nose, brother to brother. Perhaps dragging him home kicking and screaming was going to have to do. He would not lose his brother.

"I have my Faith," Lester said back coldly. "I love her, and I didn't think loving her meant losing my family. I had to make a quick decision, for her. I love her, Leon. I can't breathe without her. It's something like you can never know."

Leon's anger deflated.

"I have an idea. Then have her submit to our faith." Leon hated the sound of desperation in his voice.

"You haven't lost me, and she will not submit to living an Amish life, not after…" His words fell short.

Leon sensed there was a lot his brother was withholding.

"I will be leaving soon, and I'm not sure when I can speak with you again. I can't tell you how much I appreciate you coming here, finding me. It helps but doesn't change my plans."

"You're in trouble, aren't you? That's what all the moving around is about. What have you gotten yourself into?" Leon backed away; his head shook from side to side as it all came clear. Lester wasn't running from family; he was running from danger.

"I'm not in trouble," Lester said in a sharp tone. He ran his finger through his sandy hair, cropped shorter since they last saw each other. In jeans, Lester looked taller, larger somehow. His gray t-shirt, some university Leon had never heard of, was ragged and worn.

"She is," Lester said, alerting Leon to attention. "Faith

didn't come from a family who would jump in a car and travel hundreds of miles to find her just to see that she was okay. I have lived a beautiful and blessed life, and you have proven that to me today." Lester swallowed and shifted his feet. "She has never sat at a supper table and laughed about the day's events. No one has ever read her a bedtime story or taught her how prayers can heal."

"So read her a book, say a prayer, and then come home," Leon said, his impulsive nature couldn't stay contained as his heart pounded in his chest. Lester was in love and was protecting her. Leon knew the feeling, but how did loving and protecting Faith help Lester from losing his faith in Gott, his place in their family?

"She didn't know *Gott* even existed until I met her."

"*Gott* wouldn't want you to abandon your faith," Leon said with less anger, slowly seeing his reckless brother in a new light.

"*Nee*, He would not," Lester said. "*Gott* wouldn't have wanted me to leave her behind for her family to find, either. You don't understand Leon. They are not good people."

"Why do they want to find her if they don't care for her?"

"She saw something she shouldn't have." Lester began pacing the small room. After a few moments, he stopped and looked at Leon. "I found her in Hank's barn one morning. I about jumped out of my skin." His face grew dark, angry. Both hands rounded into fists. Leon had done the same when he thought Tabor might get bold with Hannah. It was obvious his brother truly did love this woman.

"I never saw anything so horrible in my life. Her *daed* beat her bloody, and I'm pretty sure that brother of hers pretended he didn't know where she was, but Faith said he was the one who drove her out to Miller's Creek and dumped her off."

Leon watched the expressions dance over his brother's face, listened to him, and tried piecing it together for himself.

"He dropped her off, to you?"

"*Nee*, to fend for herself," Lester said. "His brotherly love only extends so far."

"You did not know until then?"

"I had seen her plenty, in town. We actually spoke many times. I tried to get her to go out with me," Lester touched a finger to his nose and winced. "She refused me."

Leon didn't believe in coincidences.

"What did she see?"

"I can't tell you that *bruder*. All I can tell you is I won't abandon her. I saved enough to move us. I've been working at a trailer factory. She works here, babysitting during the day and caring for an older couple most evenings. But neither of us will feel safe until we get further away. And since you found me so quick, well, it's only a matter of time until they find her."

"Where will you go?"

"West," he said. "I found work out there in a small town. Nothing's too costly, and I get to see mountains, so I hear." Lester shrugged. "They won't come looking that far." He huffed. "That would require effort. I trust you to keep this between us."

"What about our parents? How do I tell them I failed bringing you home? Lewis and Luke depended on me."

"And you found me, *bruder*." Lester moved closer, placing a hand on Leon's shoulders. "There is no failure here for you. We are no longer *kinner*. The blame is all mine. You have done exactly what I knew, and everyone knew, you would. Try. It is who you are. You care about something; you don't let go."

Leon felt unbidden tears start to surface.

"It is why I love you so much."

"This cannot be goodbye," Leon said. His heart ached as each word passed through Lester's lips. Was he really leaving his whole family behind for Faith?

"It is so long, for now," Lester said.

But that wasn't good enough. Leon wanted assurances.

"I will write once we've settled. I know *mamm* will cry." Lester lowered his head, his own heart clearly breaking, knowing what this would do to her. "Because of me, she will cry and there is nothing I can do to stop that." He looked at Leon again, part desperate, part determined. "Tell her I will write. Don't tell them about the circumstances. I know they will all just want to find a way to fix it, and trust me, if it was fixable, I would have done it already."

"Do you really love her this much?" Leon asked in a dry voice. *More than us?*

"I do. I love her this much," Lester said with certainty. "And unlike me, *bruder*, I am all she has in this world."

The fact broke Leon's heart, just as he suspected Lester hoped it would. No one deserved to be alone. He suddenly thought of Hannah. Though their circumstances, their very upbringings were as opposite as the ocean was to the desert, they, for one reason or another, weren't alone. Faith didn't choose her lot in life, nor, according to Lester, had she chosen to fear for her life. Hannah was surrounded by family, friends, and a whole community, and yet loneliness was what he saw behind the heartbreak those emerald eyes betrayed.

Did she fear having feelings for him, knowing we were never promised a tomorrow? Was she afraid he would try to change her? Leon let the thought provoke him right now. Two days since he had seen her. Two days away from the scent of apple blossoms. Yeah, he missed her. Missed her so much it had him by the throat. Lester's conundrum made a lot more sense now.

"Then I shall let you go only on one condition."

Lester lifted a brow, and then a slow grin formed on his lips.

"Only one?" Lester teased.

"For now." Leon grinned back. "You do the right thing by her and marry her. Don't live like this. If you love her as you say you do, marry her. *Gott* will not allow for this,

Lester." Leon motioned a hand over the room. No, *Gott* would not abide with this living arrangement his brother had.

Lester yanked him into a hug, squeezed so tight Leon felt the air burst out of him in a crushing force. When Lester pulled back, he looked at Leon with something more like admiration than surprise.

"We married three weeks ago. I know right and wrong, and so will my *kinner* if *Gott* sees fit to bless us with them." Lester held his brother's shoulders with two strong hands. "But I will share that news with our parents in due time. First things first, and that is getting Faith out of here."

"Then I want to meet my sister-in-law before you go. You will have dinner at Marcus's tonight, and we will say our goodbyes then."

CHAPTER TWENTY-FIVE

Hannah looked out across the orchard, beyond the trees heavy in fruit, toward the rise of the hill. Still no Leon, she grumbled inwardly. The sun had risen hours ago. Hannah and Millie had fumbled through chores. Still air, hot and daunting, had her already perspiring through her pale chore clothes. Flip-flops were the footwear of the day, despite the need for sturdy shoes, climbing the ladder.

With another angry huff, she turned her back on the hill, on the man who didn't show up when she needed him most, and began harvesting the Lodi apples. More than ninety trees bore the yellowy-green fruits that hit the taste buds tart but was swallowed down sweet. *Mamm* preferred them for her applesauce and though shelf life was short, according to the local grocer, Troyer's orchard never had a surplus of them left after their season. The local grocery store owner and she had a deal, made long ago with her father, and Hannah needed to keep it fulfilled.

Last year, at least her *schwestern* had helped, but this year, only her mother stood at her side. Addie was tending to the busy roadside stand. Summer was their best time for selling vegetables, jams, jellies, and early apples. Ivy was at the bakery doing her part to help her family. Hannah suspected it wasn't much of a hardship. It could not be ignored how just a few months had turned a pestering little sister into a humming young *maedel*. Ivy loved her work it seemed. Deep down, Hannah was glad for it. Just because she tied herself to the orchard didn't mean her sisters had to as well.

She glanced at her mother in a neighboring tree. Still strong, beautiful, and just as determined as Hannah these days to see the orchard prosper.

"I'm sure he has reason for not being here. I just hope nothing bad has happened." Millie reached up, plucked another fruit, and gingerly laid it with the other in the small basket cradled between ladder and stomach.

With a fresh basket in hand, Hannah climbed the ladder, grumbling every rung on the way up before leaning her body against it. "How are we going to harvest everything this year without him?" She hated complaining, especially from her own mouth, and clamped it shut. She didn't need Leon Milford.

"He will be here. If not today, then tomorrow," Millie said without even a hint of worry.

If she knew more than she was sharing, Hannah wished she'd share now. "You don't know that," Hannah said. "He doesn't care. He thought he was some big help," she continued her rant. "Well, he is nothing more than I knew all along. Unreliable," she ground out the last word between clenched teeth.

"I didn't know you were so concerned with what our hired hand cares about," Millie shot her a look between thick branches.

"A cow. Did he really think a cow would earn him favors?" Hannah stretched between her own branches, yanking and pulling with a fueled temper. "Just because he can tidy up the place doesn't make him a martyr. It's his job. He's getting paid to do it." She shifted and sought out a new limb to plunder. No, if given the choice, she was certain

Leon would have never done all the things he had willingly.

Except those swimming lessons. He didn't have to do that. She thought about the last words they passed between them. What kind of man did that; awaken something in a woman's heart with no intention of nurturing it? Well, she huffed, she wasn't wasting another minute thinking about those looks, or the way her heart skipped when he nursed her splintered finger, or... *Stop it, Hannah.*

"Hannah," Mamm said. "Stop searching for reasons to not like him. If you worked half that hard seeing the good in him, you might be more concerned as to why he didn't come today."

A hot breeze brushed over her. She didn't want to think that something could possibly be wrong, but now that *mamm* planted the seed, she did. What if his parents were unwell? What if he was in an accident? Her heart kicked up a notch as she worked out several scenarios, now flashing through her thoughts.

"This is *narrisch*," she blurted out. She was not going to let herself worry all day about Leon Milford. "He is most likely fishing *faul* under a shaded elm." Well, he would find himself searching for a new job, that much she knew for sure and for certain.

Basket full, she descended the ladder carefully. On the hill separating farm and orchard, deep emerald grasses blanketed the ridgeline and now sported milkweed, daisies, and wild mustard. Eight baskets already dotted the ground beneath the tree, so she went to load them into the wagon.

"What is that?"

Hannah had heard it too. She pushed a full basket into the wagon flat and followed her mother's gaze.

"Finally," Hannah muttered. He was finally here. They both could hear the sound of a buggy in the distance. Why she let herself get all worked up for nothing, Hannah hadn't a clue. She would have to remind him being late for work had its repercussions.

When the horse crested the hill, Hannah was dumbstruck. She squinted into the sun; surely her eyes and the light were playing tricks. Instead of one of the workhorses or Marva, Leon's horse, Hannah watched a beautiful white gelding, once belonging to Hank, appear at the top of the ridgeline.

"What in the world?" She stiffened. Levi at the reins only added to the confusion. Just because the two were twins didn't mean Hannah couldn't bespeak the many differences, including the way he sat and held the reins. Then, as if that hadn't borne enough confusion, behind Levi more horses peeked, and Hannah soon realized she was being taken over by what remained of the Milford half-dozen.

"I should have known," she muttered snarkily. As the wagons neared, Hannah skimmed quickly over the faces and found not one of them belonged to Leon. She watched numbly as Leon's *bruders* and *mamm* stepped down and began pulling crates from their wagons.

"Well, we have been blessed this day. The Milfords have come to help us harvest," *Mamm* said, smiling ear to ear as she approached. *Mamm* didn't seem as shocked as Hannah at this invasion.

As blue eyes all focused on her, Hannah's throat went dry. Sure, more hands would be great, getting the harvest in and meeting the grocery buyer by Friday, but that wasn't the point. How could Leon just leave her without a word but send his family?

"Three days," Luke said, closing toward her. "Three days should do it." He sat four stacked vegetable crates down. She had always liked Luke. His straightforward approach to things, his quiet nature, but it was that smirk smeared over his face she was unsure about right now.

"Three?" Hannah finally managed a word. Luke simply chuckled and scooped up one of the crates. "I'll take Lovis and Levi and start over here. You can handle the womenfolk."

He smiled and aimed for the neighboring row of trees, leaving her with more questions than his presence already offered.

"We brought a few more ladders," Irma announced with a wide grin.

Dressed in dull gray and an apron front dusted with wear and use, Irma gave *mamm* a hug and the two walked off, leaving Hannah momentarily stunned. Leon's family was here, helping with the harvest. And for three days, that's what they did.

Hannah worked alongside the Milford half-dozen, minus one, every day. Each morning after the sun had risen in the sky, they came. Each afternoon when the sun made its descent, they left, and not once had Hannah dared ask the questions disturbing her. Leon's whereabouts remained a mystery. One thing she knew, without asking, was the hired help didn't care any more about the orchard than he did her.

As they rested under the Stellar trees that wouldn't ripen fully until September, Hannah sat next to Lovis and ate her turkey sandwich in relative silence. Lovis carried a strong resemblance to both his parents with soft eyes that followed his brothers' movements closely. He was gangly, like Ivy, but more observant.

Across from them, *mamm* and Irma chatted. They had plenty to chat about. *Mamm* talked about living in Miller's Creek her whole life. Irma shared tales of a colder, tighter-stitched community before becoming a transplant. One was skilled in raising sons, the other, practiced at raising daughters, and yet both smiled with equal affection when speaking of *kinner*.

Today, as a Wednesday sun bore down, John Milford came. Hannah could see where Leon got his strong work ethic. Even in his years that Hannah suspected well succeeded her *mamm*'s, Leon's *daed* could clear a tree as quick as his eldest *sohns*. There were a few moments, Hannah was sure, he goaded them too. Leon had his humor as well as that drive to treat everything like race. John was a comical type which didn't match his burly build at all. It was true one could never judge a book by its cover, she mused as he sported another tale of his offspring's ventures on her.

"Then he just jumped in. Silly fella thought he could swim because he said he could," John laughed as he finished another story of his six ornery sons. Hannah had to admit she was enjoying them. Especially the ones that spoke of a fearless little boy who hadn't a care for danger.

"I guess it's sink or swim for some," Hannah said with a laugh. It was clear they were missing Lester, so many of the stories thus far included him. Hannah felt her heart go out to both of Leon's parents. Perhaps being given so many freedoms after years of tight rules under their old community, made it hard for one to resist further exploration.

"That's what our Leon said," John said. "He is made of common sense too."

She flinched in the compliment. That grin was Leon's.

"Your family farm is the most beautiful sight I have ever seen, and I have seen my share of beautiful places. No wonder *mei* Leon wakes so early and *kumm*s home with such a smile on his face," Irma said without being prompted.

"A man cannot help but like beautiful things. It is in their nature," Lewis said before standing.

"*Mei* Eli," *Mamm* said, "wanted a home that his generations would always have. It has been in his family for many generations."

"He always said..." Hannah smiled, "...it was the closest to heaven one could get until reaching it." Hannah never took for granted a single blade of grass, or a branch that fed her family. It was a gift her father had given her. She had a choice, as did everyone, but living this life, the one she loved whole-heartedly, was all she could ever hope for.

She turned toward Leon's mother again, this time noting the small scar on her face. It did nothing to take away from the beauty of her. Irma was fragility and strength both.

Hannah never knew a woman could be both. It was inspirational and touched her somewhere deep. Hannah considered her own plight. Lord knew it was hard being the strong one all the time.

"All of them are *gut* helpers. They know when one is in need. I am glad you were in need while Leon is off doing who knows what this week." Irma looked to her as if needing answers.

She wished she could do something to ease Irma's pleading eyes, but she couldn't.

"Leon, I am certain, would rather be here." As soon as the words left her lips, Hannah hoped Irma didn't take her the wrong way.

"I know he would. *Danki,* Hannah." Irma patted her arm. "I feel better knowing he would but wish he would come home. I hate not having my *kinner* near." Irma stood and began putting away what remained of the noonday picnic.

"I'll go fetch us some water to take back to the wagons." Hannah rose and shuffled off toward the wagon. They were nothing alike she mentally fussed. She would never abandon someone in need or break a promise. Leon had disappeared, abandoning her in the middle of the harvest, and left no reason for it.

"You are angry with him, ain't so?"

Hannah turned to find Lewis standing behind her. The spouted cooler in her hand jerked, spilling half the water she had just collected from a larger ice cooler.

"Sorry. Let me help you." He rushed forward, quickly twisting the lid back on. "Sure is hot today," he said.

"*Jah,* it is," she said coolly. "It wonders me how I will ever repay you all for helping us." Lewis was not just eldest, he was biggest. Not just in size, which he was, but something about him spoke authority, leadership, and maybe even a hint of forwardness. All would serve him well as Miller's Creek's new minister. The longer she looked at him, the clearer she saw it. He was the kind of man who got answers when asking questions. No wonder Jenny had turned a new leaf and become a more pleasant person.

"We agreed to it." His smile softened all his more serious features. "I see your head spinning wanting to know, and yet, you haven't as much as asked."

Hannah swallowed. Her throat felt like sandpaper. Lewis cocked his head, awaiting her question. Well, just because he was now her elder and church minister didn't mean she would crack under his pressure.

"Just ask. You waited three whole days to do so."

"*Ach*, fine." She rolled her eyes. "Why? Why did the Milfords decide to miss work and duties of their own, for three days, to harvest our apples? Why, is our hired man missing?" Hannah stuck out her chin and straightened her shoulders. Unlike Leon, this Milford didn't find her stubbornness so amusing.

"Leon is out of state," Lewis said flatly and slightly leaned closer. "He went to fetch our *bruder.*"

Hannah gasped in knowing.

"Our parents don't know where he is. They only know that he is helping a cousin in need for a few days."

Lewis leaned even closer. Goodness, he really was tall.

"Don't think harshly of him. Leon would never shirk his duties without cause."

So, he hadn't abandoned her for fishing, just for Lester.

"It is none of my business," she said. She felt her skin flush and pulled the cooler from his hands.

"Isn't it?" Lewis smirked, his dark eyes sparkling in humor before he walked away.

Dumbstruck, Hannah stood there trying to rationalize Lewis' two simple words.

"You should rest, *dochder*. We have so much help you should not be working as hard as you have of late. You are looking a bit…"

"*Jah*, I know." Hannah finished. She didn't want to know what she looked like currently. Both caught sight of Lovis helping Ivy lift a basket into the wagon. Wednesdays were Ivy's one day off during the week, but she hadn't complained once all day about helping. At their right, Levi grumbled, spilling a few apples as he slid his overfilled crate into a wagon.

"They really don't look much alike at all," Irma said absent-mindedly.

Nee, Hannah thought, they didn't. Levi's smile was too soft, kind, whereas Leon's was playful, dangerously so. Leon was taller too, she reasoned. Over the season, Hannah had noted many things about Leon she found not so horrible. Like how he always carried his plate to the sink, or how he always removed his shoes at the door, dirty or not. Hannah prided Irma for the gesture. Raising six boys, Irma probably molded more than a handful of respectful traits into them.

"You should have heard John and Lovis talk about Leon. He apparently, like our Ivy, has a fondness for saving poor animals." *Mamm* laughed. Hannah would never get used to her mother's new laughs. It had been so long without them.

"Once he found a kitten needing saving and hid it in his room even after one of their neighbors came looking for it. Her cat was yellow and when Leon heard such, he went and painted it white, so it didn't match the neighbor's. It was a funny story; the way John tells it." *Mamm* shrugged.

"Who knew he had a soft spot for kittens?" Then again, he held a soft spot for moody females too, she mused.

Hannah couldn't help but join her mother in full laughter. Just thinking about hiding catnip in his pockets made her smile. *If only he returned, that was.* How long did it take to find a wayward brother and bring him home? She chided herself on the selfish thought. Leon was doing the right thing, and just because she missed having him around didn't mean…she missed him. Her breath caught in her chest. Yes, she really did miss him and there was no pretending she didn't.

"Leon asked them to *kumm*," Hannah said. "He had to

leave Kentucky to help a cousin."

"*Jah*, I reckon that was obvious. Leon would never have left us…"

Mamm peered up at her eldest daughter. "He would have never left you in a tight spot. I do feel he has *kumm* to love this orchard as much as you."

Hannah remained tight-lipped.

"Irma talks highly about him. He reminds me of your *daed*. He was a man who didn't sit idle either."

Hannah's heart drew to a stop at her mother's words.

"Leon is nothing like *daed*," Hannah said, feeling insulted.

"Well, *nee*, he has not a red hair on his head," *Mamm* said, a whisper of laughter still on her breaths, "but he never stops. He can out eat most men and out work them too." *Mamm* leaned closer. "And to tell you the truth, I remember a time when Eli Troyer liked kittens too."

With that, Millie trailed off, leaving Hannah to her own thinking.

CHAPTER TWENTY-SIX

Under a threatening sky, Hannah sat along the creek bank as a rare northern wind snaked between the trees. Cicadas were growing more anxious, and frogs tried to compete. She didn't give much mind now. Her attention turned to watching lightning bugs dance along the shores.

Everything had been fine before Leon came into her world disturbing it. Now, nothing felt as it should be. A tear slipped down Hannah's cheek. The season was half over. The busy harvest now held everyone's focus. Hannah loved the rush, the busyness, but nowadays she was beginning to love other things too. Long talks, passing witty banter, and Leon's flirty smiles.

Leon had made promises, and for the most part, he had kept them. But in all their talks and quarrels and words pasted between them, he never mentioned she would need him.

One short cicada season had changed her. "Seventeen years," she said with fresh appreciation toward the noisy insects. They had their summer, and now it would be seventeen years before another cicada season sprouted. A tremble started in her belly, working its way up the rest of her.

"Seventeen years," she muttered beneath sobs. Their wait she couldn't comprehend at the moment. No wonder they made so much noise. Would they too suffer the melancholy surely to follow? Would they mourn the loss of a few short weeks? She would never have a partner like that, a life with a family of her own. Just the orchard and legacy left for her to cultivate. And Leon would move on, find someone who cherished his goodness without fear or walls, and build a life.

As thunder rumbled in the distance, Hannah stood, straightened her dress, wiped the tears from her eyes, and made her way back home. Crying over things out of her reach was foolish. Cicada season would eventually end, and life would go on.

Ivy and Addie sang in the kitchen while *mamm* set the table. Hannah didn't have much of an appetite but took her place at the family table as expected.

"Luke said he would come by and deliver the last of the apples in the morning," *Mamm* said, taking a seat. All heads bowed for the silent prayer.

"Hazel said I could have a few days off to help you start the applesauce," Ivy said. She reached for a warm biscuit and slathered on more strawberry jam than one biscuit needed.

Hannah remained silent, maneuvered her food around her plate, and nibbled at a sweetened carrot so mamm wouldn't notice and fuss. Ivy was too old to remind her to control her sweet tooth.

"I can't believe Levi was able to help too. Hank depends on him so, but it was nice he was able to come help this week," Addie said, her tone whimsical and smitten.

"He would make you a fine match. Eli would have liked him." *Mamm* patted Addie's arm in approving affection. Hannah's head jerked up at her mother's words. She opened her mouth to protest none of them could know *daed*'s thoughts on such matters, but the beaming on her sister's face, the slight rosy blush on her pale cheeks knowing she had her mother's approval to court Levi, had her closing it again.

A knock sounded, and despite being in no mind for company, Hannah stood to answer it, putting some distance between herself and her family happy with their lives, new jobs, and possible interests, all reminders of just how lonely and dark her future would soon be. Levi was a great man, and Addie would be lucky to have him. Ivy loved working for Hazel and Rose, and *mamm* was beginning to spend more time in the company of others. Hannah would just as soon crawl under a rock.

Hannah opened the door to find a hand jerking back quickly. He was aiming on knocking again. Her heart beat kicked up a notch, and the urge to jump into Leon's arms almost overtook her. Almost. What kind of woman jumped in a man's arms, especially one who had no interest in her? If he had, he would have told her before running off.

They stood in silence, gazes locked. She had missed him, but seeing him standing there right now, she felt it too. Her bones softened, making it harder for her knees to keep her up.

"I'm sorry," he said in sincerity. "I was longer than I thought I would be."

He stepped back, pulling his hat from his head. Under both blue eyes, she could see the color of a weary traveler and something else. A man who looked defeated.

His clothes were wrinkled, and he smelled of smoke, cigarette smoke, she corrected. He needed a hot shower, a soft pillow, but instead, he was standing in her doorway. The low hum of an engine prompted her to peer around him. The car sat in the drive, a cloud of smoke drifting out of the driver's side window.

Sensing where her thoughts had gone, he said, "I haven't been home yet," he said.

Her heart melted and her blood warmed, but Hannah couldn't ignore the part where he hadn't told her he was leaving.

"You left without saying a word," she said. His head lowered as if a child being scolded.

"There was no time," he said, looking at her again.

"How much time does it take from your precious day to simply tell those who pay you to do a job, that," she shifted, waved an arm in the air, "you won't be back to work?"

"I had to leave in a hurry. It was important." He took a step closer, brows gathering. He had no idea Lewis had told her where he had gone to.

"And we weren't?" She leaned to see past him and then straightened again. Aside from a driver, she could barely make out in detail, the car held no other shadows. Just as she suspected. Lester was not with him.

"And I see you failed whatever you were hoping to accomplish in Ohio too." She tried to remain steady, but her own harshness made her ears ache.

"At least I tried, I would rather fail than never try."

Was he asking her to try?

"I made sure you had help."

He looked down at her and Hannah felt the fast pumping of fresh adrenaline that was making her slightly dizzy.

"My family has spent days helping you, and we both know you and I couldn't have accomplished half that. I did not leave you. I'm right here. I seen to your needs, even before my *bruder*."

And he had.

"It's not your job to do so. You will be gone after the harvest." Could he not see it? That she alone was responsible for her family's future, her father's orchard. That no matter how he stirred her heart, she feared he too would leave her standing alone.

Recognition flickered in his eyes. "He trusted you with it," he muttered.

She felt the sting of her vulnerability being sliced into.

"I have never had such placed on my shoulders." His voice grew deep and slow. "But he would never expect you to go at it alone. I am here."

Hannah bit back a sob as reality offered her a hard slap. Leon was here with her.

"I know you miss him wonderfully so. I know you think my finding Lester wasn't more important than being here and helping you."

He held her gaze, but weariness hung heavy in his voice. She had worn him down and for that guilt now was making her nauseous.

"I'm sorry you don't trust me." Shoving his hat back on his head, Leon turned to leave.

Her chest began to ache. It felt like panic. Yes, she was panicking. He was leaving and she was letting him go.

"*Nee.*" Hannah stepped out of the house behind him. Her heart raced with every step he put between them.

"*Jah!*" He barked over one shoulder, aiming for the car.

"No!" Her final and last command if he would only stay. "Leon, I…I…" *Apologize*, her heart screamed. "You're right."

Leon froze.

"About all of it," she said as he turned to face her again. "I miss him, and it hurts. I need him to help me and there is so much I still don't know. If I make a mistake, it could all be lost to us…forever." No longer could her tears be held back, her sobs be silent. "I am so angry at *Gott*, at those men who were responsible for letting so many die that day." She clutched her belly with her fist, too weak to stand tall now. "I'm so tired, I can't think some days. And Lester did come first. He is your *bruder*, your *mamm* misses him terribly. And…I'm sorry for saying what I did. If that was Addie…" she wept harder, incapable of finishing the apology, the reasons, and excuses she owed him.

Leon spun and marched up to her. His heart was broken in

two that he forced her to see what everyone already knew. Hannah needed this for herself. She needed to let go, spill out all the things weighing her down. She needed to face what ate at her gut for the last two years. He placed a hand on her shoulder, squeezed slightly, and leaned toward her. Tears on her face didn't belong.

"Hannah," he whispered before his lips crashed into hers.

Leon was careful, cradling her face in both hands. She was strong on the outside, but it was the inside he wanted to nurture. He expected her to push him away, but to his shock, Hannah accepted the kiss. Tears and hot breath mingled between their first surrender, and he felt her yield as two small hands grasped his shirt in tight fists. To her, Leon imagined, it was knowing she wasn't alone, finally feeling his love.

To Leon, it was heaven and possessive and nothing like he expected. A man grew taller when his love was returned. Leon pulled back first. They were both breathless, but it was the way her green eyes grew soft, somber, looking up at him that filled his soul. He could spend the rest of his life kissing her, holding her, and reminding her she was never alone.

"I wasn't finished," she muttered.

He smiled. "Well, it was the best way to shut you up," he said playfully, touching their foreheads together. To Leon's amazement, she laughed.

"And now, I know how to shut you up too," she said just before placing her lips on his again. This second kiss was softer and so much sweeter.

"I still hate you," she whispered.

"I hate you too." He chuckled and pulled her to him and simply held her. She fit in his arms, her head on his shoulder. He hadn't even suspected how wonderful it would feel to be a man and be held too. Leon looked toward the house and the beady-eyed door with a mangy cat licking an outstretched leg underneath.

Millie would probably come out of the house any second

threatening him with his life, but Leon knew this, his hold, his protectiveness, his love, was what Hannah needed from him most and what he needed to offer despite all the strengths that forged him.

Hannah had busted his lip, bruised his cheeks, smashed his ego, and stolen his heart. It wouldn't be easy, he measured, loving a woman whose heart ached for something she could never have again, but Leon always did like a good challenge. The way he figured it, *Gott* had made him just for this purpose. To love Hannah Troyer.

CHAPTER TWENTY-SEVEN

Leon woke, climbed out of dreaming, and rolled out of his bed. Still dark, but habitually how every day started, even for men who barely got three winks of sleep thinking about a woman. *The* woman, he corrected and smiled as he rushed through a shower and donned fresh clothes.

After talking with his parents late into the night when he had returned home from Ohio, Leon was surprised to find both understanding. They didn't blame him for Lester not returning and just as Lester predicted, *Mamm* had cried. *Daed* led them into a prayer for the son they may never see again.

Leon wanted to wait at least a week or so before springing his intentions on them, but he had never been known for his patience and told them about his upcoming baptismal classes and about Hannah. God made her for him and him for her. No other could ever complete him so well. *Mamm* agreed with his thoughts, his choice, though a grown man didn't need his *mamm*'s approval to ask a girl to marry him. But given that she did, Leon was glad. He had also given his mother something to smile about right now. Surely, her heart was torn between rejoicing in one son's happiness and losing another to the world. Lester was right, that we could only be responsible for our choices.

"You heading over to the bishop's today?" *Daed* asked when he stepped into the dimly lit kitchen. Leon nodded, combing his fingers through his wet hair. "I could tag along. If you want support for those big ideas of yours, that is." *Daed* winked and then burst into a laugh.

"Now, John, stop." Irma scolded her husband.

"I just can't help it. Our Leon…" John chuckled again.

"You say it as if I'm the shock of all your *sohn*s," Leon said, ignoring his father's typical banter, and took a seat in front of a warm, steamy breakfast.

"You each shock us in different ways," *mamm* said with a slow smile and a lifted brow.

"Your *mamm* once slammed my hand in a door," John said, tossing a cunning grin toward *mamm*. If Leon wasn't mistaken, she was blushing. Those rosy cheeks had nothing to do with preparing breakfast. Footsteps overhead signaled Levi and Lovis were waking.

"You were being bold." *Mamm* waved a spatula toward him. The absence of the wooden spoon, accompanied by that smile on her face, was enough for Leon to gag at the flirting. It was one thing to be considering new methods of flirting with Hannah, another to watch your parents do it so openly.

"Well, I asked for a kiss, and she said no and slammed the door in my face," John said.

"It was our first date," *mamm* said before turning her attention back to Leon. "He was too bold. I think your heart knows what it wants and your intentions for her, her family, are *wunderbaar*."

Leon was glad she agreed. Today, he would talk to the bishop about his plans for the Troyers and for all their futures.

By evening, Leon had everything in order. He was not the type to get nervous, but as he walked up the porch steps of Hannah's home, sweaty palms and a racing heart suggested otherwise. He gave the beady-eyed door three firm knocks and took a step back, careful not to trample a one-eared, one-eyed mangy cat that was starting to think it might like him after all. Who would have thought just months ago as he stood on the step and was greeted by a flea-bitten critter and Hannah's all-out fury, that he would spend a summer helping her? And what a summer it had been so far. He smiled like the fool he knew himself now to be. He learned something new, apple growing too, and was eager for more.

Hannah answered the door. Her dark blue dress and fresh apron highlighted the sun-kissed fleshy parts revealed under elbow-length sleeves. Her *kapp* was fresh and crisp, bringing out the deep earthy hues of autumn and sunsets in her hair. Leon didn't care if she was dressed in her best or a chore dress, she still made his heart skip beats.

Removing his hat, he set it aside on the porch rocker and reached for her hand. "*Kumm* with me. I've something to show you." She giggled as he pulled her outside without awaiting her response.

"Leon, where are we going? *Mamm* and I were in the middle of…"

"Oh, that can wait, this cannot." He shot her a smile and kept her moving forward. "Trust me, Hannah. Your *mamm* already does." He winked.

"That's because she doesn't know you paint horses when no one is watching." Hannah chuckled.

When they reached the forgotten concrete, the pad that sat idle near the front of the property, her hand pulled from his.

"Leon," she took a step back. "I don't like being here."

"But you only see it as something he left behind. Hannah, I need you to see as it will be." He encouraged her forward. She let him bring her to the center. "Stand here."

Hannah didn't ease, the tenseness in her shoulders revealing her apprehension. She knew he was hoping they could finish it. But the money wasn't there. That was why he figured she let the whole thing slip out of mind. He planned on convincing her it could be done.

"All up and down this side, booths, a restroom at this end. Ammon Plank has volunteered to see to all the plumbing."

Hannah's hand covered her heart as she stood on the reminder of a dream. One she had envisioned just as *daed* described it.

"At this end, Hank Fisher and Lewis will be displaying their goods. My *bruder* has a knack for woodworking it seems."

Was he saying others wanted to see the market finished as well? She shook her head, trying to grasp what was happening.

"Shelves, dressers, bedroom suites," he said. "It works better for them since they need plenty of space."

Leon watched her expression, but Hannah couldn't offer anything but a blank one right now.

"Then here," he pointed toward the northern side of the platform, "*Mamm* and the other women will display their quilts. So far Eliza Lapp, Mirim Plank, *Aenti* Emma, Lily Peachy, and a couple from the next district will take turns tending it. You won't have to worry with that, *Mamm* agreed to handle it for you. I think it excites her now that she has more time to spare."

Leon took a few steps toward her. "You will be too busy running an orchard to handle who works a quilting booth."

He floated her a grin.

Her vision blurred. He was handsome, and more so when he was eager and determined. Leon was also finishing what *daed* had started.

"Millie can sell her jams and jellies here, and Addie her honey." He came closer. "There are others who want to join, but until you decide how much space we need for our produce, we can't move any further." She could see it, envision it, just as *daed* had. Pumpkins and squash in full display. Maybe sell mums alongside them. Crates and baskets of Troyer apples.

"Wagons out front too. For pumpkins and apple baskets," she said in a shaky breath, holding his gaze.

"Only open on Saturdays."

He moved in, leaving just a couple feet between them. Leon lifted his hand and brushed a calloused thumb over her cheek.

"The bishop doesn't want it to get too big so as to pull many from their duties and families. It is a perfect location this close to the main road."

She could hardly breathe.

"He suggests auctions, large gatherings, and perhaps the mud sales here."

"*Daed* wanted that," she muttered. Leon took her hand, ran a thumb over the top, but didn't break eye contact with her.

"He was a smart man. Bishop Schwartz asked that ten percent of all sales be added to the community fund."

"Ten percent?"

"It's fair, my dear, and no more than a biblical tithe, for a new school and to help families still suffering."

"We will be helping," she said, finally seeing the full of it in his eyes.

"*Jah*, we will. This is what your *daed* wanted, I think. It wasn't just for him, or your family, but for the community. He wanted to do something to help all, to see everyone prosper, gather happily together."

"He did want that," she said, no longer sad when bringing him to mind.

"Hannah Troyer, you are the most complicated woman I ever met."

She felt a smile threaten despite a few lingering tears working their way out of her.

"You busted my lip, my face, my pride, and all that pounding cracked my heart right open. I have never seen a more lovely future made than the one you and I will have," he said.

Her heart leaped.

"Will have?" Her voice rose above a whisper. "You want a life, here, with me?"

"I do," he said and scooped up her other hand. "I started baptismal classes and soon will take my baptism. There will be nothing standing between us soon enough."

"But this was just for the harvest. You wanted to work with Lewis, remember? You grew up on a dairy farm and…"

"And I have mastered a hundred other things since. I think that works in your favor *lieb*," he winked and gave her hands a gentle squeeze. "Hannah, I love it here. The air, the space, the whole lot of it."

"You do?" She couldn't believe it. He really wanted a life growing apples and mowing grass and plowing fields?

"If you'll have me, I'll even let you be the boss in the orchard."

She gasped at the proposal given with no hesitation.

"Say you will marry me; spend the rest of your life helping me build something beautiful with you."

"I…I…"

"I'm not letting you say no." He grinned challengingly. "We both know it. And you can't keep affording my enormous talents anyway," he said. A grin tickled the corners of his lips.

"Is that the best you can do? You know some wise man

once told me that there are bugs that wait seventeen years for the perfect mate. Come back then, and we will see if you still want to put up with me."

"*Nee.*" He kissed her. "I can always do better, but…" He laughed. "Do you really want to wait seventeen years, my dear?" She melted into him. Seventeen years was a very long time to go without Leon's kisses.

"Well, since seventeen years is so far off, then, *jah*, I will marry you." She kissed him back. "I still hate you," she whispered, a grin playing on her lips.

"I hate you even more," he said before dropping his lips onto hers again.

Epilogue

One year later

It was crowded, and Ivy didn't like hospitals. The strange smells, mixed with her overwhelming anxiety right now, were enough to make her gag. She focused on the tiles, the tiny gold blotches in each one, and began counting.

"Oh, would you men stop with all that pacing?" Hazel glared at them, and multiple pairs of boots clapped to an abrupt halt on the white-tiled hospital floors. "All that stomping about ain't doing a body any good."

"They're just worried, *mamm*." Lydia patted her mother's leg.

Ivy knew how Hazel felt. She glanced about the open room. Black bonnets and black felt hats filled the waiting room. It warmed Ivy's heart to see so many here for Hannah and Leon, praying and supporting one another.

"The Lord is with them, I tell ya," Hazel said looking at Millie Troyer sitting across from her as she spoke. "And he made certain Hannah was made strong for this day, rightly so."

Ivy could see she was speaking more to herself than a room full of family and friends. Hank Fisher offered Hazel a cup of something, and Ivy found herself grinning for the first time since her sister realized some minor morning back pain was something more.

The small Pleasants County Hospital wasn't equipped for new life deliveries, but ever since Hannah Milford's seventh month of her pregnancy, Doc Richmond saw to it a neighboring doctor would be on call when the big day came. And though four weeks too soon, life was coming whether Hannah was ready or not.

"It is early is all," Irma said in a shaky tone, her hand clasped tightly onto Millie's.

The two were about to be grandmothers and both looked to be sick.

"You know more about twins than I do," Millie looked to Irma to say something comforting.

"Levi and Leon were three days late. I can't know what this means."

"But the Lord does," Hazel said.

"Hazel's right. *Gott*'s will. Let us pray," Lewis said, quieting all doubts.

At the sound of the double door swinging open, all heads lifted as Leon burst into the room. He was dressed in blue from head to boot. Ivy rose and joined everyone. She held her breath and tried measuring the distraught look on Leon's face. Was he in shock, all wide-eyed like that? Acidy bile began rising up her throat. The life of her sister and her possible nieces or nephews were at stake.

"Leon?" Millie asked and his eyes darted between her and Irma. Suddenly, a slow flicker of reality washed over him, and with it, that all too signature Milford smile.

"*Mamm*, Millie," Leon said. "Hannah is fine. More than fine. She is smiling, laughing, and more beautiful than the day I married her. And you are both now *mammi*'s to the strongest, healthiest, and sorry for being prideful, but it must be said." His chin lifted boastfully. "The most beautiful set of red-headed girls ever to be born."

Thankful prayers shot up mingled with relieved sighs. Ivy dropped back into her seat as everyone crowded around Leon. She couldn't help but cry happy tears as the air rushed in and out of her.

When she felt a hand touch her shoulder, Ivy lifted her head to meet Hazel smiling down at her. "Did you doubt it? Told ya the Lord knows what He is doing," Hazel said.

"I was so afraid for her, for all of them." Ivy brushed a sleeve under her running nose. "But Hazel, I don't think matchmaking is for me. I have never been so tense in my life." Ivy blew out a trapped breath.

"*Ach* now, child. We are just getting started. The Lord has work to be done here."

"Then I'll let Him do it. I have two nieces to love. I'm not sure I'll have the time. Hannah will need me."

"But not all the Milford half dozen have been matched, yet. And there is the matter of those Lewis boys. Even they deserve love, Ivy. Don't you think so?"

Ivy shook her head. It was hopeless to go against the woman. At least helping Hazel would keep her out of her crosshairs.

"Then, there are you and Addie still yet."

Hazel bumped her shoulder, a fresh look of cunning in her eyes so soon after worrying over Hannah as she had. Ivy's eyes widened, and Hazel chuckled menacingly. It was no secret that God's will moved a lot faster when Hazel put her influence on it, but Ivy wasn't about to let Hazel Miller and her disturbing ideas work on her.

Suddenly, it hit her. Working for over a year with the local matchmakers had taught her a thing or two for herself, and match-meddling worked both ways.

"Fine." Ivy straightened and looked the elder in the eye. "You might try your hand at me, but we both know…" Ivy glanced across the room at a poor innocent Hank Fisher just looking for an exit and smiled. "You *will* still marry before me, Hazel Miller."

ACKNOWLEDGMENTS

When I began creating the setting of Miller's Creek, Kentucky, I never imagined so many would fall in love with this beautiful place dear to me. Though fictional, Miller's Creek has many actual places that are part of my home and community. Twin Fork Lake was a favorite swimming hole of mine growing up.

These first books in the series are also about the healing and togetherness of a community devastated by multiple loses. Though the tragedy is fictional, it was strongly encouraged by the disaster that took place on April 27th, 1978 at Willow Island, West Virgina. 51 men lost their lives that day and hundreds were forever without them. Our family was strongly affected by this disaster, but they had their faith, community, and wiliness to keep on keeping on. I admire many of the women who withstood the storms that followed.

I have been blessed by readers who are faithful and supportive and give me a reason to keep on writing about the wonderful people who live between the pages of Miller's Creek, Kentucky. The Amish communities surrounding me have been wonderfully supportive as I continue filling pages. I have been welcomed kindly into their world and treated with respect and trust that I will represent them honestly and fairly. I hope to never disappoint.

About the Author

Raised in Kentucky timber country, Steele is a best-selling author who writes in favor of her rural surroundings. Her books are peppered with humor and sprinkled with grace, charming all the senses to make you laugh, cry, hold your beath, and root for the happy ever after ending. A storyteller at heart, she enjoys coffee indulgences, weekend road trips, and researching her next book.

Author links:
https://mindysteeleauthor.wordpress.com/
https://www.facebook.com/mindy.h.steele
https://www.instagram.com/msteelem07/
https://www.goodreads.com/au-
thor/show/14181261.Mindy_Steele
https://amazon.com/author/mindysteele
https://twitter.com/mindysteele7

Troyer Chicken Casserole

½ pound of bacon, cooked and crumbled
1 pound chicken, cooked and diced
1 Tbsp olive oil
1 package of Hidden Valley Ranch dressing mix
8 oz of cooked pasta, spiral or shells
1 cup mozzarella, shredded
½ cup cheddar, shredded
Salt and pepper to taste
14.5 oz jar of Alfredo sauce.

Directions:

Cook bacon and chicken and set aside. (You can use chicken strips and real bacon bits to quicken the process)

Coat your baking dish with olive oil and add cooked and drained pasta. Now add bacon and chicken and sprinkle with salt and pepper.

In a separate bowl, combine Ranch dressing mix and Alfredo sauce. Mix and pour over dish. Sprinkle with cheese and bake until cheese is melted fully.

Hannah's Apple Orchard Pie

2½ cups of apple pie filling
½ cup of sugar
3 TBSP Flour
1 (3 oz) cream cheese
1 cup sour cream

Crumb topping
½ cup flour
¼ cup sugar
2 TBSP butter

Directions:

Pour apple filling in 9 inch pie shell.

Combine sugar, flour, add sour cream and cream cheese. Blend well. Put on top of filling.

Top with crumbs and bake at 425 for 15 minutes then reduce heat to 350 and continue baking for another 25 minutes.

Dear Reader

If you enjoyed reading Cicada Season, I would appreciate it if you would help others enjoy this book, too. Here are some of the ways you can help spread the word:

Lend it. This book is lending enabled so please share it with a friend.

Recommend it. Help other readers find this book by recommending it to friends, readers' groups, book clubs, and discussion forums.

Share it. Let other readers know you've read the book by positing a note to your social media account and/or your Goodreads account.

Review it. Please tell others why you liked this book by reviewing it on your favorite ebook site.

Everything you do to help others learn about my book is greatly appreciated!

Mindy Steele